The Rideshare Chronicles

Volume I

The next ride could spell
DISASTER

Part of the
Murder Mindset series

Amy Janece

The Rideshare Chronicles: Volume I is a work of fiction. Names, characters, places, and incidents either are the products of the author's imagination or are used fictitiously. Any resemblance to actual persons, living or dead, events, or locales is entirely coincidental.

Cover art and design: Parvez Ahmed

Cover image/model: Michael Houston

Published in the United States By
Less Ordinary Lives Publishing

ISBN: 978-1-952973-00-0

eBook ISBN: 978-1-952973-01-7

DEDICATION

To Michael. Thank you for your friendship, honesty, loyalty, non-judgmental existence, and for your unrelenting encouragement. The countless hours of sharing stories and thoughts to make this actually come to life are appreciated more than any words that I could ever string together (and we both know I can string together a lot of those). Thank you for being my confidant and co-conspirator in this project. More than anything, thank you for being you.

CONTENTS

ACKNOWLEDGMENTS

There are several wonderful people in my life that helped me make this dream come true.

First off, thank you to my editor, Karyn Doran. Your comments, edits, sharp eyes, and fantastic use of the English language have helped me more than Google or software ever could. I'd also like to thank the beta reader team: Mary Studebaker-Reed, Karen Craigo, Jennifer Dean, and John Doe. The suggestions, questions, and input from all of you was invaluable.

Mom, thank you for your relentless support, your time in helping me with technical and website stuff, and your astounding belief in me. I am blessed to have you.

To my boys, thank you for always giving me inspiration, hope, and teaching me what love is. Your arrival altered the course of my life and I wouldn't have it any other way. I love you guys more than words could ever possibly express.

Brittany, thank you for listening to me bounce from pride to fear to excitement to worry and everywhere else throughout this adventure. I am eternally grateful for you.

Julia, you are always an inspiring young lady. Thank you for allowing me to be a part of your journey.

Arianna, thank you for the amazing photos and your encouragement. I'm grateful to have you in my life.

Thank you to Michael Houston, Melvin Lamont Cravin, Tristana Bennett, and Cindy Holbrook for your part in making the trailer come to life. Special shout out to Pee-Larr Handley for your hand in our first try. And last but not least, thank you to he who wishes to remain unnamed for your part as well. Y'all are seriously appreciated.

To the rest of my family and friends, I have not forgotten you. Your support, or even your doubt, has helped to shape me into who I am and given me the persistence to keep working to make my dreams come true. Thank you for your contributions.

The Rideshare Chronicles

Volume I

The next ride could spell
DISASTER

PROLOGUE

SEPT 2018

For the average person, one of the most prevailing daily concerns and discussions is what's for dinner. Mine is if I'll be assaulted, yelled at, spit on, or even covered in a stranger's vomit by the end of the night. No, I do not work in the ER, and I do not get hazard pay. I'm just your average single father, struggling to make ends meet.

Just as I completed that thought, the magical alert went off letting me know it was time to go pick-up the unknown. As I tapped the screen, which acknowledged that I was accepting the risks that came with the mission ahead, the only briefing I got was the name and location for pick-up.

In my mind, I'd like to believe that I'm some sort of secret operative or a spy. Unfortunately, it's nothing that glamorous. I am just your ordinary, run-of-the-mill Rideshare driver. My imagination occupied the time I spent trying to locate my passengers. I felt like a creep as I scanned the crowd, intently looking for someone, yet I have no idea what they look like. I was hoping they would see me and flag me down quickly since they at least had a photo of me.

Since that didn't happen, I pulled into an empty spot by the curb to begin the five-minute countdown waiting for them to find me. If they didn't show up, I would be able to cancel the ride as a no-show and be compensated for my time.

Time was running out when my phone rang. "Hello?" I answered it, even though I knew that I was about to hear a pre-recorded message.

"This is a call from your passenger," said the annoying robotic voice.

"Hello? Where are you?" slurred an intoxicated, irked woman. There was drunken giggling and belching in the background.

"I'm at the Rideshare pick-up zone outside of the Flamingo and Cromwell." I probably sounded slightly robotic and irritated myself, since this seems to be a recurring conversation that I take part in several times a night.

"Why are you there? I'm in front of Caesar's Palace," she whined.

Sigh. Welcome to another busy Friday night of Rideshare in Las Vegas, Nevada. Rideshare is an ingenious app-based service where people drive their own personal vehicles to usher others around for pay, kind of like turning your car into a taxicab in your spare time. It's been challenging for the Rideshare services to get into certain cities, such as Vegas. I believe it's all because of money and politics; the taxi business is huge here.

As with all newer technology, there are some hiccups sometimes. The GPS pinging the wrong pick-up or drop-off location is one of them. Although user error also causes some of these issues; especially when the user is inebriated and not terribly familiar with Las Vegas. At least this passenger seemed to know where she was. It's not uncommon to hear things like, "I'm at the front," "I'm at the big casino," "I'm by the big entrance sign," or "I'm by the sign that says casino." In most cases that describes all or most of the main entrances to any given property, which might mean four or five different options that are not easy to get from one to another on the outside.

If you've never been fortunate enough to visit the city known as "Sin City," let me explain a few things. The properties on the Las Vegas strip are huge. Our blocks are roughly one mile long, which is not your typical "city block." The area commonly referred to as "The Strip" is the 4.2 mile stretch of Las Vegas Boulevard where the infamous properties feature hotel rooms, casinos, shopping malls, condos, offices, attractions, convention centers, and numerous other ways to entertain you and take your money. Most of the casinos have nightclubs and even daytime beach clubs set up at their pools to give you another way to drink and spend money. It's a little bit different than your typical nightclub scene in other cities. For one thing, there is no last call. Sin City really is a twenty-four-hour town.

All of the large properties have specific zones where

we're allowed to pick you up, and nowhere else. This is supposed to cut down on unnecessary traffic jams, make it safer, and help us to find each other more quickly and easily. Most of the properties have several different entrances with the same or similar signage. Just to make it more fun, they seem to change the designated pick-up and drop-off locations randomly. (Insert sarcasm here.)

And, NO, we cannot pick you up on the main street, which is Las Vegas Boulevard, in front of the properties. That comes with an incredibly expensive fine that I, like many of my fellow Rideshare drivers, cannot afford to pay.

Back to my night…

"It'll take me a few minutes to get to you. Or you can go ahead and cancel this ride and request a new one. Just make sure that your pick-up location says Caesar's Palace."

Flamingo and Cromwell share a driveway that is set up fairly conveniently for pick-ups and drop-offs, except that you have to go a block east of Las Vegas Boulevard to the next street, Linq Avenue, to access it. They block off the entrance from the Boulevard on the weekends. Caesar's Palace is on the west side of Las Vegas Boulevard with the main entrance being accessible directly from the Boulevard, across the street from Flamingo and Cromwell. Even though the properties literally face each other, separated by just six lanes of traffic, it takes at least five full minutes to get from one to the other with no traffic if you hit all three of the stoplights favorably.

She pleaded, "I've already been waiting forever, so can you just hurry up? Please," she added desperately.

"Yes, ma'am," I replied dryly. The nightclubs were starting to shift, so it was busier than normal as some were winding down, others were just getting started, and many club-goers were simply club hopping. It wasn't quite 2:00 a.m.

While it should have only taken about five minutes to get to Caesar's, it took seventeen minutes due to the traffic. In addition to this being a busy weekend and time, the Las Vegas Metropolitan Police Department (LVMPD) had blocked off the right lanes going north and south on Las Vegas Boulevard for the night. That wasn't enough, though. There were also some additional lane closures due to construction. I'm not sure who is in charge of this kind of stuff, but it seems incredibly backwards to me.

I hoped it would be a decent ride and that she would give me a nice tip since I could have cancelled the ride, received my three dollar and seventy-five cents cancellation fee, and probably caught another ride coming out of Cromwell, along with not having to deal with all of the irritation. We don't get paid for our time or mileage to pick up a customer, only the time and distance when they are actually in our vehicles.

I finally made it around to the strip side of the fountain in front of Caesar's main entrance, where the Rideshare pick-up zone is located. A group of four young women stumbled to the back of my car to compare my license plate to their phone. They blended in with the other clusters of women in short, skin-tight dresses (mostly black) and high heels that most of them are not proficient in walking in. They reminded me of baby giraffes.

I had been listening to a song talking about a Player's Ball where the pimps and their best whores party. I amused myself with the thought that only the pimps in their impeccable, brightly colored suits, furs, and feathered hats were missing from this scene. I envisioned the top ladies of the night to resemble a lot of the attractive young women who pour out of these clubs nightly.

Three out of the four were wearing the uniform black dresses, but one had on white, which made her stand out even though she wasn't the most attractive one in the group. The crisp white dress seemed to enhance the deep summer tan on her skin. She was petite, with honey-blonde hair and fiery emerald eyes.

She was the one who opened my front passenger door.

"Cassie?" I asked, to confirm that I was picking up the correct passenger.

"Yes. Forgive my friends, they're a little drunk," she said hurriedly. She hiccupped and fell into the seat. I was thinking she might have been more drunk than she realized.

The other three climbed into the back seat. Two of the young ladies seemed to be half alert, while the third looked like a zombie. The two were giggling and talking about the men who tried to pick them up. The other girl looked at me and mumbled, "Don't worry. I won't throw up in your car."

I pointed to the controls in the center of the car ceiling behind me and informed them that they could control the rear temperatures there. The zombie rolled down her window "for fresh air," which made no sense considering it was still over one hundred degrees outside and a cool seventy-six degrees in my car.

I watched her from the corner of my eye every time I glanced in my side mirror since rolling down the window seems to be a consistent factor in those who have thrown up in my car (and the cars of the other drivers I often talk to). I wish I didn't know these telltale signs the way that I do.

I confirmed the address with Cassie, which was in a smaller neighborhood of custom-built homes in the southwest part of town, roughly fifteen minutes away. We proceeded with the customary small talk.

"So, are you from here?" I asked. It used to be easy to tell who lives here and who was visiting based on their destination. Many tourists are renting homes through services such as AirBnB or staying with local friends and family. At any given time, we have just as many visitors (or more) as we have residents here. The last report I read from the Las Vegas Convention and Visitors Authority claimed over forty-three million people visited our city last year. Just over two million people claim the greater Las Vegas area as home, including North Las Vegas and Henderson.

Cassie said, "No. I live in Tennessee, but we're here…" - she paused and looked back at the other girls. They all busted up laughing, and she finished through fits of giggles, "We're *supposed* to be here for a bachelorette party."

I was intrigued. That was a bit unconventional. "Uh-oh. Where is the 'supposed to' part coming from?"

Most of the conversations I've had with the majority of my passengers are pretty routine. Every once in a while, I get to learn about other places, this city I call home, other people, and of course through it all I learn more about myself.

"The bride got into trouble at work at the last minute and couldn't come," one of the giggly girls from the back explained.

"So y'all decided to just make it a girl's trip, huh?" I asked, amused.

"Yep. Everything was already booked and paid for and we already took our vacation time," said the other giggly girl.

I maneuvered onto Highway 215 West from the I-15 South and glanced in my driver side mirror just in time to see the zombie hanging out of the window behind me expelling everything from her stomach.

Great. This is exactly what I need tonight, I thought.

I pulled over onto the shoulder of the highway to let the girl finish emptying her stomach without assaulting the other cars with her spent dinner and what seemed like an entire bottle of cheap vodka.

"What are you doing?" demanded Cassie with enlarged eyes and a look torn between confusion and terror.

One thing I've always been concerned about is women feeling afraid of me, or even men being intimidated by me, especially in the close confines of my vehicle. I'm a larger man, standing 6'4" and weighing a solid 275 pounds. I'm biracial, though by looking at me you'd be hard-pressed to figure out what my ethnicity is. I can pass for just about any race. My head is shaved bald (thanks to the thinning hair) and I have light brown/hazel eyes. What many passengers might not realize, is that the Rideshare companies all do a thorough background check on us and make us take selfies occasionally to confirm our identity. Passengers see photos of the driver and car, as well as have our license plate numbers to confirm who we are. In addition, we are tracked via GPS from the beginning to the end of each ride.

Because of her frightened look, I was slightly sympathetic. I do not wish to scare my passengers in any sense.

"Letting your friend finish," I said dryly and pointed behind me.

"Really, Crystal?" She sighed in exasperation and threw her head back dramatically against the headrest, looking up at the ceiling of my car.

The rest of the ride was pretty quiet except for a few whispered apologies. I just cracked the windows and continued on to their rented house. Roughly ten minutes later the girls were home safe, and I was Googling twenty-four-hour do-it-yourself car washes. Of course, the closest one to me was fifteen minutes away on the east side of town.

As I drove that way, hoping to salvage at least a part of my weekend earnings, I thought back to how this journey began…

I'm just your average Rideshare driver, Scott Benson. I'm a forty-one-year-old single father of five. The older boys (twenty-two and twenty-one) live together in California, and my eighteen-year-old daughter lives in Texas with their mother. My eight-year-old daughter and seven-year-old son are with me four to five days a week and spend most weekends with their mother's family. (That means two baby mamas to deal with if you're keeping track.) Those kid-free nights are my money nights. I also work seven days a week from 2:00 p.m. to 10:00 p.m. at a small retail shop in North Las Vegas that's been in my family for more than thirty years.

I got myself into a severe financial hole a few months ago where I was on the verge of losing the little bit that I have. My old SUV kept breaking down on me, causing issues for me to get my kids to school and for me to get to the shop. My house was a couple of weeks away from going into foreclosure and all of my utilities were on disconnection notices. I wasn't really able to draw a wage from the shop due to business being slow and major repairs that needed to be made. I really needed to buy a reliable car but couldn't figure out how to make it work.

A friend of mine, Alyssa, had been driving with a couple of the Rideshare platforms and suggested that I give it a try to get out of the mess I was in. I don't mind sacrificing TV time to have the extra income to support my family in the way that I deem appropriate. My old SUV only qualified for food deliveries and ate up more in gas than I could reasonably expect to make in a night, not to mention the reliability concerns I had for the truck.

I did some research and settled on a low-mileage, year-old Dodge Journey. It has a third-row seat, which qualifies me for the larger (more profitable) rides, but still has a four-cylinder engine so it's pretty good on gas. People frequently ask me if it's the official Rideshare vehicle because it is apparently common. I laugh it off, but the vehicle is really practical for me.

I've been able to put out a few fires in my financial world and reasonably get by while working about thirty hours per week between the nights that my kids aren't with me and the late mornings after they go to school, until the summer break, that is.

I started thinking about compiling some of these Rideshare experiences to put together a coffee table type of book after some interesting experiences I've had, as well as the ones I've heard about from other Rideshare drivers. I've done over one thousand rides in the past six months. I'm not sure if I'll include my personal details, including this explanation, because I'm pretty sure the rides are far more interesting than my life story. I think I'm pretty close to being able to compile the book now. I started keeping notes and writing about the best rides in detail about a month after I started driving so that I wouldn't forget anything.

I'm frequently asked if I'd recommend this gig to others. I typically ask a few questions or simply let them know that if you enjoy driving, have at least a little bit of patience, and like people it can be a terrific way to make some money. It can also be incredibly entertaining if you enjoy people-watching, far better than any reality TV show in my opinion.

As for Las Vegas, it's already a city like no other, filled with some of the most interesting characters you could ever hope to come across. Well over half of the residents of the valley - including North Las Vegas, Henderson, and all of the suburb communities - have migrated here. The locals call us "transplants." I've personally been here for about thirty years.

My guess is that about half of our residents hail from our neighbor California, mostly due to our drastically lower cost of living, no state income taxes, and considerably less traffic.

Most of our visitors rarely see much of our city since conventions and advertisements all start and stop on the strip. Contrary to popular belief, "Sin City" actually has quite a bit to offer families and those who aren't interested in gambling, drinking, clubbing, or general partying. You'll meet very few "locals" who actually hang out on the strip regularly. Most of us have our favorite spots away from the strip or we venture downtown to the "Fremont Experience," which is also commonly referred to as "old Vegas."

You can drive in any direction from the center of the strip for twenty-five minutes or more and still find neighborhoods that resemble any other city with parks, schools, libraries, grocery stores, etc. Even with all of that and the tremendous growth we've experienced over the past two decades, we are still on the small side for a major American city; we're just spread out quite nicely.

CHAPTER 1
SHARED RIDE FROM HELL
SUNDAY, APRIL 1, 2018 2:00 A.M.

How did I manage to get a drug-taking, drug-dealing, gang-banging, and God-fearing woman all in one on Easter Sunday? The irony in this one was beyond me.

I just started driving about three weeks ago, but I think I'm getting a pretty good grasp on things now. The orientation they had me attend was less than an hour long, including the fifteen-minute video that explained "everything you need to know." Uhm, yeah, okay.

The video plays while they're talking to you and you can follow along on your app on your phone. Everything was glossed over and explained so quickly that I felt a little lost. Looking around at everyone else only made matters worse because they all looked like they had it down. I was too proud to ask anyone or speak up. After the video we all got into our vehicles to line up for the vehicle inspections. I've always been self-employed, so formal training has never existed in my line of work. I figured that must be why I was missing something.

To add insult to injury, they offered a ride-along with a seasoned driver. I really would have liked to take advantage of this, but my pride got in the way. They all said the same thing after each portion, "Don't worry, you'll get it." That really didn't make me feel any better.

I decided I'd rely on the couple of people I knew who had already been driving. They all gave some information and tips and finished with the same line, "Don't worry, you'll get it."

I was quite discouraged, but I had no choice other than to get out and try to figure this stuff out on my own. I turned to the anonymity of the internet and looked up videos on YouTube made by complete strangers, silently begging for their help while hiding behind the screen of my phone so they couldn't judge me. I learned enough to get my nerve up to at least turn my app on and take my first ride.

The strip is both a blessing and a curse for us. There are several people looking for rides at any given time. However, it takes quite a while to get familiar with where all of the pick-up and drop-off zones are and how to easily maneuver among them using back streets and alleys. So they tell me.

Some drivers will turn their apps off (to "unavailable") to get back to the strip, or to get away from the strip, when they drop off their passengers. I am currently one of those who get away from the strip as fast as humanly possible. It brings about all of my insecurities in driving.

One of my first rides had a pick-up at Circus Circus, one of the older hotel and casinos still standing. I haven't been there in at least nine years. The passenger called me to find out where I was. Somehow, I got through the conversation and found her, though I'm still not sure how. I didn't even know how to respond to her because truth be told, I had no idea where I was or how to even begin to explain it.

Most of my rides so far seem to follow a fairly simple routine, or what seems to be normal. I greet each passenger and ask how they're doing. Some are very talkative, and we have great conversations about anything and everything. Others are very quiet, so I'm quiet too. I just go with the vibe that the rider gives off.

The thing that has surprised me the most so far is just how much the city has grown and how much goes on here. I thought I had a really good grasp on my city, but apparently there's much more than meets the eye.

I had my first really unusual ride tonight, which is what prompted this whole explanation. It was a shared ride, which is a newer option where several passengers who are headed in the same general direction will end up in the same ride, like a carpool, to save the passengers some money and maximize the time of each driver.

I picked up a young man in his early twenties at PT's, a local chain of gaming bars that serve beer, hard alcohol, and light food while providing entertainment via a jukebox, pool tables, and video poker. I picked him up around 2:00 a.m.

Before the young man was shoved into my car by his drunk friends, I had already received the notification that we had a second passenger added to the ride. Because the shared ride is a newer option, I asked the young man if he was familiar with the concept.

His reply said it all. "Aww man, that's what they ordered for me?"

I explained that he could cancel the ride and order a solo ride and I'd move on if he didn't want to share. I also informed him that when people order rides for others, they almost always choose the shared option because they are a bit less expensive than the solo rides.

In a positive, up-spirited tone he said, "Well, maybe it'll be a hot chick!"

I just shook my head. I was concerned with the fact that I'd have to manage an interaction with two individuals who did not know each other and attempt to keep the entire conversation and ride pleasant and peaceful for everyone. At 2:00 a.m. What do I do if they get into it? They didn't cover this in any training.

We pulled up to an apartment complex to get the second passenger just a few blocks away from PT's. She was nowhere to be found. I started to call her to establish contact to I could cancel the ride with pay. As the phone began to ring, a fairly unattractive middle-aged woman stumbled toward the car. The young man had a look of severe distaste in his eyes and turned his head in disgust. She was clearly inebriated or under the influence of something.

Just great, I thought. Not only do I have two complete strangers that are obviously from different walks of life and age groups, but they're both intoxicated as well. I pushed my nerves aside. I needed the money, after all.

Once she was settled into the car, I asked her how her night was going and how she was. She responded with, "God is good." Religion, politics, money, and sexual preferences are my least favorite topics, especially in these rides when I have multiple passengers who do not know each other.

I tried to change the subject to something more uplifting and less controversial. She ignored me and started to address the man, who was sitting up front beside me. She asked, "Where're you guys headed tonight?" When she didn't get a response from him, she turned to me. "What's wrong with your cousin?"

I said, "Ma'am, we're not related. He's another passenger, just like you." He put his headphones on and turned the volume all the way up to drown her out.

She said, "Well he doesn't have to be rude. If he doesn't want to talk, he can just say so."

I sighed in my head. This is one of those disasters I'd been concerned with. "Ma'am, he doesn't want to talk to you, so I'll talk to you. What would you like to talk about?"

She asked, "Do you accept Jesus Christ as your Lord and Savior?" Before I could even answer she slurred, "That xanny I took just kicked in. Man, I'm loaded."

I found this to be incredibly ironic. Seriously, this lady just went from super religious to super high? I kept that to myself and said, "Well, I think it's beautiful that you do."

She said, "God is great and you need God in your heart. God bless us all."

I couldn't help it. I asked her, "Did God bless the narcotics and the alcohol that you took?"

She said, "Sometimes it's just hard. Sometimes I need the drugs and alcohol to get through."

I replied, "When things get hard? That's what I thought God was for, not pills and alcohol."

She continued by telling me that it had been really hard on her lately. Most of what she said was unclear due to the mumbling and substance-induced distortion. The irony did not escape me. I was relieved that she was fading out though, so that I didn't have to entertain that conversation any longer.

We arrived at the first stop and the gentleman got out of the car. In a very sarcastic tone, he looked at the female passenger and said, "God bless you."

That woke her up and set her off. She opened the door and started climbing out of the vehicle - at nearly three in the morning - and started shouting in front of this man's house. "God has blessed me, you need God!" She was getting angrier and angrier with each moment that went by.

In an attempt to defuse the situation, I requested that she get back into the car and close the door so that we could continue on to her destination. She ignored that and continued to yell at the man, even though he was long gone inside of his house.

In a more aggressive tone, I stated, "One way or another I'm leaving. You can either get in the vehicle or stay here to continue discussing this with the gentleman who is no longer there."

She got back in the car and closed the door so that we could continue on our way. She explained to me that she has a relationship with the Lord and that man was so wrong for the way he talked to her and so on and so on. Within about five minutes she was fast asleep, and I was relieved. I was still severely confused on how she could partake in the drugs and alcohol and judgment of others and at the same time claim to be so religious. Seemed backwards to me.

As we approached her destination, 628 West Craig Road, I recognized the entrance to Craig Ranch Park immediately. I was familiar with this part of town, so I was originally thinking that the GPS was taking me to the apartment complex behind the park, maybe trying to take me through the middle of the park as a shortcut. However, it said I had arrived at my destination when I got to the park entrance. At that point, I realized the pin on the map was in the center of the park, not at the complex behind the park. I woke the woman up, telling her we had arrived at her destination, and I clicked the "finish ride" button.

She was extremely groggy and disoriented. She looked around through the dark, tinted windows of my vehicle and began to demand, "Oh no, this is not my destination. Where did you take me? This isn't my home. Take me home." She found an all-new level of aggression.

I explained that we were at the destination she put in the app and pointed at my phone, which is mounted in the center of the car so passengers can easily see my GPS. She didn't listen to a single word that I was saying, but she continued to insist that I take her home. Instead of trying to fight, I simply asked her where her home was.

When she actually registered what I was asking, she told me that her home was on Craig and Cheyenne by the AMPM gas station.

I was getting incredibly impatient but tried to keep my composure. "Ma'am, those streets run in the same direction. They both run east to west." I really wanted to tell her she had to go. Her and Jesus.

She said, "I know where I live. Right behind that gas station on Craig and Cheyenne."

I repeated that they run in the same direction several times, adding that there are several AMPMs on both streets. I began to get more frustrated, being that we were sitting in a dark parking lot at the park arguing for over thirty minutes at this point. I told her, "Tell me where you live, and I'll get you home." I pulled out of the park.

She just kept repeating that she lived behind the gas station on Craig and Cheyenne. I pulled across the street into a gas station that was well lit and still open. I suggested that we go inside in the light to try to figure out where she lived.

The woman got very angry and hostile, speaking with a harsh tone and a great deal of profanity. She told me, "All I know, cuz, is that you're gonna take me home. NOW!" When I pulled into a parking stall in front of the gas station she continued, "Naw, cuz, you're not going to get me out of your car so you can leave me here."

How did she know that as soon as she got out I was planning on driving off to get as far away from her as possible? Was she reading my mind? I was going to leave, and in good conscience, knowing that she was in a well-lit place of business that was still open so she wouldn't be alone.

My thought skipped back to her. Did she really just gang-bang on me? She was dressed in all blue and the use of the word "cuz" in the way she kept spouting it is gang slang on the west coast. At that point, I realized I was dealing with a highly unstable individual. I mean, super religious, drug and alcohol abuser, and a gangster, all in one? I shook my head.

I had no choice but to wait for her to give me more clues about where she lived as she continued to just sit in my car and talk and talk. Finally, she mentioned another street, Michael Way, which ironically, I am familiar with. There is an AMPM gas station on the corner of Cheyenne and Michael Way. I let her know that I thought I knew where she stayed and began to head in that direction.

She handed me a business card saying that I could charge the ride to that card since it was a different address and she'd take care of it. I looked at the card. It was a referral card that merely offered a discount towards rides if you signed up as a new rider. It held no cash value and there was no way for me to actually receive any kind of compensation for this ride. I was so frustrated at that point that I just wanted her out of my car, at all costs, so I was willing to do the ride for free.

The only other alternative I could possibly think of was calling the police to ask them to come get her out of my vehicle. Then I thought of how incredibly absurd that would be, being that I have a great deal of size on her. I thought the police would probably spend more time laughing at me than actually being of any assistance. That did not sound like a good option. That situation was something I never thought I would encounter as I was thinking women would be more nervous getting into my car, yet this woman refused to get out of my vehicle. I could not even begin to process what I was actually thinking and feeling about the entire situation.

As we approached the gas station, she got excited, pointing to the upstairs of the neighboring apartment complex saying, "There. I live right up there."

I pulled into the entrance of the apartments and asked if the location was good for her.

She said, "Okay. I'm finna run up these stairs and sell these drugs real quick. I'll be right back. Wait for me right here."

I could not believe that this woman really thought I was going to sit there and wait for her and why she thought that I would even want to be a part of anything that she had going on. Before I opened my mouth to object, I realized it was best to just let her disappear and then I would do the same before she had the chance to return, instead of debating the situation with her for thirty minutes like we had just done at the gas station. My heart was pounding because I kept thinking she was going to glance back every few steps. As soon as I saw that door close behind her, I could not get away from there fast enough.

As I drove away, I turned my app off. I didn't want to chance the woman ordering a ride and it pinging me back to her; besides, thinking about that ride only upset me even more once I put together that I actually made about seven dollars during the more than two hours I spent with her. I decided to go home. I only had a few hours before I planned on picking up my kids so they could celebrate Easter Sunday.

CHAPTER 2

THROWUPPER #1

SATURDAY, APRIL 7, 2018 6:30 A.M.

I had been working all night, since 10:00 p.m. after closing the shop. The rides were coming in pretty steadily, so I kept on working. In between rides I would chat with my friend Alyssa, who drives on a similar schedule to mine. It really helps to have someone to talk to and relate to. Throughout the night, our calls had been cut off several times by a woman I have been seeing - and I use that term loosely - for a few months, named Veronica.

When we go through certain moments in our lives, we don't realize how much they'll change the course of our lives. The moment I met Veronica was a major turning point in my life, even though I didn't realize it at the time.

With all of my day-to-day obligations and responsibilities, I didn't go out of my way to approach or even attempt to date women. I just didn't have the time. This situation was not any different.

It was a Sunday afternoon, which are typically slower days at the shop, which makes it a great day for the tedious work, such as pricing, re-stocking, organizing, and labeling the items we received over the weekend. As I found myself going through the motions, I looked over and saw my children busy in their makeshift work area I had created for them. At first glance, customers, friends, and family think the kids are tortured, being "stuck" in the store with me all the time. We - the kids and I - know that it is exactly the opposite of that.

When it comes to a small retail business, space and utilization of the space is a big factor. My store is not the size of a Walmart. I don't have the luxury of unlimited space, or opportunity to use it in whichever way that I choose. I keep a carefully limited amount of entertainment and practical items, from old video games and toys to T-shirts.

I did manage to carve out one hundred square feet, roughly a ten-foot by ten-foot area, where I managed to squeeze in two complete computer workstations with full accessibility to the internet and four shelves, which allow the opportunity to store and play board games, put together crafts, and space to complete homework and studies, while maintaining a level of privacy, or seclusion, from the rest of the store and customers.

As I glanced into their area, they were so preoccupied with YouTube and various other activities that I might as well have not even been there. I found my thoughts drifting away from the task at hand.

I didn't believe that I would do well in corporate America because I actually find enjoyment in some of the tedious parts of running a small business. It reminds me of when I was a kid, when it was just me and my father building the store. Just before I finished my trip to la-la-land, she walked in.

My first thought when I laid eyes on her was that my store was visited by an angel. If you would have told me that there was a halo hanging behind her, I would have believed it. That is, until she spoke.

She began firing words off at a rapid pace that was difficult to keep up with. She began asking me a million questions about James, my sole employee. She expressed concerns about his capabilities, maybe due to the way he carried himself or his image. I will admit that at first glance you would most likely ignore him and write him off as a panhandler, but he's actually incredibly intelligent and very capable of accomplishing several things.

I'm not a huge fan of having conversations about people, especially when they aren't present. I find that to be rude and disrespectful.

When she initially asked about him, I referred her back to him. I told her, "I believe that you should go speak to James about James."

She began to explain her situation and why she was asking me about him. I did understand her concerns, so I said, "Yes, he is capable of the work he said he could do."

She started throwing questions at me that I believed were too intrusive for me to answer about another person. She asked, "Why does he refer to himself in third person? Is he on something? Are you sure he can fix this for me?"

I spent about fifteen minutes taking in this assault of questions and constantly referring her back to James before she finally got the hint. She stopped asking about James and started asking about me. She seemed to be incredibly agitated and it seemed like her mind was racing in twenty different directions, all at the same time.

I asked, "Why don't you just take a deep breath and relax?"

For some reason, she found that to be very intriguing. She replied, "The sound of your voice is very calming."

I had no issue with answering questions about me. I actually found it to be kind of refreshing that she was interested in me. Veronica made it crystal clear that she was married and had a boyfriend on the side. Even with all of this attention, I didn't believe any flirting was going on. I had never had an issue with maintaining platonic relationships, so I welcomed the conversation.

She began to talk about herself and express how people didn't understand her. She said that some of her ideas are pretty far out there. She mentioned that her therapist couldn't decide if she was delusional and crazy or a genius.

I encouraged her to open up and to feel free to express herself. I welcome conversations that are different, out there, or abstract. I believe that a lot of the topics she brought up were some sort of a test to see how I'd respond because she paid very close attention to my facial expressions, gestures, and mannerisms. This didn't make much of a difference to me because I have great control over my reactions to my emotions.

After she became more relaxed and comfortable, she expressed her interest in galactic travel, space stations, and the future of humanity. I found all of this to be incredibly fascinating, as I am a big fan of *Star Trek*.

We talked about all sorts of subjects for the next few hours. Then she hit me with that fatal question. "Are you single?"

"Yes," I answered.

"Why are you single? If you're such a great catch, why has no one scooped you up yet?"

I told her, "I'm single by choice. I don't need to be with anyone or be in a relationship. I am committed to my children and my work."

I did find her to be attractive physically, as well as interesting intellectually due to the things and subjects that caught her attention. I thought this was a great combination, even if she was married, with a boyfriend on the side.

She told me how refreshing it was to meet someone who was genuinely single because her boyfriend on the side was actually married to another woman.

I blurted out, "You have a very confusing, complicated situation. It sounds very stressful."

By that time, it was getting late in the evening. She had obligations to fulfill, and it was time for me to shut down the store and get my children home for bed. I had already spent time I couldn't really spare interacting with her.

I think she was surprised that I didn't ask her for her phone number and wasn't pursuing anything beyond our initial conversation that we just had.

She told me, "I don't get to this side of town very often, so I don't know if I'll ever see you again."

I replied, "If it's meant to be, then we will see each other again."

As I was locking the doors, she said, "Are you kidding me? You're not even going to ask me for my phone number?"

I answered, "No. I didn't have any intention of doing that."

"So you don't even want it?"

I reminded her, "You are a married woman, with a boyfriend on the side. So what would be the purpose? What would be respectful about me taking your number? Even if I took it, I wouldn't call."

She said, "I don't give a shit about that."

I said, "Well, if you'd like, you are welcome to have my number."

She looked at me with a puzzled, strange expression. She said, "Alright. What is it?"

I gave her my number and figured that maybe I'd hear from her one day, or not. I got into my car and my thoughts drifted back to my reality, as I thought about the things I had to take care of at the house.

I think I might have made it about twenty-five feet out of the parking lot when my phone rang. I had a long drive ahead of me, so we continued the conversation throughout my drive. The children were happily watching their tablets, so the conversation didn't take anything away from them.

She told me, "I don't want the conversation to end, but I don't like talking over the phone like this, I prefer to do it in person."

I said, "Well, I just got home. You're welcome to come over and continue the conversation if you'd like."

She snapped back in a seriously sarcastic tone, "I bet you would like to get me to your house. What's next? You're going to ask me to your room?"

"Never mind. Forget that I asked. It was merely an invitation, with no insinuations beyond that."

Over the next several weeks we became somewhat close. I enjoyed our conversations and the subjects that she brought up, while she enjoyed the limitless attention that I gave her. She didn't mind being on the phone and being patient in between my customers at the store or my passengers at night

She started to express a great fondness for me. She started asking how I felt about her. I always answered that I enjoyed talking to her and I enjoyed her company. Somehow that translated to me having feelings for her in *her* mind.

Maybe I should have seen the warning signs coming. I did tell her directly that I didn't have feelings for her. I do not beat around the bush and I do speak my mind. I thought it was pretty clear.

She began to make excuses to show up at the store or visit me, which I welcomed at first. Naturally, the more time we spent around each other, the closer we got. One evening, during a long conversation, we crossed the line; or, should I say, *she* crossed the line.

It started with her brushing against me, or "accidentally" making contact, which then grew into her kissing me. She implied that she wanted to do more. Physically, I was interested. I was also concerned, though, due to the complexity of her situation. I did not want to have any problems that could disrupt the delicate balance that I currently had in my life.

I told her I didn't think it would be best for us to continue. She said she wanted it, and we continued.

Over the next couple of months, it was as though we were involved in a simulated relationship in her mind. The interesting conversations we used to have and the topics we used to discuss seemed to never come up anymore. Now, the major topic was about relationships, or her telling me how we aren't going to "be together" long-term and we wouldn't have a chance at working out. I could only think: we aren't together now, so what's the difference?

She asked if I'd be willing to uproot myself and move across the country with her, because her career was taking her elsewhere. I had always been honest and forthcoming with Veronica. I never led her on to believe that I would make any such changes, and I never said anything that even kind of implied that I'd be willing to adapt to whatever she wanted, but I believe that in her mind, this is what she was thinking was going to happen.

This turned into extremely unpleasant conversations every other day. There seemed to be a cycle. She called several times per day, back to back to back. I expressed that I was busy and I'd talk to her later. That didn't seem to be suitable for her, as she called me right back. She asked why I was treating her so poorly and why was I acting like I was going to just discard her like yesterday's trash. I always told her that I was not interested in the kind of interaction that we were having, and she told me how we'd never work out. I asked her what the point of us even discussing this was. Her response was always that we're just finishing this up so that we can go our separate ways.

What began as a fun and interesting interaction had turned into something obnoxious, irritating, and undesirable. I attempted to avoid the phone calls, but she would just show up at the store. I had been concerned about the extent she was willing to go when things didn't go her way, so I was trying to be civilized while I figured out the best way to exit the situation.

Then, she told me, *again,* that we were not going to work out. I asked her how we could speed up the process. Since we were not going to work out, what reason was there for us to even talk? That question sparked a three-hour discussion that I didn't even have to participate in. I don't believe she desired any response from me anyway, besides just listening.

Listening is something that I never have a problem with, until repetition sets in. When she began repeating the same conversation every fifteen minutes, all I could think was: what have I gotten myself into? I've seen all of the classic movies, such as *Fatal Attraction,* and it always seems to end badly for the person who is being obsessed over. Not to toot my own horn, but it felt like I was being obsessed over. I have a lot to live for, so I needed to tread very carefully since I had no idea how far Veronica was willing to go if she truly believed that I had wronged her or hurt her in some kind of way.

I don't understand how she found this amount of time to call, talk to, and obsess over me. She has three children, her own business, a husband, and a full-time boyfriend on the side.

I decided to put my phone on silent so that Veronica's calls wouldn't disturb my passengers. One of them asked me if I needed to answer the call after her name lit up my phone for the fifth time during the very short, five-minute ride.

Overall, it had been an incredibly busy, productive night. I was starting to wear down a bit, but I believed I had another hour or two in me. Besides, I had a bonus offer for the week if I could meet a certain quota of rides by the end of the weekend. I only had tonight and tomorrow night to make it happen, since I would grab my kids Sunday afternoon.

I got pinged for a shared ride at Money Plays, a local bar on West Flamingo and Decatur, a couple of miles west of the strip. I pulled up and a tall, thin man got into the front seat. He couldn't have been more than twenty-three years old. After pleasantries, he appeared to pass out. We got pinged to grab a second passenger at the Orleans Hotel and Casino on West Tropicana. It was a short seven-minute drive down Decatur at that time of morning with no traffic on the streets.

I pulled up to the Rideshare pick-up zone outside of the Orleans and two young women, about the same age as the man, walked up to the car and got in the back. They were both dressed like they just stepped out of a 1950's sock hop. They told me about an event they had just attended and they were tired but happy because of how much fun they had. Their energy was refreshing, and Veronica hadn't called for a couple of hours. I was thinking the conversation should help me get through the rest of the ride so that I could grab an airport run back to my side of town and call it a night and get a few hours of sleep.

The girls were supposed to be dropped off first. Their destination was off of Lake Mead, about nineteen minutes away. I headed east on Tropicana toward I-15. We were sitting at a red light in the left-hand turn lane when I noticed the young man going in and out and making the gurgling and choking sounds like someone who's about to get sick.

I immediately started rolling his window down and told him to get out to throw up. He looked me in my eyes and said, "No, I'm o-" and began to vomit before he could even finish. He cupped his hands around his mouth and finally looked toward the window. I didn't even get it rolled down all the way. Now there were chunks of vomit on my window, in my window frame, and all in his hands. I was utterly disgusted. I felt horrible for the young women in the backseat. I usually welcome the longer rides as they yield higher earnings, but I couldn't wait for this man to be out of my car and out of my presence.

I wasn't sure what the proper thing to do would be at that point. I could pull over and kick him out of my car, or I could continue the ride. I guess I could have offered for the young women to order another ride, but that didn't occur to me at the time. I think I was so focused on my anger toward the man, and on keeping my composure, that nothing else could penetrate my mind. If he would have vomited in my direction or gotten any on me, I think I would have lost it. Rideshare certainly didn't offer any training on throw-uppers.

The man was incredibly embarrassed and kept apologizing. I think he was crying because he started to wipe and rub his face and eyes. All I could think was that his eyes were probably stinging as well. I rolled down the other three windows as it smelled pretty bad. It was sixty-six degrees, so it was a little chilly out. It was a bit uncomfortable to be traveling down the interstate at sixty-five miles per hour with the windows down, but it was the best I had at the moment to make things somewhat more bearable.

At some point during the fifteen minutes it took us to get to the Lake Mead exit, one of the young ladies handed me a plastic bag and said, "Just in case." I thanked her and handed it to the man.

He once again tried to reassure us that he was fine, even though we didn't believe it. As we pulled up to the light at the end of the off ramp, he began the gurgling and choking sounds again. I looked at him and he said, "No, I'm okay."

I very sternly told him, "Outside or in the bag. Your choice. Or you have to go." He chose to utilize the bag, then the crying and apologies started all over.

Within five minutes we pulled into the girls' apartment complex and they got out. They looked like they pitied me. Interesting, since I felt bad for them.

I looked at my GPS and we had another ten minutes until I'd get to the man's house. He was all the way up on the hill off of Hollywood, near the Air Force base. I silently prayed to any God who would listen to please not let him throw up in my car again. I hit the button that lets them know not to send me anymore rides because I would be off duty after this one.

We pulled up to his house and he begged me to wait so he could try to clean up the mess he made. I obliged. It's not like I could grab another passenger at that point anyway. He came back outside with a container of disinfectant wipes, a rag, a roll of paper towels, and an empty plastic bag to use for trash. I realized he was making more of a mess than he was cleaning it up. He was still drunk, swaying, and almost fell a couple of times.

I thanked him and told him that I had to go. I was completely disturbed, disgusted, and pissed off because I have a bonus this weekend that I'm probably not going to hit. I was hoping to get an airport ride from that side of town to get paid to head back towards home.

I drove all the way home with the windows down - a very chilly forty minutes. As dead-tired as I was, I couldn't even go to bed. I knew that I had to clean my car inside and out before I laid down or the sun would heat up the valley and bake all of it into my car. I don't even clean up my kids' messes at this point because they're old enough to know the signs and make it to the restroom, yet there I was cleaning up after another grown man.

I submitted a message to Rideshare with photos of the car. Because he started to clean it up it didn't appear to be as bad, so they only gave me a forty-dollar clean-up fee. I was disappointed. It took me two hours to clean it up and I still had to get my car detailed before I could drive again.

I did also inform Rideshare that the girls should not be charged. I can only imagine what a nightmare of a ride that was for them. I don't know if they got their ride for free or not, but I sure hope so.

I showered and went to lie down. The light from my phone caught my attention. It was Veronica. I just sighed and turned my phone off. I needed some sleep.

CHAPTER 3
SEAT HITTER
FRIDAY, APRIL 13, 2018 3:15 A.M.

I was on the phone with Alyssa because neither of us had rides when she got a pick-up at the Stratosphere. I decided to stay on the phone because it was Friday the thirteenth, I didn't have a ride yet, and I could mess with her a little bit. We occasionally do this. If she's in a ride but I'm not, I'll give her suggestions on what to say or play a song that I know she can't resist singing, or comment on her passengers to try to get her to laugh. She does the same to me. It keeps us alert and entertained, as the slow times between rides can really wear you down. It's also a safety thing. She's an attractive woman, and it just seems like someone knowing where she is and what's going on with her while she's working alone at night might be useful at some point.

She confirmed that she had the correct passenger, though it was in his mother's name, and went through the same customary pleasantries as I do. We've actually been able to learn a lot and be supportive of each other. We were both more comfortable driving the strip, even though neither of us prefers it.

The man she picked up was slurring, so he was drunk. That isn't uncommon at that time of night. We definitely run the gamut on drunken people from the emotional drunks, aggressive drunks, sleepy drunks, talkative drunks, horny drunks, etc. The man said he had a really long, bad day and got quiet. She later filled me in on the details of the ride that I couldn't hear through the phone.

He had put his headphones on so she just continued on the ride in silence, turning her radio up a bit. She made her way over to West Flamingo and continued heading in that direction. Out of nowhere she heard a loud thunderous noise. He was hitting the back of the passenger seat. She snapped her head around to look at him. He shook his head as if to clear out the fog and stars he must have been seeing. Then he slumped back and passed out again. She continued driving west, figuring his bad day was probably the result of gambling losses or an issue with a lover. They had about twelve minutes left until they would reach his destination.

A few minutes later she sensed movement from the corner of her right eye. He flung himself across the back of the passenger seat and wrapped his arms around it, hugging the seat tightly. She adjusted so that she was leaning against her door, as far away from him as possible, and watching him out of the corner of her eye. His hands and arms were way too close to her for her comfort. She fingered the .380 pistol she keeps in her door pocket purely for self-defense. Nevada is an open-carry state, but the Rideshare companies frown upon drivers carrying weapons of any kind. Some of the platforms will even kick you off if they receive reports of a weapon. She's really quiet about having it in her car, but it made her feel a little bit more secure.

By that point, I had a passenger of my own. She whispered to me that she might have a problem and gave me her cross streets. I was glad for once that my passengers were relatively quiet so I could listen to her ride and try to figure out if I needed to call the police or make my way toward her when I dropped my passengers off.

As she was finally pulling into his apartment complex, he started furiously hitting the back of the passenger seat again. He came to when she stopped the vehicle inside of the complex. He asked, "Where did you take me?"

Her tone was as stern as I've ever heard it when she replied, "To the address your mother requested." She pointed to the GPS on her phone. He put up a bit of an argument, which she wasn't entertaining. She told him, "You need to get out now. If this isn't the correct place call your mother and have her order you another ride."

When we discussed the ride, I suggested that if she's ever in another uncomfortable situation like that to pull over. Tell them calmly and coolly, "You have two choices. Knock it the fuck off or get the fuck out." She doesn't mind using profanity and I believe that those words spoken confidently from a woman will end most of that nonsense. I added that if they refuse to get out or comply, she can simply step outside of the vehicle and call the police. I believe they'll respond promptly, especially given that she is a woman.

Overall, she hasn't had any issues as a female driving alone at night. She actually prefers nights, which works out well for us to keep each other company. We swap stories over the phone or when we have the opportunity to meet up for coffee breaks in the middle of the night.

Oddly enough, despite it being the thirteenth, I didn't have any usual rides that night.

CHAPTER 4

THE YEAH YEAH MAN

SATURDAY, APRIL 14, 2018 2:20 A.M.

It was just another late night with me hustling the streets of Las Vegas, chauffeuring people around to earn some extra money. I found myself traveling west on Tropicana, away from the hustle and bustle of the strip. I got pinged toward Tropicana and Jones. As I approached my pick-up spot, I realized I was pulling into an upscale trailer park. There was a young man standing at the entrance of the trailer park in a Smith's grocery store uniform awaiting my arrival. Knowing that there's a Smith's less than a block away - less than a leisurely five-minute walk - I was thinking it would be a quick ride.

The man was incredibly pleasant, well-spoken, and young. He was dressed neatly with his shirt tucked into his trousers. I asked, "Are you Jason?"

He replied, "Yeah, yeah. I'm Jason."

"How are you this evening? Are you on your way to work?"

"Yeah, yeah. I'm going to work. Yeah, yeah. I'm doing good."

Looking at his uniform, I asked the obvious, "Do you work at Smith's?"

"Yeah, yeah. I work at Smith's."

I finally looked at the destination, which said twenty-eight minutes until our arrival. I asked, "Are you going to the store right here on the corner of Trop and Jones?"

He responded, "Yeah, yeah. I work at a different one. Yeah, yeah. It's in Henderson."

It was late in the evening and I might have been delirious, but I started to see a pattern with all of his responses. Every time he began to speak, he started with "yeah, yeah." I shook it off and thought I must have been hearing things.

I asked, "Why do you work so far away when there's a Smith's really close to your house? That seems like it must be inconvenient."

"Yeah, yeah. I have to go a long ways, but they don't have any spaces open for me at this one right now."

At that point, I knew for sure that I really was hearing "yeah, yeah" with each statement. I asked how long he's worked at Smith's.

"Yeah, yeah. I've worked for them for two years," he answered.

I asked if he liked working there.

"Yeah, yeah. I like it."

I took another look at my passenger, since I didn't believe I was in the *Twilight Zone*. I could see the headlines in my mind, "The Rideshare driver serial killer, the 'Yeah, yeah man.'" I refused to believe that he was going to start every single thing he said with "yeah, yeah." I decided that I was going to see if he would change the way that he spoke.

Then I looked at him again. He was clean cut with little wire glasses and looked just like every serial killer I've ever seen. I was thinking I was going to end up on the news the following night as another victim.

I decided to try to encourage more conversation to allow for more involved responses, and therefore hoped to eliminate the "yeah, yeah" pattern. I asked, "So what department do you work in?"

"Yeah, yeah. I'm just kind of all around the store." Hmm...okay.

I asked, "Do you drive?" I was thinking this seemed pretty obvious since he was in the car with me. The answer would likely be no.

"Yeah, yeah. I don't have a car," he said. He was not showing a great deal of emotional reaction to anything. He didn't sound like he really got excited about anything either. All of that just added up to him being the "yeah, yeah serial killer."

I continued my questions, just trying to elicit a response other than yeah, yeah. I was also working at stimulating a conversation with more than these short responses that seemed robotic.

"So you've worked for Smith's for two years. What did you do before that?"

"Yeah, yeah. I was at Albertson's before."

Well, another failed attempt is what I thought. I turned back to him, "So do you plan on trying to move to a different part of the store, or maybe take on more responsibility in the store?"

"Yeah, yeah. I can work anywhere."

"How do they treat you?"

"Yeah, yeah. They treat me good."

"How's the pay?"

"Yeah, yeah. I like the pay."

I was feeling like it was a game of tug-of-war. Did he realize that I was wracking my brain trying to get him to say anything other than "yeah, yeah" and he was just messing with me?

I took a wild guess that he didn't have any children, so I asked, "Do you have any kids?"

"Yeah, yeah. I'm single and don't have any kids." By that point, I realized I was losing the game of tug-of-war and he was completely beating me.

I realized that because my next question began, "Yeah, yeah. Do you like using Rideshare?" I didn't even do it on purpose. I think I had literally been beaten into submission.

He responded, "Yeah, yeah. It's always nice."

I thought, did we just bond? Did we just become the yeah, yeah brothers? As we got closer to his destination, I realized that I was not going to win this battle. I was just hoping that his destination would be his final destination so I wouldn't have to take him all the way back home. The Smith's we were going to was not even open for business at that hour.

It was really dark in the parking lot. There were no cars and no one was around. It may have been in my head, but it didn't even seem like any of the lights worked. My mind took off on its own, recalling every single horror film I had ever seen and every news story I could think of that involved some kind of horrific murder. I suddenly wondered if this man lured me here under the guise of him going to work, knowing no one else would be here, just to kill me, rob me, and take off with my car. Or maybe he would just take me into the freezer in the back of the store and torture me, then grind up my body and put it out with the high fat beef. Many serial killers that I've read about don't seem to do it for the money, but just for the thrill of it. Those who do it for the money are even referred to as hitmen instead of serial killers. I suppose when you do something for profit you are a professional, which typically comes with more esteem.

I snapped back to the possibility of him killing me. What would my kids do? Who would take care of my little ones? Would Rideshare alert anyone if my trip wasn't completed? Or if I somehow just stopped responding to the app? Could this really be the last moments of my life?

My mind was still going down this dark, twisty road when I realized he had gotten out of my vehicle and left me to torture myself with my fearful thoughts. I'm a big guy. I shouldn't be concerned with another man overpowering me to torture me. I shook my head and proceeded on to the next passenger.

CHAPTER 5
THE *REAL* NASA
WEDNESDAY, APRIL 25, 2018 12:30 P.M.

I actually had a very pleasant evening with Veronica last night. She stopped calling all of the time and went back to the desired conversations and interactions that we used to have. I didn't even try to kid myself into thinking that her obsessive behavior was a fluke, but I figured I could at least enjoy her while her behavior fit in with what I was open to experiencing. We were incredibly compatible physically, and I was stimulated by thought and intellect. I just didn't have any desire for some sort of relationship beyond platonic and sexual. Having that sexual release the night before helped me get my day started with a little pep in my step.

I picked up a woman from a dispensary on Sunset and Green Valley Parkway, which happens to be a really nice, prestigious neighborhood. She appeared to be in her mid-fifties and looked as though she had lived a rather difficult life, or at least battled with some serious habits. She had the loose, saggy skin of someone who's been smoking her whole life and the skin was shriveled up around her mouth and eyes. Her teeth, at least the ones she had left, appeared to be in very bad shape. She was incredibly slim and picking at the sores and scabs all over her arms. The sight of her made me shiver.

I confirmed her name and destination near Tropicana and Boulder Highway, which was about fifteen minutes away if we didn't encounter construction or unusually heavy traffic for that time of day. We started the small talk and chatter, and she seemed to twitch and have some sort of a tic in her face as she processed my words and spoke her own.

I pretended I didn't notice it. Driving for the previous month or so had allowed me to strengthen my patience and understanding, as I'd encountered several people from different walks of life and some with severe tics. This, in addition to working in North Town for over twenty-five years, had exposed me to nearly every kind of personality you could imagine.

One man made a horrendous noise or nervous laugh after each sentence. I don't even know how to begin to describe it properly, but it sounded something like a horse being slaughtered by a giraffe with both of them expelling an ear-piercing, horrendous noise simultaneously.

A year or so ago, marijuana became legal in the state of Nevada. Since then, we got several trips going to the dispensaries for tourists who were happy to legally partake, and locals who had incorporated the visits into their regular routines. I always say that Vegas is a great city to live in (or visit), as long as you at least have *some* control over your vices. You can literally get *anything* you want here, any time of the day or night, relatively quickly and effortlessly. I mean anything. Drugs, sex, gaming, alcohol, food, or anything else you can possibly imagine along with the things that you wouldn't even begin to conceive.

She began to commend me on the good vibes coming in the ride. I wasn't sure how to respond or take that, so I asked her, "Have you had bad vibes coming from previous rides?"

She responded, "Sometimes. Not all of the drivers are positive and uplifting. Some of them get really weirded out or bothered by some of the comments I've made."

I told her, "I can handle any kind of conversation because I'm very open-minded."

She started to explain, "I know about the *real* NASA, because that's where my girlfriend worked, behind the scenes NASA, not the NASA that the public sees. Do you know about that?"

"Please do continue to share. I cannot say that I'm familiar with it."

She took the stance that we were discussing something serious and taboo, like assassinating the president. She said, "Well, not everybody is ready to hear this. And I'm not sure if you can handle it, because this is really heavy." Her eyes were bulging so big and wide, like they were about to pop out of her head.

My facial expression didn't change, and I showed no emotional reaction to her statement. She continued, "You can find proof of it on the internet," with great agitation and hostility. "There's pictures! Pictures that people have caught of planes frozen and glitching, just like in *The Matrix*. When the planes glitch, they're frozen in a single spot and don't really move. As a matter of fact, you can look it up and there's a video that shows this. People have recorded video for up to five minutes where a plane is not moving. It's not flying, it's not hovering. It's not a spaceship or helicopter, but an actual passenger airplane that people have claimed to be on. I know three people that have been on one of these planes. But, besides that, my girlfriend worked at the real NASA and would tell me about all of the things that they don't want us to know."

After she said that, she pulled out her phone to attempt to show me one of the videos. While I was still driving, mind you. I didn't dare give her the inclination that I wasn't looking at the video and certainly didn't remind her that it probably wasn't the safest thing to do while actively driving. She was trying to show me this video from the backseat.

I made eye contact with her phone, but for all I could tell she could have zoomed in on an ant climbing across a picnic blanket. It was incredibly blurry and nothing in the picture was distinct enough for me to make heads or tails of it. As the story progressed, her emotional state became increasingly erratic, so I did not dare question or challenge or show any doubt whatsoever to the picture that she was showing me.

Just then, when I wasn't sure what to say, I was saved by the bell. Her phone rang. It just happened to be her girlfriend, who used to work for NASA. The *real* NASA.

It's really difficult in these situations to refrain from mocking these passengers, at least in my own head. It is the entertainment that helps me get through some of the more difficult and challenging rides. I really do think that she believed everything that she was telling me. As the story went on, however, the details and evidence led me in the opposite direction.

Her girlfriend's voice, which I could clearly hear even though the phone was not on speaker, sounded like a chain smoker who hasn't left the couch (or a cigarette) in over twenty years. She definitely was not well-spoken or articulate enough to get into NASA from what I know, especially the *real* NASA.

The two women went back and forth for several minutes, which seemed to take the focus off of her sharing about the real NASA and the matrix that we are all stuck in. The nature of their conversation was about the edibles and purchased items from the dispensary. I thought that talking about weed and the products that go along with it gave people happy, relaxing thoughts and conversations. Her conversation seemed to get her more agitated.

When she got off the phone, she began to tell me about all of the things that were wrong with her girlfriend, health-wise. She went on to explain that her girlfriend was part of the original ten with NASA. She said it was the ten families that they did "things" to. But these families were also privileged to know about the real NASA and the matrix we live in.

I wondered how we got back to this subject. I was under the impression that the phone call with the girlfriend diverted us from this topic.

Then she asked me, "You've heard about the NASA Ten, right?"

"I can't say that I'm familiar with that," I replied.

She said, "Wooooo. That's really spooky stuff. And anyone that knows about it isn't safe."

I said, "I don't wish to put myself in danger, but if you want to share I'll listen," just as we were pulling into her complex.

I figured that she could not possibly share enough details during the remainder of this trip because the complex is not that big. The multiplex that I took her to was formerly known as the Budget Suites. They are all-inclusive daily, weekly, or monthly rentals that don't require a great deal of verification or identification. This attracts all different walks of life, and typically the less desirable ones. They are commonly filled with drug addicts, prostitutes, people on the run, and criminals of all other sorts. This further took away from the credibility of her story, at least in my mind. I thought that if you're so privileged to know about the inner workings of NASA, you'd be in a much more prestigious location or facility.

She guided me to her unit and got out, tilting her face up towards the sky, squinting and twitching. I avoided making eye contact to discourage further conversation and began to turn around to get out of there expeditiously.

That was definitely a ride to share with Alyssa, but I received a phone call that distracted me from calling her. It was another friend, Adam.

Time and time again, I sit back and realize that I am incredibly lonely. I mean, I have my kids, my *dependents*, but I don't have anything like a companion. I'm gone all day, so having a dog is completely out of the question. I really don't see the purpose in reptiles. They're kind of creepy with their looks, and I certainly didn't want a venomous pet. I'd hate for something to happen to one of my children. The thought of a girlfriend or dating seems so distant and absurd to me, especially with my time commitments. What would we do together? She could watch me sleep, since that's all the time I would be able to really give her.

I ran into a good friend of mine, Adam, a few weeks ago. He began to tell me about his new fish tank that he acquired. I said, "Fish tank? Like, you have a goldfish?"

He laughed. "No. I feed my fish goldfish."

I realized that my experience with fish and understanding of them was pretty narrow. I was taught to fish when I was a kid but did not find very much enjoyment in it. I always felt bad for the fish, watching them squirm with the hook going through their mouths.

As I was asking about his fish tank, he pulled out some pictures. I didn't realize that you could have such beautiful fish with an amazing background in your home. He began to explain, "Each of the fish has their own personalities. They're great to watch. The best part is that their whole world is self-contained, so they require less maintenance and attention than a hamster or a cat."

I guess he saw the look of wonder in my eyes. His next comment was to suggest that I get some fish. I said, "I'm far too busy for that. I don't have time to try to squeeze in cleaning fish bowls."

He said, "If you get the right size tank and setup, you might have to clean it once every six months."

In my ignorance, I asked, "What do you do with them? Do you pet them?"

He laughed at me, again. He said, "No. You never touch them. The movement, sound, and the sight of the water are very calming. It might even help you relax a little."

In a very dismissing manner, I said, "I'll think about it." I excused myself from the conversation.

Here we are a few weeks later and the same friend is on my phone and adamant about meeting for lunch. I reluctantly agreed, even though I knew deep down that I should be working. I'm glad I went. We caught up and enjoyed a nice lunch.

He brought up the fish tank again.

I said, "I'm still thinking about it. I'm not sure if I'm ready to take that on." I didn't want to admit that I still wasn't sure I could actually keep them alive, not to mention how broke I was. How could I take on anything else that *costs* me?

He said, "Well, come look at something with me."

Ironically enough, the restaurant we were at was right across from Trop Aquarium, so we went inside. I found the selection and variety of fish to be mind blowing. Some of these fish were the size of my head. Might I remind you, I have a very large head. They come in all kinds of colors, and surprisingly they all had a distinctively different look to them.

As I walked down each aisle, the fish kept getting more and more interesting. I couldn't resist the temptation to look at the prices. They had a sword fish that was the length of my forearm for only seventy-five dollars. I've always thought those fish were really cool looking. Before I could get carried away with the thought of really doing this, I thought about the tanks and all of the other things I'd need; these tanks must cost thousands of dollars

Adam found me wandering the aisles. He asked, "What do you think?"

I couldn't even hold back my excitement. I responded like a kid in a toy store. "They're great! I can't believe there are so many different kinds of fish. I knew about catfish and bass and trout. But I don't even see any of those. There's no way I'd be in a position to get one of these expensive tanks and have a setup like this."

He said, "What if there was a way? Would you be interested?"

"Interested? No, I would love that. But I don't want to get my hopes up."

He told me, "I'm going to make a few calls. I'll get back to you later."

I thanked him for lunch, and for introducing me to the fish, as we parted ways.

A few days later, Adam called. He said, "I have a friend who's getting rid of his setup. He'd like to give it to you."

I asked, "Give?"

He said, "Well, he's selling it. But I'd like to buy it for you."

I quickly said, "I can't let you do that. It's too much."

Adam dismissed my rebuttal quickly. "He's not asking for much. And I believe that you would really enjoy it and give the fish a good home. I'd like to see that. You've done a lot for me, so I'd like to do something nice for you."

I reluctantly agreed to take the fish tank. We arranged for me to go pick it up on his next day off.

When I arrived, I was pleasantly surprised to see that the man was giving up several large, beautiful fish with the tank. I spent the rest of the afternoon setting up my own fish tank, with Adam's help of course, and forgoing work. That night, I got the best sleep that I had gotten in a very long time. I'm not typically easily persuaded by others, but I was glad Adam was persistent about this fish tank. Life seemed to be finally looking up.

CHAPTER 6

BIG, BEEF BURRITO

SATURDAY, APRIL 28, 2018 4:00 A.M.

I found myself doing a pick-up at the fruit loop, which is the area that most of the homosexual nightclubs are concentrated in. I picked up four passengers, one girl and three guys. The girl may have been the only other one in the car that was heterosexual, besides me. She was also the most masculine out of the bunch. When they got in, they were full of energy and their hands were full because they had just made a purchase from the taco truck outside of the club.

As they settled into my car, they were still going back and forth with their discussion about their night in the club, talking about dancing, gyrating, and things of that sort. Then one of the gentlemen decided to invite me into the conversation.

He began, "I'd like to apologize for making your car smell." He must have realized that the odor from his food container could be offensive to a person who is not eating. "Would you like some of my *big beef* burrito?" he asked, with a great deal of emphasis on the big beef.

I told him, "No, I'll pass. But thank you."

He said, "Well, if you don't want some of my *big beef* burrito, I'll gladly buy you your own *big beef* burrito if you want to go back."

The gentleman who was sitting in the front seat was flipping from side to side so he could address the people in the back seat. When he wanted to speak to the person directly behind him, he swung to his right to speak to him over his right shoulder. Then, when he wanted to address the person in the middle or to the left of them, he flipped around to the left side, but in a very exaggerated manner.

I tried to change the subject by addressing that gentleman. I asked, "How are you doing that without getting dizzy?" He kept flipping from side to side so fast that it almost made me dizzy and nauseous.

Immediately, the gentleman in the back who kept offering me his big beef burrito, which by the way, I don't believe he was referring to his actual food, interjected. "We're fine, we've been dancing and twerking all night. Do you know how to twerk, Scott?" Of course, he said twerk and my name with an emphasis, so it sounded like ttwweeeerkkkkuuuhhh and Sssscotttuh.

I responded, "I do not know how to twerk. I believe I'm a little bit too old for that."

He said, "You're never too old! I can gladly teach you how to twerk." I suppose he realized that conversation was going nowhere by the look on my face or my body posture. He went back to offering me some of his big beef burrito.

With four passengers in the car, one of whom was constantly speaking to me and offering me his big beef burrito over and over, I began to get very uncomfortable. I figured that one way to shut the conversation down was to let him know that I'm a vegetarian; thus, I do not enjoy beef.

It had quite the opposite effect. He began to get more aggressive with saying big beef burrito. He told me, "It's such a shame that you don't get the opportunity to enjoy a *big beef* burrito. I could not imagine living my life without enjoying *big beef* burritos."

I think after I said that I was a vegetarian he said big beef burrito more times than before, and no one else in the car seemed to have a problem with this gentleman offering me his big beef burrito. You would have thought that this ride took over an hour, at least it felt like it to me. In actuality, it was less than two miles and less than seven minutes.

It was the longest seven minutes of my life. I've never felt so dirty and violated as I did by his thoughts. I could only imagine what he was doing to me in his mind. On second thought, I'd rather not.

Upon exiting the vehicle, the gentleman extended an invitation for me to join them up in their room at the Excalibur. He said he was still willing to share his big beef burrito, with a smile and such a nice tone. Then he licked his lips slowly while looking me up and down.

I respectfully declined, though I did not share with him how much that made my skin crawl. I felt like I needed a shower, or an acid bath. I maintained my professional composure, as I'm concerned with my ratings and finances and need this gig to pay the car note I just took on.

I called Alyssa to share the experience with her and ask if this is completely abnormal or if this sort of behavior is common for women to encounter. She laughed so hard she was snorting and crying. She couldn't even breathe to get a full sentence out in response. I wasn't sure if she caught something that I missed or if I should feel humiliated for sharing.

She said, "For me, and most of the women that I know, that wouldn't even be out of the ordinary. Honestly, I get hit on several times per night. Most guys think that's okay. I just shrug it off." She started laughing again, then added, "Welcome to being a woman, Scott!"

I tried to take it a little less seriously and personally, but it still irked me. I told her, "I really feel sorry for you women and all that you endure. That conversation was completely out of line. I don't get how a grown man can think that's okay when his advances are clearly unwanted."

Up until this point, I'd never had anything so direct when it comes to homosexual activity, only mild insinuations. I'd had men ask if I was seeing anyone, to which I've replied yes, I'm not interested, or I don't share your way of life, depending on the situation. I've always been respectful, but it's not my get down. I've had men discuss their significant others, spats with their lovers, and things of that nature.

I even had a gentleman tell me it was his birthday and sing opera to me - Ophelia if I remember correctly - and tell me (repeatedly) that he just needed some kakkah (his exaggerated version of the word cake). I told him cake usually doesn't go well with liquor. He looked me up and down, licked his lips exaggeratedly and said "no, *kakkah*" (I later learned cake is sometimes used to refer to booty). He also asked me what my opinion was of his rendition, looking for a thorough critique. I'm not sure what about me made him think that I was familiar with opera, but I responded, "Sounds good to me." He respectfully backed down when I changed the subject.

I'm slightly uncomfortable in situations like that because I honestly don't know how I'd react if a man touched me inappropriately. Prior to Rideshare, I hadn't really participated in any conversations regarding homosexuality. I'd excuse myself or end the conversation. I was starting to wonder if any heterosexual people used Rideshare. I'm big on personal space and do not welcome being touched without an invitation anyway. I do respect free will and encourage all to be themselves, as long as I'm not infringed upon because, at the end of the day, we all have our own lives to live.

CHAPTER 7
BACKWARDS THURSDAYS
THURSDAY, MAY 3, 2018 11:45 A.M.

Thursdays are my long days. I get up to get my youngest kids off to school, drive, work at the shop, then drive Rideshare some more until I'm so exhausted that it's just not safe anymore. I started the morning with a fairly fun ride, which helped set the tone for my day.

I picked up two couples from the Golden Nugget downtown, which is in the Fremont District, or "old Vegas."

When I pulled up, they looked a little unsure and fidgety. I rolled down the window and asked, "Ride for Abraham?"

One of the men hesitated, looked down at his phone, and said, "Yes. Are you Scott?"

I said, "Yes," thinking obviously. They have my name, a photograph of me and my car, and the license plate number.

They slowly opened the door and climbed in, still

displaying a great deal of hesitation.

I began by asking, "How's the day treating you guys?"

One of the gentlemen said, "We're fine." After a pause and glances amongst themselves, he added, "But are you okay?" with a strange tone in his voice.

I told them, "All is well with me." They continued to look at each other, seeming to be a bit puzzled. Then I asked, "What brings you guys to Vegas?" I was just trying to get to a normal state of conversation.

I got the short, abrupt answer of, "Vacation."

I asked a few more general, generic questions as I do with most of my rides. But each response that I got was equally as short and abrupt as the first. I began to wonder if they had a chip on their shoulder or if there was some sort of issue with the ride.

My rule of thumb is typically three questions. I take it as a hint that the passengers just don't want to converse with me if their answers are short and dry or they aren't too into the conversation. Without being pushy, I allowed an awkward silence to set in.

After driving a few more blocks, one of the gentlemen asked me, "Does everyone drive backwards in Las Vegas?" I can honestly say that was the first time I had ever heard that question. I usually don't get caught off guard with passenger's questions, especially about the city.

From his tone, I couldn't tell if he was being funny or if there was a real issue. I began to replay our interactions from when they first got into my vehicle to try to figure out what he meant or what he was implying. I hadn't seen anyone driving backwards and their unusual behavior seemed to insinuate that the issue was with me.

The best response I could come up with was, "Backwards?" with a questioning tone.

He replied, "We were watching you drive to us to pick us up. It seemed odd because your car was moving backwards on the app."

I was still unsure as to whether or not that was just his humor, or if he was possibly new to Rideshare and unaware of the kinks and glitches that can come up with the app and service. Of course, he could have just been irritable and wanted to take it out on the driver, whom he'll likely never see again.

At that point, what did I have to lose? I said, "We always drive backwards on Thursdays. It's almost a state law. I'm sure the police are just too busy right now to come down here and address all of these folks who aren't driving backwards." I held my breath because I wasn't sure how he'd respond, but I knew that I really wasn't in the position to get another bad rating or have another complaint. I couldn't afford to get kicked off of the Rideshare platform.

The entire group started to laugh. That response relieved a lot of pressure. I cleaned it up by explaining, "The service and the app is constantly evolving. There are a lot of hang ups as they continuously try to improve the service. For example, I'll be driving down a straight road and the GPS will suddenly flip the map upside down and tell me to make a U-turn. It gets really hectic and crazy, especially in areas like this. I believe it's due to the high demand and influx of requests for Rideshare all at once."

One of the other passengers responded, "That's such a relief! We thought it was a little bit early for you to be drunk."

I told her, "Fortunately, there is no last call out here. So alcoholism can begin and end at any hour. Personally, I make it a rule of thumb to have no whiskey before lunch." There was an awkward pause. Then everyone in the car broke out into another fit of laughter.

The ride progressed with more cheeky humor and lightheartedness. As we were rapidly approaching their destination, the couples shared with me how much they loved our city and wished they could come out here more frequently. They talked about how each time they have come how new and exciting it is, and how much has changed since their last visit. Although Vegas does not have any preserved or historical district, we compromise by having a face lift every few months. There is always a new attraction or something fresh and exciting to see, even if you're not addicted to the slot machines and gambling.

As I pulled into Boca Park to let them enjoy their lunch, I suddenly had an idea and stopped abruptly. I told them, "It's not too late for you to get the full experience of backwards Thursdays. So I can drive the rest of the way backwards if you'd like."

We all got a good laugh as we pulled up to the restaurant. I was so relieved that the ride that began with me so unsure of how the passengers were responding to me ended up with such a fun and lighthearted exchange. This reminded me of how grateful I am for the positive experiences and really cool people I have been exposed to while doing Rideshare.

That ride was one of the many that made me laugh and enjoy driving. It really started my day off on a good note; however, I was met with some rather unpleasant news when I got to the shop.

My phone rang. The number wasn't saved but looked vaguely familiar. I answered. "Hello?"

"This is Miss Franklin, with the D.A.'s office. Is this Mr. Benson?"

"Yes, ma'am. How can I help you?"

She explained, "I'm calling in regards to a request in the case involving your children."

That confused me. I asked, "are you sure you have the right person? Because I have a court order from Family Court, so I didn't think I'd be hearing from you guys again."

She verified my name, the children's names, and their mother's name.

Baffled, I told her, "I was under the impression that our case was closed and we didn't have any issues, so why am I being contacted?"

"It states here that the mother is requesting an adjustment and is asking us to review the case."

Again, I repeated, "I do have a Family Court order that states that we do not have any support either way, so I don't understand what this is in regards to."

Miss Franklin reminded me that either parent can request a review at any time, even if you do have a court order.

I said, "Okay. So what exactly are we addressing here?"

In a hostile tone, she stated, "It's an order for support that has come across my desk."

I told her, "with all due respect, I am not trying to be confrontational. I do understand that you're just doing your job, and I would like to assist with that. If I may be a little more forward, my children's mother has not really been involved very much since the implementation of our court order, so this is catching me by surprise. She is actually suffering from different mental ailments, and I'm honestly not sure if she's actually in a position of being able to know what's best for our children. The entire time I've been co-parenting with her parents, not her."

Miss Franklin then advised me to type up what I had just explained to her and submit that to the D.A.'s office as my response. She gave me her email address. She added, "This way, I can add your response to your file while the case is under review."

I asked, "Is there anything else that I can do to assist with this whole situation, besides typing up that letter?"

"Just check your mail. You'll be receiving several correspondences from us."

I was a little beside myself after that phone call, so I reached out to the children's mother.

Once she answered the phone, I asked, "Is there an issue? In what way do the children need support that I am not providing?"

She abruptly hung up and continued the conversation via text, stating that she was on the phone with the D.A.'s office. I found that to be a bit coincidental; nonetheless, I continued with the conversation over texts. Her wording was strange, and she was implying that she was somehow coaxed into the custodial arrangement, which we actually sat down and filled out together.

I asked her what the difference was now, and what had changed. She said I hadn't provided proper daycare.

There was nothing but pure irritation and frustration going through me. I took a few deep breaths, trying to pull myself together. In my mind, I thought, how raggedy can you be? How pathetic is this whole situation, since she's the one who hasn't even been around for the past two years? How would she even know what type of daycare has or hasn't been provided? The last time we even had a conversation about our children she was begging me not to take them away since she was in a mental facility.

Our situation is definitely not typical. I have my children with me at the shop after school Monday through Wednesday. Their grandparents pick them up Thursday, then I get them again Sunday. I try to keep our routine as normal as possible, but it can be difficult to juggle all of it. I take time from the store for every school event, field trip, and any other special event that comes up. I'm present for *everything*. So how could I not be providing adequate daycare?

Somehow, for some reason, this was just another silly game she wanted to play. I decided I would do my best not to allow this game to affect what I had going on in my life, or my children's. I knew in my heart this is all about money and she was looking at my children as though they are an ATM. She was trying to take advantage of the court system favoring the mother and always assuming the father is a deadbeat. I also believed that she was trying to provoke me into saying something that would hurt my case or give her just cause to take further legal action. Because of this, I contained all of the rage I felt inside of me and respectfully ended the conversation. Inside, I was thinking, man, I really hate this fucking bitch.

CHAPTER 8

THE BREAKUP

SUNDAY, MAY 13, 2018 12:15 A.M.

I picked up a couple outside of Caesars Palace. They were playing tourists after an incredibly expensive dinner at Gordon Ramsey's Hell's Kitchen. I'm always curious to hear one's opinion about the different restaurants and attractions around the city. I file the information in my memory bank in case a future passenger asks about the establishment or wants recommendations. It also helps to offset the uncomfortable situation where we sit in a vehicle with complete strangers in dead silence.

When they first got in, they seemed to be in the middle of a rather heated discussion. In situations like this, it's always tough to tell if I should intervene, talk, try to change the subject, or simply drive as though I'm not in the car with them. Being that they were strangers to me, I wasn't sure if that was how they normally interact together, or if there was a problem.

Even the fun, happy people can have me

questioning myself, because I've offered little jokes or conversations that didn't go over too well. This can add a lot of pressure on a man who is simply trying to make a living to support his family. If my ratings drop, I won't be allowed to drive Rideshare anymore. This really stresses me out sometimes. Alyssa and I talked about these things, but I didn't share everything that I was thinking. I mean, how could I? I'm supposed to be a man. Men are never supposed to second-guess themselves but are always to appear to be completely confident and in control.

At times, I hear Alyssa struggling with directions or running over curbs or making other mistakes, and her passengers just laugh it off when she apologizes. When I make a mistake like that, I get dirty looks or comments and they act like I'm beneath them. I think that women have it easier than men when dealing with other people and being allowed to make mistakes. They actually go to comfort her, whereas they go to scold and belittle me. What a blessing it must be to be born with boobs.

The gentleman, Chris, ordered the ride. He cut off the woman with him and addressed me, asking how my night has been going. That snapped me back into the present moment. I answered, asked about theirs, and the small talk ensued.

As I was going through my normal questions and small talk, I got a weird vibe that things didn't seem happy with this couple, at all. I let my conversation trail off and they resumed talking among themselves, so I just sat back and concentrated on the drive. Obviously, I can't help but hear the conversation taking place a foot behind my head, but I also know how to stay in my lane and respectfully stay out of others. My only rules, if we can call them that, are do not disrespect me and do not disrespect my car.

She was very animated. Even though she was sitting directly behind me, she was leaning in towards him and I could see her hand movement and body language, on top of hearing the pleading tone in her voice. She was throwing her hands up, gesturing that she was desperate and almost begging.

He said, "No, I told you I don't get down like that. I don't like that behavior, and I don't choose to be around it. You knew that."

She said, "But, I wasn't really that bad. I thought we were okay. I thought we were having a good conversation and a good time."

From the conversation, I gathered that they had dinner with the gentleman's brother and the brother's wife.

He said, "I told you, I don't do loud. I don't do ghetto. I don't do messy. You were all of that, and I'm done."

She started crying. "But, Chris," she sniffled, "she brought up the situation with Cheryl. I didn't bring it up."

I could see him out of the corner of the rearview mirror. He just turned his head to stare out the window. He didn't flinch or blink, as she continued.

"Chris, don't do this. I love you. I didn't start it, and

I didn't want to be rude when she brought it up. I just wanted them to like me."

Apparently, she had just recently been introduced to his family. She knew some of the same people as the sister-in-law. Chris didn't really care for the sister-in-law's behavior. He had warned her, but she thought he was playing.

That was my first Rideshare breakup. I wasn't sure if I should offer the young woman a tissue, or just turn up the music. It was slightly uncomfortable for me.

She kept sniffling, saying his name, and pleading for another chance. He just quietly stared out of the window, as though she wasn't even sitting next to him.

Right on time, the song "Love Don't Live Here Anymore" started to play. I thought the timing was impeccable and kind of enjoyed the irony. I made eye contact with Chris in my rearview mirror and he nodded at me as if to say leave it playing, then looked back out the window. She started bawling.

Just as the song was ending, we pulled up to his luxury apartment complex in Southern Highlands, a nice master-planned community in the southwest. He handed me a tip, told me to have a nice evening, and walked off toward his apartment. It was as if she became a ghost in the middle of the ride and he no longer saw her or acknowledged her presence.

She fumbled out of my car, still balling her eyes out and calling his name.

I didn't have much time to feel bad for the young lady, as my phone dinged for me to go pick up the next passenger. My mind did wander during the next few minutes. I thought about how many relationships may have ended, or even started, in the back of a Rideshare vehicle?

CHAPTER 9
THE EDC UNICORN
FRIDAY, MAY 18, 2018 1:00 P.M.

This weekend is EDC (Electric Daisy Carnival), which is a huge techno dance music festival that has taken place every year in Vegas since 2011. The music is commonly referred to as EDM (Electronic Dance Music). Think Woodstock, only a modern-day rave. The more colorful and unique your attire is, the better. Every single participant that I came into contact with was friendly, peaceful, and all about love...and being high. Maybe a more apt description is Woodstock on steroids.

I'm not into house, techno, or dance music whatsoever; however, I am intrigued and think the festival would be a delightful place to be, just for the energy. On the flip side, there is a lot of extracurricular stimulation and it seems most (if not all) participants partake in it.

This is one of the busiest weekends of the year. It used to take place in June, which was perfect for many partygoers because school is out. This year the event was moved up to May due to the extreme desert heat, which had contributed to deaths in prior years. Many of the popular stimulants taken during the rave actually heat up the body. That, combined with excessive heat, dancing, alcohol, and very limited water, serve as a recipe for disaster. They do have water stations and have done everything they can to promote safety, but many people don't realize their body has had enough until it's too late. Younger crowds don't typically worry about drinking water or staying hydrated, especially when they're partying.

The event was set up at the Las Vegas Motor Speedway, about ten minutes past the last bit of civilization in North Las Vegas. There are only two ways to get in and out of there, so traffic is something else. If this year was anything like the prior few years, there would be over 135,000 people expected on each of the three days.

I decided to make sure I was available to drive as much as possible that weekend. According to the drivers I'd spoken to, some drivers refused to work this week because of the drugs and traffic. There are also a lot of surges expected since it's all about supply and demand with many people trying to be at the same place at the same time.

I got a ping to pick someone up at the Hyatt Place near the airport. As I was navigating through the crowded parking lot I was scanning the crowd for my passenger. I find that I do that often. I'm looking through the crowds at the people as if I know what my passenger looks like. I always laugh at myself when I realize this. I probably look like a creep to the crowd.

There was a woman in a small, white thong bikini with her skin and face painted blue. I don't know if she was trying to take on the Smurfette character or some other new age anime character, but I saw her as Smurfette. I was hoping and praying she wasn't my passenger. I didn't know if that blue body paint or whatever it was would stain my seats. How would that work? I wouldn't be able to pick up anyone else. I would lose out on the money for the day because I'd have to have my car detailed. Would they even pay me enough to get it cleaned properly? How did she even get her entire body that consistent shade of blue? As I slowly rolled past her, she didn't even look in my direction, so I was safe on that mess.

I'm not sure what some of these people were thinking when they got dressed and actually got the courage to go outside looking like that. Were they high before they even got dressed? How did they even put these outfits together? I was thinking maybe they just rolled around in honey and ran through a costume shop or their closet to see what would stick. A good chunk of them didn't even seem to match, though a lot of the groups seemed to have some kind of theme to them. Maybe they bought one Halloween costume and split it up among seven people? The original costume didn't appear to be the right size, though. Maybe they were buying children's costumes. I'm not sure how these people were being permitted to walk around the city like that? Wouldn't it be considered indecent exposure? Or is it just being overlooked because of how much money the festival brings? That doesn't make sense though because from what I've heard, most of these people shack up and barely spend any money on food even. I believe fast food is their primary source of nutrition while in Vegas. I didn't get the impression that many of them spend very much money while they're here, other than their festival tickets.

I shook my head and continued inching my way through the crowd. I feasted my eyes upon a beauty queen reject. She was slender, but badly built. Not toned at all. Skinny doesn't always mean attractive. Her face looked worn like she had some years on her, though I got the impression that she was young. She was wearing a sash like the beauty queens wear. I'm not sure what was holding it together or keeping it in place. When I say she was wearing a sash, I should mention there were no clothes under it. Somehow it wrapped around to cover parts of her. A large, silver star-shaped pasty covered her exposed breast and a matching silver thong covered her lady parts. I was so caught up on what she wasn't wearing that I didn't even bother reading the sash. She was also covered in glitter. Much like Smurfette, I was hoping she wasn't my next passenger. All I needed was glitter all over my seats. That stuff never comes out. My younger daughter loves crafts with glitter and gets it everywhere, causing me to look like I spend all of my spare time in strip clubs.

Next up, in proper character fashion, was

something I'd like to refer to as Big Bird. It looked like he glued giant yellow feathers on himself, and then stood in front of a fan so most of them blew off. They only covered patches of his body, in no distinguishable pattern. Thankfully his manhood and ass were covered. I wouldn't even want to see all of that. He was not a small nor fit man. I definitely didn't want him to be my next passenger. What if the feathers came off in my car? Then I'd have a mess and another man's ass to look at. No thank you.

My ride ended up being two young men who were going to one of the shuttle stops. To reduce traffic, there are several tour buses that go to the Speedway from a few different points around the strip. These passes sold out this year, so many people had to find other ways out to the festivities, which was a good thing for me.

One of the men was dressed in hot pink shorts and a tie dye tank top with a smiling sun on it. This wasn't so peculiar, especially since I've seen plenty of women walking around in neon-colored fishnets, a clashing neon-colored tutu, skimpy tops, and furry, clunky boots.

The other man, however, had the most unique (and disturbing) costume I had seen so far. He was sitting on my seat in nothing but a jockstrap and unicorn headband. I'm not sure if he really thought it was a cute outfit or if he was too high to realize he wasn't wearing *any* clothes! If you're unfamiliar with the term "jockstrap," it's also known as an athlete's cup. It includes a hard shell that is supposed to cover (and protect) a man's "royal jewels" but doesn't cover much else. This man had his bare booty cheeks on my backseat. I was so grateful he sat back there, and not right next to me.

I was tempted to ask where he found the unicorn headband (for my daughter), but I really didn't want to invoke a conversation that might make me uncomfortable. So I didn't say anything. I was just silently grateful that he sat in the back and that it was a short ride.

On second thought, my kids sit back there. What will they be sitting on? There's no telling what was on his ass. I decided to let those thoughts leave me because all it was doing was grossing me out. Besides, there would be plenty of other booties on these seats before my children got back in my car. I made a mental note to get it washed before I pick up the kids, though. I had a feeling it would be a very nice weekend between earnings and entertainment. Let's hope so, anyway. I could use the break.

CHAPTER 10

THE EDC EXPERIENCE

FRIDAY, MAY 18, 2018 11:00 P.M.

I had been enjoying the upbeat, positive vibes of the EDC participants, along with the astonished comments about the scenery for those who were not in town for the festival. I actually went to open the store a little late because the rides were just too good to pass up. If it wasn't for a customer calling me, I might not have made it in at all. I got a little carried away with the surges and back-to-back rides.

My day had been going so well, that it was hard not to look at my app and wish I was out driving instead of working. When there are fewer drivers available than ride requests coming in, the passengers pay a surge price. That means a five-dollar ride may turn into ten dollars without any additional time, miles, or wear and tear on my car. It's not always double; the increase really depends on supply and demand. It's an ingenious business model, and I'm grateful that Alyssa turned me onto it.

I shut down the store an hour early to get back in the streets. My first ride out of North Las Vegas went all the way to the MGM, on the south end of the strip. That was an excellent way to start my night, especially since I had already exceeded my daily goal with the pre-work rides.

My next ride was a shared ride. The first group had three guys. I'm not technically supposed to take more than two in a shared ride. I wasn't sure how to handle the situation and figured it wouldn't hurt since I do have the third-row seat. I explained that they would need to order a regular ride the next time, but I would allow it this time unless we ended up getting more passengers to the point that I needed that third seat to remain legal. In that case, at least one of them would have to get out.

I picked them up at the Excalibur, catty corner to the MGM. The group consisted of three Caucasian males in their early twenties. I believe two of them were a couple. They sat in the middle seat together and huddled up, whispering to each other. The third guy sat up front with me.

We immediately got dinged to pick up another passenger at Harrah's. The two guys in the back decided to move to the third row. The new couple, a black guy and white girl from Ohio, also in their early twenties, sat in the middle row. They all made introductions and everyone seemed happy. That was my first ride going all the way to the event. I knew there would be some traffic, I passed it heading south on the freeway earlier. I figured there would be no worries, since I do make money by the mile and by the minute. Besides, I thought, the traffic couldn't be as bad as others had made it seem, since they do this event and other major events at the speedway every year. I would think they must have the traffic situations handled.

The guys in the back were offering alcohol and drugs to the couple in the middle. They explained that it was their third year attending the festival and it's best to pregame so you arrive ready to party. The couple was brand new to EDC, and chose to partake. I'm not exactly sure what they were doing, as I was focused on driving; besides, the guy in the front seat was talking to me.

I decided to let the young folks do their thing, as long as they weren't smoking or making a mess in my vehicle or being disrespectful to me.

The guy in the front started telling me how he cannot order Rideshare anymore because he was kicked off of the platform. We barely got onto the freeway heading north when we hit the traffic jam. It was standing still, barely moving a few inches every few minutes. As we were just sitting on the freeway, I was half listening to the guy in the front, while being mindful of the passengers in the back of the car. I was listening and watching for anything abnormal so that they didn't leave a mess in my car.

As it clicked that he was saying he was banned from ordering Rideshare, I had to inquire as to why. Especially since he was in my vehicle. From my understanding, it takes a lot for the Rideshare companies to deny service to a passenger. That's their bread and butter. Instead, they'll make it so that any driver and passenger who have issues with each other will never be matched together again. I suppose that works, except that a passenger leaving false negative feedback or making erroneous accusations against a driver should be booted after the first offense so that other drivers don't have to endure the same, in my opinion.

His long, drawn out response regarding his ban on the Rideshare platform didn't make any sense to me. He was talking in circles, and just saying he had a misunderstanding with a driver. This news disturbed me a bit since I have no idea what to expect from these passengers, and they were doing drugs and drinking alcohol in my car. If we got pulled over, I would be the one taking the rap for all of it because it was my car and I was the one driving. That made my nerves bad.

After about an hour and a half, we finally made it to the Cheyenne exit, which was less than ten miles from where we originally got on the freeway. I had to pee, and so did the lone female passenger. We had been listening to techno music, blaring, the entire time. My head needed a break. I was happy to continue the ride, though, because I could see a big payday coming off of that one. I mean, I was already ninety minutes in!

We went inside of a small, local joint called Dotty's. There are several of these bar/casinos all over the valley. They started freaking out because the girl was wearing fishnets and booty shorts and a tiny bikini top. She was so intoxicated she didn't even hear security trying to stop her. They looked at me. I looked at her boyfriend. He told them she just needed to use the restroom.

The bartender spouted off, "We don't have public restrooms. You have to buy something. Is she even old enough to be in here? I need to see IDs for everyone."

I flashed my ID, bought a water, and used the restroom. Roughly ten minutes later, we all reconvened at my car. One of the guys from the backseat, the one in a skirt and heavy eye makeup, was leaning against my car looking like he was about to fall flat on his face. I asked if he needed a minute. His partner said he'll be fine and shoved him back in my car.

We got back on the freeway and proceed to inch our way north. My head was pounding as they kept playing one electronic sound after another. I held my composure though because I might get a huge tip. Besides, I thought, the ride should be well worth it either way.

We finally made it to the speedway exit three and a half hours later, only to find another line in front of us. The girl was behind me hanging out of the window because she thought she might get sick. She wasn't sure what the drugs were doing to her; she was barely functional. Her boyfriend was holding her and telling me that she was fine. The guy with the eye makeup started whining, asking how much further. I explained that we were still a couple of miles out according to the GPS. He said he needed to use the restroom and just wanted to walk the rest of the way. I explained that they could get out, but the app wouldn't let me close out his ride until after the couple's ride was closed out.

He got incredibly frustrated and snapped at me, "Then I guess you'll be paying for my ride!"

I responded, "No, sir. That is not how this works. You are welcome to get out whenever you'd like to, but the app won't let me close your ride until their ride is closed out. I cannot control that."

The girl's boyfriend was asking her if she was okay to walk so that they didn't cause any issues. She was attempting to slur, "Yes," but nothing audible came out. The guy in the front seat was telling his friends to just wait.

Then the girl wanted to walk, the guy in the front seat wanted to get out to pee, and the guys in the back wanted to stay in the car. This circus went on for the remainder of the two hours it took us to get to the gate.

I was gritting my teeth and my entire body was tense because that ride had taken a serious toll on me. I was concerned about one, or all, of the passengers getting sick in my car, becoming violent toward me, or having some other kind of reaction to the substances they were using. If you're not a fan of dance music, that constant throbbing for over five hours is enough to make you want to cut your ears off and poke your eyeballs out, even though your eyes have nothing to do with the intense throbbing inside of your skull.

I smiled as I hit the "end ride" button on the app, thinking that at least I was making good money to sit there through all of that garbage. I knew I wouldn't be getting a tip at that point, at least not from the three jackasses, so hopefully the ride fare would kick my night off well. It took me roughly five hours to get them safely to the festival.

I checked my earnings, only to see that I made an entire fourteen dollars and fifty-three cents. Are you kidding me? How does that even add up? I thought that there had to be some kind of mistake. There was absolutely no way that could be correct.

I furiously sent an email to the support team requesting an adjustment in my fare. I also called Alyssa to see what her experiences were for the night. She told me that she was on her way home. She had dropped off two carloads and was done with it for the night. She didn't think that the time, frustration, and effort was worth the minimal fare she earned. Every driver that she talked to was on their way home after long wait times, and garbage income.

By the time I reached the gate to leave the grounds, an hour and fifteen minutes later, I received the response email from support telling me that they adjusted my fare. It was now seventeen dollars and eighty-six cents.

I don't think Alyssa, or anyone else for that matter, has ever heard me cuss the way I did just then. I turned my app off and headed home, cursing the entire way. Now I know what it's like when someone leaves a two-cent tip for a waitress. I seriously did not understand how I could sit in all of that traffic, for all of that time, and earn pennies on the hour. I don't even think that covered my gas to get out there in all of that traffic.

On top of all of that, I had to endure the rudeness

and shenanigans of the passengers. I decided that it would be best for me to go home. There was no point in trying to salvage the night, as my mood was foul and definitely not welcoming to any more strangers being in my car with me. I thought, I might just sit out the rest of the weekend. I really couldn't afford it, but I couldn't afford to stroke out because of my blood pressure spiking either. I was *losing* money by working. I thought, fuck this Rideshare stuff; I can't keep doing this.

CHAPTER 11

THE BAG LADY

SATURDAY, MAY 26, 2018 12:45 P.M.

It was a brand new weekend and most of the EDC patrons had made their way home. The city seemed to be back to its own kind of crazy. My Friday night was fairly fruitful, but nothing abnormal to talk about. I did have throwupper number two last night. He was a local. I picked him up outside of MGM and took him home to Southern Highlands, in the southwest.

He asked me to pull over. I obliged. He got out and threw up on the side of the road, then got back in and told me he felt better and we could continue. It wasn't much of an incident, and since he got it all outside, I didn't report him.

I was able to get a couple of hours in today before opening the store. I felt pretty good about last night's earnings and ran until four in the morning, yet still woke up completely rejuvenated at ten.

I did a few rides around the strip as the pools were

open, it was warm outside, and people were pool hopping at the day clubs. I picked up four Asian nursing students at the Cosmopolitan and took them to their hotel, SLS.

All four of them had impeccable makeup, heels, bikinis, and short little see-through dresses, skirts, or shorts on. The one in the front was talking to me about their experiences at the pool parties, saying it was a much-needed break from their nursing finals. The three in the back were laying on each other for support, with the one behind me completely slouched over.

The young lady sitting directly behind me sprang up and said, "I'm not feeling so well. Do you have a bag?"

I told her, "Yes," as I handed her a plastic bag. I added, "If you feel like you're going to be sick, please let me know and I'll pull over." As I spoke, I maneuvered the vehicle over to the right lane so I could try to pull off or turn if she did give me the signal.

Then I heard it; throwupper number three.

She asked, "If I got it all in the bag, are you still going to charge me?"

I just shook my head. "As long as you got it all in the bag, and *take the bag with you,* I won't charge you."

I had to turn my app off to double check the car after they got out. I stayed true to my word and did not report the ride since she did remove all trace of her incident. I decided to just go to the store and open up a little early. Hopefully the night would be better.

I really needed this Rideshare gig to work. I was still a couple of months behind on almost everything and my stomach was constantly in knots. I couldn't talk to anyone about any of this because I'm a man. What am I supposed to do, cry on someone's shoulder? What am I supposed to tell my sons? I had told them their entire lives that they need to be men, suck it up, take care of their responsibilities, and make stuff happen. How could I possibly let any of them know what I was going through?

I also had to fly to Texas the following week to watch my middle child, my oldest little girl, graduate from high school. I couldn't make this trip without a really good weekend with Rideshare. I could never look her in her eyes again if I didn't show up for the most important day of her life so far. How could the words, "I'm proud of you," mean anything at all if I can't even make it out there? I felt like a complete failure and hypocrite.

I tell my kids to make smart financial decisions, but I was a fraud. I had to turn all of this around before they saw it or questioned me. I'd never lied to them, and I wouldn't start now. But, I had let them believe that I'm a far better man than I am. That's the only way I could figure to try to teach them to be better than me. I felt like I was losing it a little. Maybe this was what they refer to as a midlife crisis?

I'd always thought that women who kept journals or diaries were crazy as hell. Now I'm seeing that it can be slightly therapeutic. I mean, seriously, who could I open up to about this? I'd say my closest friend is

Alyssa, but a man doesn't complain about his situation. A man doesn't cry about it. A man just does what a man has to do to take care of his family and make it work.

CHAPTER 12

SUGAR DADDY

SUNDAY, MAY 27, 2018 2:00 A.M.

I had been ping ponged across the city since I closed the shop at ten. It was a relatively quiet day at the shop, which only emphasized my financial concerns. I had been working and doing pretty decent with Rideshare. It's been a great way to redeem my experience from this morning. I was on the phone with Alyssa, as we seemed to be taking turns having passengers.

I picked up a gentleman in North Las Vegas; a local. He was drunk, very jolly, and a little hard to understand between his heavy Spanish accent and inebriated slur. As soon as he got in the vehicle I tried to verify his name to make sure I had the correct passenger. He didn't even respond because he was too busy making a phone call, trying to arrange to get a seat at the poker table at the Cosmopolitan. The destination I saw on the phone was not the Cosmopolitan.

I asked him, "Can you please verify your

destination?" I had already started the ride and was driving toward the strip. As I was talking, I heard Alyssa laughing uncontrollably. She was making comments about me getting another drunken passenger in my ear.

"No, no. I just make another seat. I have seat reservation at property, but I am going Caesar's Palace. That is destination in app." He finished up his phone call.

I began my usual small talk. "How's your evening going?"

"My wife no like gambling. You pick me up at corner because she no like me to go to casino. She think I go to store, so you can not pick me up at my house." Ironically enough, as soon as he explained, his wife called.

He kind of stonewalled her, and just pacified whatever it was that she was saying, asking, or demanding. They hung up, and he turned his attention back to me.

"Pinche wife. I don't know what her problem is. I work and pay bills, and I just like to play. Why she no understand?"

I attempted to sympathize and point out, "Sometimes women just don't like us to gamble."

He said, "Maybe instead of gamble I just go to strip club." My ears perked up. I knew that we get a kickback when we drop someone off at the strip clubs. I haven't been this fortunate yet, but Alyssa had.

I encouraged the thought. "Maybe that's exactly what you need tonight."

He said, "Well, I am already drunk. I have no one to watch out for me." He paused, as if searching his brain for a way to make this work. "Will you come in and hang out?"

At that point, Alyssa was laughing again. She said, "Look at you, making friends."

I was trying not to laugh as I responded to him. I was also trying to figure out what he meant by come in and hang out. I said, "I'd love to, but I have to work because I'm trying to earn money."

He quickly interjected, "I pay for you. And I pay you. Come in and stay with me. Then take me back home. I give you one hundred dollar."

I was adding up the time, and thought that would be fair for the evening, depending on how much time he wanted to hang out there. The only problem was, how much money would I spend having a drink or two, getting a lap dance or two, and hanging out? It would not be a good idea to take the money and spend it, and still be out a night of work.

Before I could respond, he said, "I'll buy drinks. You just come hang out."

I thought, is this guy reading my mind? I weighed my options, thinking about all of the pros and cons of going with him or not. I had planned to work about eight hours, and only had about four hours in. I hadn't really enjoyed myself or let loose since I started driving Rideshare, and it had been a while since I had any attention from a woman. I hadn't been to a strip club in a few years. I really could use a little break from my rigorous routine. The hundred dollar offer really did sound appealing.

Alyssa was laughing again, and I heard her ask, "Wait, what? Did you really just get a sugar daddy before me?"

I graciously accepted his offer. "Sure, I'll come hang out. Which strip club would you like to go to?"

He said, "We go to the Crazy Horse Three."

I said, "Okay," and began to drive in that direction.

At that point, common sense might have been lurking through the fog of alcohol that invaded his brain. He began questioning our deal and my integrity. "Are you really going to stay? You not going to leave me?"

I said, "No. I'll stay the whole time."

"And you take me home?" he asked.

"Yes."

He said, "We no have to stay that long. Just a couple drinks and a couple dances. Then go back home."

I said, "No problem. It sounds fun. I used to have a lot of fun going to strip clubs."

We pulled up to the club and I parked. We were walking towards the door when skepticism set in again. He was nervous and seemed a little unsure. I told him, "Don't worry. You can just pay me when we're done, so then you'll know that I'm not going to leave you."

He said, "Are you sure?"

I said, "Yeah, that's fine. Just please be honest and make sure that you live up to your end of the deal."

I think that gave him a great sense of comfort. At that point, I was the only one with something to lose. I really couldn't afford to spend the night out, even if I was partying and drinking on his dime, because I needed to be working to make money to pay my bills that were still stacking up. I told myself that the worst case scenario was that I'd lose one night of work, but on the other hand I could really use a little break since my schedule had been so demanding the last few months.

Once I was mentally clear and preparing for a fun, relaxing evening we hit a roadblock. I didn't meet the dress code. The bouncer looked down at my very comfortable basketball shorts and informed me that my attire was not permitted in this establishment. I completely forgot about that. Most of the strip clubs in Vegas don't allow basketball shorts. They are extremely practical for driving since they aren't restrictive and I'm sitting in the same position for the better part of seven or eight hours.

I told my passenger, "I'm so sorry. I didn't even think about the dress code."

He said, "Is okay. I'll just go gamble."

I thought, it's okay for you, but not for me. Now I have to work the rest of the night, right after I got into a relaxation mindset. I was checked out mentally and ready to have a drink. Not to mention I was already counting on the hundred-dollar tip that I was sure I would not be getting now.

I asked him where he'd like to go, since he had reservations at two casinos. He chose the Cosmopolitan, so I took him there.

As I dropped him off, still not quite ready to go back

into drive mode, he handed me a forty-dollar cash tip. At least the cloud of this experience had a silver lining. I figured that would be a great head start on what I'd like to make for the evening. Plus, I was being responsible and working instead of spending my time playing around. And, I'd always have this memory of the one and only sugar daddy that I almost had.

My call with Alyssa had cut off during the ride. I tried to call her back, but she sent me to voicemail. That only happens when she has a passenger in the car that can see her phone. Two seconds later, she called me back. I heard drunk giggles and "Hi, Scott!" from what sounded like a car full of women.

Alyssa said, "I was just telling my passengers that you'd tell me to tell them that you love them, and they asked me to call you back." She was laughing.

I told them, "I do love you."

They laughed and said goodnight to Alyssa. She told me about their ride.

Alyssa picked up two pretty young women from a local bar in the far east corner of Henderson. She took them to another bar near Green Valley Ranch casino. During the ride, they started talking about music and concerts. One of the young women said she likes country music. Alyssa told her she didn't have any country in her playlist, as she prefers hip hop and R&B.

The young lady told her, "Play something. If I like it, you'll be rewarded handsomely."

Alyssa had been playing "Cake" by Trey Songz for a few days, which is a lesser known song of his.

The girls squealed with delight and asked, "Trey Songz?"

Alyssa answered, "Yes."

The country fan said, "I've never heard this one before."

The other girl said, "I just seen him in concert! Look," as she showed Alyssa footage that she had recorded on her cellphone. "We were *just* talking about him an hour ago. I love him." She swooned.

As they pulled up to their destination, the country fan handed Alyssa a hundred-dollar bill. She said, "I told you you'd be rewarded nicely if you played something we'd like."

Apparently, that was when I called.

I told Alyssa, "How is it that I was supposed to have a sugar daddy, and you ended up with a sugar mama?" We both laughed.

Although it ended up being a lucrative night for both of us and I was happy for her, I couldn't help but think it was unfair. I could have really used the extra money. I had a lot going on and little kids to support, and she was just going to end up wasting it on one of her pointless endeavors with Mr. Wrong.

CHAPTER 13

THE MASSIVE COMBUSTION

THURSDAY, MAY 31, 2018 1:13 P.M.

This was my last day to drive before I took off for Texas to see my oldest daughter, the middle child, graduate from high school. I was incredibly proud of her and all of her achievements, so I wouldn't have missed this for the world. Of course, I couldn't really afford this trip. I had to make arrangements to get my older boys out there, as well as my mother, grandmother, myself, my younger two kids, and I tried to arrange for my father to go.

I booked all of the travel and the hotel and somehow ended up paying for everyone's hotel rooms, in addition to the airfare for myself and my four children, and rental cars for everyone. I was completely over-extended to begin with, but I would not let any of my children know. It is my duty, after all, to provide for them and set the example that I wish for them to see. I had to take a high interest payday advance loan to get it together, but I wouldn't let them see me sweat.

I'd been working since I dropped off my little ones at school, around 8:30 a.m. I accepted this ride at 1:13 p.m., thinking I'd shut down after this ride to go open the store. Apparently, my nerves and my body had another idea.

I pulled up to a quaint, well-maintained home in an older part of town near downtown. I was waiting for a gentleman to come outside when it hit me. An extreme case of the bubble guts that was not going to wait for me to go anywhere to use the restroom, let alone attempt to complete this ride.

I was walking up to the door to knock when he started to come outside. He said, "Are you okay?"

I didn't realize how pale I was. I was sweating bullets and clenching my stomach, as my insides were grinding against each other and twisting and turning, causing immense pain. "I've never had to do this, and I'm so sorry, but I don't think I can wait. Can I please use your restroom?"

He said, "Of course!" He quickly led me down the small hallway with wood floors and worn throw rugs.

I barely got my pants down in time to sit down and allow the massive combustion between my cheeks before the explosion of all of the sediment released from my bowels. It was one of the worst things I've ever smelled in my life. As I was looking around for spray, matches, a candle, or some kind of air freshener, I saw the fatal detail.

My bowels were still contracting and releasing

whatever bad thing that I ate, and there was absolutely *no* toilet paper. It was a small bathroom, so I opened the cabinet under the sink, but nope, no toilet paper there either. I courtesy flushed and looked around to figure out what I could possibly do.

The only solution that I could come up with was to use my undershirt and wash it out in the sink or tub when I finished. That thought disgusted me, but it seemed to be the best option that I had.

He knocked on the door. "Are you okay?"

"Yes. I'm sorry; I'll be another few minutes." How could I tell this man that, not only did I blow up his bathroom, but I needed to wash my shit out of my shirt in his sink? I was so horrified. I do not like to defecate anywhere other than home, as it gives me anxiety. I have a whole routine and typically need to be naked. My bathroom is set up for my bizarre antics, this one was not.

He said, "I am so very sorry. I realized that I am out of toilet paper and forgot to grab some. I can ride my bike to the store really quick to get some. I am so sorry!"

I just shook my head. I had assaulted this man's bathroom, and *he* was sorry! "I was just going to use my undershirt and wash it out. I am sorry to do this to your house!"

"No, don't ruin your shirt! I'll be right back. It's only a few minutes away."

I was just sitting here, hanging out, with my pants around my ankles and the smelly, sticky, horribleness of human waste hanging onto my booty cheeks

I fiddled with my phone for about ten minutes while waiting for him to get back. He set the toilet paper outside the door and walked away so that I could open the door to retrieve it with a small amount of dignity.

Once I cleaned myself up, I went outside to take him where he needed to go. I felt so bad for wasting his time, making him go to the store, and for defiling his home. I opted to tell the Rideshare company not to charge the man for the ride. It was the least I could do for his help in getting out of my shitty situation.

To make matters worse, I had been dealing with an onslaught of text messages from Veronica all day. She has gone through cycles similar to this, but never this aggressive. It started around five in the morning. I had way too much on my mind to deal with and she was not helping the situation. I had to take the Bluetooth out of my ear because there was a slight beep noise to notify me when I had an incoming text message. Although it was slight, it was happening every couple of seconds. One, five, or even fifty beeps I can handle. But we were going on over four hundred beeps, and it was just *too* much.

It was amazing how such a small, slight tone that most people would ignore becomes a massive, migraine pain that you just can't block out. Even looking at my phone brought a feeling of pure disgust over me. Something as normal as a regular phone call was unbearable because all I could hear was that persistent, annoying beep.

In less than twenty-four hours I was supposed to be

participating in one of the highlights of my entire life. There was no reason for me to be this irritated and frustrated right now. Money was not the best, as usual, but I'd grown accustomed to that. Finances was something that I believed I would stress over for quite some time, maybe even until the day that I die. Something so trivial as money, a piece of paper or a digital number that we put value to, or how little I have of it, wouldn't be able to take away from this burst of pride and happiness I feel. Yet there was a *grown* person causing me this much agitation just twenty-four hours before I went to see my pride and joy walk across the stage and graduate. How did this make sense?

It wouldn't have been so bothersome if she got everything out in one message. But she sends messages to where it just fills up the preview line at the top of my screen, making sure that I have the optimum chance to see everything she wants to say. She must hold the world's record for texting speed. I wish I was exaggerating.

That had been carrying on for several hours. Between the beeps and just imagining what I could do to stop this, getting everything organized to get on this plane, and making sure that I scrounged up every dollar that I could possibly come up with to do something nice for my daughter's graduation, I felt like I was about to snap. What could I do to just make this stop? Then after every hundred or so text messages I was receiving phone calls, which I was sending straight to voicemail.

Finally, I can't take it anymore and I answered the call. With pure irritation, I said, "WHAT?"

There was a dead silence. That was the only response I got. Then she hung up.

What the hell is going on? All of that because she wanted a response? And now I answer, and she doesn't even fucking speak? I didn't get it. It made no sense at all, I thought. Once again, the text messages resumed. They were coming in every second. I started to read a couple that popped up on the drop-down screen as they came in. My frustration grew out of control. I took a deep breath and decided I was going to try a different approach. I replied to her texts with a simple message. "Please stop." I'm not one for begging. I'm fairly certain that I made it clear that I did not wish to speak to her in that moment. I was practically begging for mercy at that point.

A few minutes went by with nothing. The next text message popped up in all caps. "NO. I WILL NOT STOP. YOU'RE NOT GONNA FUCKIN IGNORE ME…" and on and on.

At this rate I would not be able to hold onto my sanity. All that I could do was turn my phone off. So much for working. So much for some extra money. I just wanted to bury my head in the sand and call it a day. I hoped none of my kids needed me. Of course, they know the shop number. But, then again, she did too.

CHAPTER 14

HOME SWEET HOME

MONDAY, JUNE 4, 2018 11:45 P.M.

I had spent the past few days in Texas with all of my children. The trip was so much more than I could afford. I didn't let my kids know it though. We all had a great time, and I was incredibly proud of my daughter. She graduated with honors and scholarships to a Texas university.

Of course, nothing in my life goes as planned. The two younger children and I had an early morning flight back home. We got up at four in the morning and made the drive to the airport. Due to some traffic, we were cutting it close. We dropped off the rental and made our way to the ticketing booth. By the time we got to the front of the line we had fifty-seven minutes to board the plane.

Since I had booked their tickets after mine, they weren't on my travel plan. And because they were minors, we couldn't check them in online or at the kiosk.

The agent took our names and my ticket, and then shook her head slowly as she clicked around on her computer. "I'm sorry, sir. But their seats have been given away because we are less than an hour from takeoff."

I just stood there with a blank look on my face. I realized it wasn't her fault, but I didn't have anything nice or productive to say. I must have looked like a sad, lost puppy. As I stared at her, I noticed pity mixed in with the natural kindness in her azure eyes. I do not appreciate being pitied, but I couldn't even think about that as I processed what she was saying. Her face had a welcoming look to it, as her features were soft, and she had warm wrinkles and lines around her eyes and mouth as though she spent a lot of her time laughing and smiling. Her chestnut brown hair was pulled back in an impeccable bun. She looked like a poster child for the fantasy grandma who always had a hot meal ready for you and cookies in the oven.

She clicked around some more, and then added, "It looks like we can put all three of you on standby. The next available flight isn't until tonight, landing at 11:20 p.m." Her news broke through my thoughts.

I sighed. "Can you please go ahead and put us on that flight?"

I reserved another car on my phone while she worked her magic. She must have really felt for me because she said, "I'm going to go ahead and waive all of the fees. It looks like you don't need any additional stress today."

"Thank you so much, ma'am."

We went and picked up another rental car. My kids were sleepy and looked at me with pleading eyes. They just wanted food, sleep, and help carrying their heavy backpacks. I felt for them, but I also appreciated and respected them for being little troopers. They didn't ask for anything, whine, or complain.

I let my oldest daughter know that we would be in town for the rest of the day. She had other plans with her mother's side of the family though. The boys were already back home since they left the night before. That left just me and my two little ones.

With an entire day to kill, I decided to take my kids to the zoo. I used it as a way to teach them to make the most of any situation, while inside my stomach was in knots. I couldn't afford the extra day off from driving and opening the store, let alone the actual cost of another day away from home.

I had no one to talk to about my frustrations. I mean, Veronica would love to listen to tell me how much of a failure I was or take it as an opportunity to think we were more than we are. I refused to mislead her that way. Alyssa would listen and then pity me. I definitely didn't need that; besides, it would make me feel like even less of a man and more of a failure. I think I already felt that enough. There were a couple of male friends I had that I was close to, but we didn't talk about these things. They would look at me like I was crazy for my thoughts, and then look at me as less of a man. So, for now, I'll just write. Before I try to publish these crazy rides, I'll have to take out these personal rantings.

I decided to feed my fish and get some sleep. I couldn't even work in the morning because the kids don't have school anymore. There goes twenty hours a week that I was working before. I seemed to be going backwards. I feel like I'm drowning, and no one knows or would even understand.

As the weeks went by, I found a brand-new admiration, respect, and healthy relationship with my fish. I'd never really been big on interior design or felt that it was an option. I believed that was something that the wealthy did. I'd always had furniture and household items that were hand-me-downs or donations.

I took an exceptionally high level of pride in the placement of the donated fish tank. I take great satisfaction in sleeping with the fishes every night, literally. The length of the fish tank is the same width as my bed, and the height made it the perfect headboard. I think this helped me and the fish become even closer. Not to mention, the sound of the water from the tank's filter running all evening puts me to sleep almost immediately.

Most nights, I don't even turn the TV on anymore. Every time I talk to Adam, I find myself asking millions of questions, much like a young child would ask his teacher at school. I don't understand everything about them that I think I should, but I am learning.

I learned that when you have more than one fish, there will always be one dominant fish that runs the tank. I would have assumed that the dominant fish would be the biggest fish. Adam made it clear that it is not always the biggest, but the most aggressive fish that will be the dominant. And that is the case of what was going on in my tank.

My dominant fish happened to be the mid-sized, orange, grey, and black pacu. Pacu's are a species of omnivorous freshwater fish that are related to piranhas. The pacu's teeth are straighter and more square, similar to human teeth, unlike the piranha's razor sharp, pointed teeth. The pacu can grow much larger than piranhas, however.

A lot of times, when I look at him, he moves his mouth as though he's talking to me. I don't believe that I fully understand the role or what it means to be the dominant fish, but I think that I'm learning rather quickly.

Every time I approach the tank with a bag of goldfish, he becomes a fish rancher. He herds each fish to a different corner of the tank, and then takes up the mass majority of the tank for himself, claiming the center. It seems a little greedy on his part when he has roughly four feet of space in the tank, while the other fish are tucked away in small corners. Each time one of the fish feels a little brave and swims out, he rushes toward them, backing them back into their respective corners.

As soon as the goldfish hit the water, you would expect it to become a feeding frenzy with each fish going after their meal. There are plenty of goldfish to go around, there is no shortage; however, that is not the case. Until the pacu gets his fill of the goldfish, not a single other resident fish gets to eat.

You would think that there would be some sort of mass rebellion. The other eleven fish could easily overtake the pacu; however, they didn't even try. I suppose this is the order in which a fish society must operate in order to work well. It's quite fascinating to watch. I watch my tank with admiration, as I see them as my extended family. When I'm mesmerized by the tank, I can relax and forget about my money issues, concerns about the well-being of my children, and all of the other things I find myself stressed about.

CHAPTER 15
DIRTY FEET
FRIDAY, JUNE 8, 2018 11:55 P.M.

So far, it had been just another average Rideshare night. I knew that it was fairly early for a Friday evening, so I was sure I could get something exciting by the end of the night. The weather was warm and it was summer time, so Vegas had an influx of partying patrons. It had been pretty busy, and I had been moving back and forth throughout the city.

I picked up an interesting group of individuals from Caesar's Palace. There were four people, one gentleman and three women. I wasn't able to distinguish the dynamic between the group at first, who were interracial and incredibly diverse, all the way down to their clothing.

When they initially got into the vehicle, I didn't even realize they were all together. The gentleman was in cowboy attire and looked like he just participated in a rodeo, all the way down to the oversized cowboy hat. Two of the women looked like they just came out of the fancy nightclub at Caesars, dressed upscale and younger than the rest of the group. The last woman appeared to be older than the other three.

None of them favored each other, dismissing the idea that they could be related, even as distant cousins. The only inclination that I had that they were actually together was the friendly nature in which they interacted, it didn't seem like a group who had just met. I've learned in my Rideshare experiences that assumptions are not beneficial to my earnings, nor do they contribute to a pleasant ride. So I dared not assume to know or understand the dynamic of their relationships; instead, I waited for them to offer clues as to how they knew each other.

The destination was estimated to be twenty-five minutes southeast, which took me deep into Green Valley, a nicer part of town. I knew it would be a lucrative ride just from the distance. Before we're able to really get going, they mentioned that they were hungry and asked if we could stop at Capriotti's, where they placed an order. They assured me that it will be fast. They also implied that I would be receiving a tip, which is definitely a motivating factor for me and incredibly needed.

It was on the way, and I really didn't mind stopping, anyway; although, on second thought, I was leaving the busiest part of the city during the busiest time of the night. The extra stop was not going to help me get back to the money pit that the strip seemed to be on these nights. Reluctantly, I agreed to fulfill their request. Capriotti's was en route to their destination, and I couldn't take the chance of receiving a bad rating due to not accommodating their request.

We pulled into the parking lot and I was lucky enough to grab a spot right in front of the door. This particular parking lot is typically really busy at this time of night. The restaurants in this plaza are typically full until at least two or three in the morning.

The conversation that I had initiated with the group had taken off without me. The gentleman got out to go inside and pick up their order, while all three women stayed in the car with me. Maybe they were worried that I'd just leave them there, or maybe they were just tired and didn't want to go in. The three women continued conversing among themselves, still excluding me. Of all the parts in the city to have a delay, this was one of the favorable locations to have one due to all of the eye candy walking around the plaza.

It was a nice night, not too hot, so I rolled down the windows. As my eyes wandered around the scenery, I caught a lovely image in my side mirror. I saw an incredibly attractive woman who was about 5'5", light complexion, very well dressed, and had the figure of a supermodel. I was lost in her beauty and didn't realize she was walking straight toward me. When I realized she was approaching my vehicle, I was thinking maybe she caught me staring at her.

She walked up to my window and said, "I know they're black," in a very hostile tone. I was caught off guard and had no idea what she was referring to. I guess I was too busy daydreaming. All of the women in the car were white, but the man who went inside was black. I didn't know if she was making reference to the man, or what she meant by "they're black." I didn't think she could even see the women in my car because she approached from behind and my windows have a dark tint.

The women in the back of my car all looked offended. One of them asked, "What did *that* mean?" She had an extremely disgusted look on her face.

Just as they asked, I happened to look down and notice her feet as she approached Capriotti's. She was dressed as though she had just come from the nightclub inside of the Hard Rock, which is across the street. Her shoes were in her hands, though. More than likely, like many women who have enjoyed a Vegas nightclub, her feet hurt so she walked across the dirty black pavement barefoot. At that point, her feet matched the dirty tar. The sight of it made my stomach turn and I wanted to vomit. I don't believe that I have any type of foot fetish, but there's something about people walking outside on dirty pavement with no shoes on that really strikes a nerve with me.

Thinking about the distance in which she had walked on that black street with no shoes on made my skin crawl. I could just imagine all of the bodily fluids and other disgusting things that had seeped into the pavement, and then were being absorbed into her body through the skin of her feet. My stunning princess instantly transformed into a disgusting, evil witch. A quick image flashed across my mind of her laying in bed next to me, as I gazed down to see black tar covering the bottom half of my sheets.

I shuddered with disgust and returned to the circumstances at hand. I realized they were making their second request for clarification on what the woman meant by her comment. I believed that the women in the car were concerned about what the woman's intentions were for their black friend, who was still inside. To put their minds at ease, I told them, "She's not talking about him."

In unison, they chorused, "What did she mean then?" They stared at me with puzzled looks.

I replied, "Look down at her feet."

Two of the women began to laugh, while the third made vomit noises. They all agreed that it was disgusting, and I certainly didn't argue with that assessment.

To make light of the situation, I decided to have a little bit of fun with them. The way I was parked didn't give them the vantage point of seeing their friend. I could see him clearly, though. He was within a couple of feet of the dirty foot woman who had just approached the vehicle. They could see just a glimpse of her.

I asked, "Do y'all know her?"

They said, "No. We've never even seen her."

I said, "Well, she appears to know your friend."

The woman on the far right side said, "What? What do you mean?" Her tone was as sharp as a butcher's knife. That made it pretty clear to me that she must have been his wife, girlfriend, or significant other. She couldn't see him at all from her position. The aggression coursed through her body and she stiffened as all of her muscles tensed up. The other two women were as silent as church mice.

"They appear to be extremely friendly, as though they've been lifelong friends. She's leaning toward him and smiling in his face. He appears to be laughing and welcoming the conversation."

They all began to break their necks to see him and see what was going on. Seeing that I had them, the opportunity to mess with them was too good to pass up. Watching the woman squirm as my words reached deep into her soul and stroked each and every one of her deepest insecurities compelled me to continue so I could observe the full cycle of her emotional anguish. I really shouldn't have taken the chance on this since a complaint could really hurt me.

Still, I couldn't resist, so I added, "Wait, why is he laughing and looking at her like that? I thought you guys didn't know her?"

His other half began to open the door. Before this went too far, I decided to come clean.

"I was just joking."

She replied, "She *better not* be touching him and talking to him like that!"

I said, "No, he actually looks like he's trying to stand as far away as he can from her. I think she's just trying to order her food. She doesn't look like she's paying him too much attention, either. Or maybe he's worried that you would notice that they were being too friendly." I paused, and then quickly added, "Just playing."

The woman acted like this put her mind at ease, but she still made her way inside. When she left the vehicle, the other two women who remained kind of chuckled a bit. We all ended up having a good laugh about that one.

I was incredibly relieved, since I was worried about this being one of those situations when some kind of major confrontation was going to take place when the dirty foot woman approached my vehicle. Thankfully, it was just a misunderstanding about a woman who decided to walk across the filthy Las Vegas streets barefoot, while inebriated.

Perhaps my expectations let me down. Even though I went out of my way to stop for them, they didn't even leave a tip. I wish passengers wouldn't dangle the false promises and hopes of a tip. I was starting to realize that when they say they'll tip me in the app or give me a big tip to do them a favor, it's a safe bet that I'll end up getting nothing. Why even say anything when you know you aren't going to tip me? I don't expect it if you don't say it, but I always appreciate it. Come to think of it, they didn't even offer me a sandwich. I wouldn't have taken it, but it would have been better than the empty promise of a tip. People really suck sometimes.

CHAPTER 16
THE VEGAS HEAT GOT ME HEATED
SATURDAY, JUNE 16, 2018 8:15 A.M.

When I opened the shop yesterday afternoon it had already been a long day. Rides were not coming in as quickly as I had hoped. The day started with the frustration of knowing it would be another hot day. It was over one hundred degrees before noon, with no sign of relief anywhere. A slight overcast or a simple breeze would help. Attempting to maintain some level of optimism, I reminded myself that at least the sun didn't directly hit the front of the building.

After a few hours, that optimism disappeared rapidly. I stepped outside to get a breath of fresh air, but quickly came to the realization that it was hotter inside than outside. It's been my experience in the past that a repair like this will be a minimum of a few thousand dollars. That seemed so far away, since I had just spent every dollar that I didn't have when I went to the graduation. I would just have to tough through it.

I reminded myself that it can't be hot forever, but the excessive heat made the day long and very draining. The heat just wears you down because you feel like you've been cooking in an oven all day long. It didn't help that nearly every customer that walked in felt like it was necessary to tell me, "Scott, it's hot in here." As if I didn't notice the sweat dripping down my own face.

As the hours dreadfully dragged by, the sun went down, yet the heat did not disappear. Finally, it was closing time. I had been pushed to my limit and just could not take anymore. On the long drive home, I was half asleep, just thinking that I'd be able to cool off inside the house.

I walked in with a great sigh of relief. I began to get things situated, and of course the first thing I did was turn on the air, knowing that it would be at least an hour before the house cooled off, but at least it would cool off. As I lay in bed, anticipating the refreshing, cold air, I realized that a few hours had already passed by, yet the cold, refreshing relief I was looking for hadn't come.

I got up and looked at the thermostat, only to see that it was actually three degrees hotter than when I first arrived home. How could it be hotter than when I first got here when the air has been on for the past few hours? How could this be happening? I reached up to feel the vent. Unless I was completely delirious, which is possible, there was nothing coming out of the slats.

This was just what I needed. No air at the shop, no air at the house, and an outside temperature that never dropped below one hundred degrees, even at night. In a panic, I realized that I couldn't subject my kids to this. If it was just me, it would be fine. I could take a cold shower, fan myself, and eventually I would pass out from pure exhaustion; however, this would be torture to my kids, and it would be completely unreasonable to put them through this. It was rare that I had them on Friday nights; however, their grandparents were out of town and their mother pulled a typical alcohol-infused disappearing act.

I pulled up Google and found a twenty-four-hour air conditioning service company. I tried to keep my optimism high, hoping and telling myself that this could be something as simple as a five-dollar fuse. The soonest they could get someone out would be several hours later, in the morning. I watched my kids turn red, as though they were sleeping in the direct sunlight. There was no chance I would be getting any sleep, and to top it all off I was feeling like a complete failure as a father.

The morning finally arrived, and just past eight the A/C repair man showed up. I managed to get a blink of sleep, maybe forty-five minutes. The man explained that the visit would be seventy-five dollars for him to assess the damage and that could be applied toward any repair. I handed him a credit card, with my fingers crossed that it wouldn't be declined.

He pulled out a ladder and climbed up onto my

roof. He appeared to be very professional. He even had me sign a document stating that I couldn't sue them if there was any damage or leaks to my roof because he had to wear cleats up there. He smiled in my face as I signed the waiver, and a few moments later I heard footsteps on the roof.

He wasn't up there for more than ten minutes before I heard another slight knock at the door. He was standing there with a sheet of paper on his clipboard. At first glance, the sheet of paper had a number that appeared to read over nine thousand dollars. He smiled and said, "Let's go over the estimate."

I replied, "What's the problem?"

He said, "We'll go over that. But here are the numbers." He used a lot of words very fast. The only ones that I was able to retain were "Twelve thousand; however, you qualify for a discount that brings it down to ninety-one hundred."

Once I was able digest the fact that he just said ninety-one hundred dollars like I should be grateful, there were a few realizations that came across my mind. The first was that this man just quoted me a price without even telling me what the problem was. Of course, that price was for an entire new AC unit. I did not understand how this happened. The second realization was that the amount of time that he was actually on the roof only allowed enough time for him to write down these numbers. His bright, white shirt didn't even have a speck of dust on it. The final realization was that he just fucked me in my ass without any lube and absolutely no reach-around, and

I paid him nearly a hundred dollars to do it.

All I felt was a sense of rage come over me. This man had the audacity to stand in front of me and hustle me. If he went around all day long making these one hour house calls, getting paid seventy-five dollars a pop, even if no one bites on the dressed up, "discounted" brand new unit for the same price as some new cars, he was making roughly seven hundred and fifty dollars a day to go around fucking people all day long.

I was looking at the bright pen in his hand, picturing myself taking it from him and ramming it into the side of his neck, and then watching the blood drip down the side of his bright white shirt, thinking that it would give me a sense of accomplishment and justice. Of course, I wouldn't be doing it just for myself, but for all of the people who he fucked over. I imagined how many people agree to the ridiculous new unit for over nine thousand dollars, which he conveniently offered to finance for me.

The only problem that I thought I might experience from the whole situation is that I would have had to find his keys and figure out how to get rid of the van he left parked outside of my house. It would have been very easy to get rid of the body. As long as I made sure that he fell inside, there would be no blood splatter outside of my home. My nice, tile floors would've made it incredibly convenient to mop and clean up his blood after he bled out in my living room. I was sure that I would be able to accomplish all of that before my beautiful children woke up.

I needed to clear my head. Thinking about that was

not helping my situation, cooling me off, or helping the fact that I would have another long, hot day in front of me with no air conditioning at work or home. I guess I should have been grateful that at least I had a working, ice cold air conditioner in my vehicle.

I told him, "I'll have to get back to you," and ushered him outside.

For the time being, I'd have to go old school and use all of the fans that I could muster. I figured I could purchase a swamp cooler for fairly cheap and just have sleepovers with the kids in the living room downstairs, where it was slightly cooler, until I could figure out a permanent solution.

I didn't know how things could get any worse. Nothing in my life ever worked out. It was always one problem after the next. When would this misery ever end? Fuck. I really just hated life.

CHAPTER 17

THE POP UP

SUNDAY, JUNE 17, 2018 2:18 A.M.

Alyssa had a rather interesting ride. Our calls were cut off throughout the night from other passengers calling, Veronica calling me, or a new love interest of Alyssa's calling her. We typically talked on Facebook Messenger rather than actual phone calls so as to not interfere with the apps. With the phone service that she currently had, she was not able to use any apps while on a phone call unless she was connected to Wi-Fi. We found a workaround by utilizing Messenger because it is another app; although, we could talk and use our Bluetooth like a regular phone call.

She picked up two young men downtown, near Fremont Street. Because she couldn't find them, she used the Rideshare app to call them so they could locate each other. Many people don't realize this, but when we call through the Rideshare apps, we don't actually get your phone number, and you don't actually get ours. The calls are routed through a third party to protect all of our privacy.

The two men were able to find her and they began their journey towards the men's home. Alyssa thought the two men were a gay couple, as they appeared to be having a drunken lover's spat before entering her vehicle. They were actually standing right outside of where she was parked, but were completely oblivious to her arrival until she called.

After the pleasantries and verification of the correct address, she began heading toward their home, which wasn't too far away, behind the Boulevard mall.

Both men were on the smaller side, roughly 5'4" and 5'6" and thin. The taller one was wearing expensive designer jeans that had been torn and ripped with great care to appear as though they had been worn for years, with a bedazzled tank top and a flannel shirt tied around his waist. The shorter man wore a designer T-shirt that probably cost more than we made in a week with similarly torn jeans. He had messy dreads and a red bandana around his head.

The shorter of the men asked her, "If you were stranded on a deserted island and could take the catalog of five artists with you, but that's the only music you'll hear for the rest of your life, who would you choose?"

Alyssa decided to play along, as this was a new question for her. "Definitely Tupac, Lil' Wayne, and Jay-Z because I love them all and they all have massive catalogs. The fourth one would have to be either Trey Songz or Chris Brown because I'd need some good R&B. It's going to be tough to choose between them.

And I'd really have to think about my last one."

As she was deep in thought, trying to figure out her final artist, the smaller man said, "Oh. So, you like chocolate, huh?"

She replied, "I guess you could say that. My kids are mixed."

Alyssa is a white woman in her late thirties who has mostly dated black men. She says she's equal opportunity, though I've never actually seen her with a man of a different race. Even though she is a white woman, or at least visually appears to be, I'm not sure that she knows that.

The little guy said, "I see. Well, I'm an adult film star. I can do things to you that you've never even imagined before. I know how to make you feel really good. Are you seeing anyone?" Being that both men were African American, I suppose he thought he had a chance at her.

To antagonize her further, I sarcastically said, "Oooh, he's gonna do things to you that you've never had done before. I bet you can't wait to see what that's like." I was really enjoying being able to mess with her because it took my mind off of the fact that I wasn't getting any rides. I could tell from her tone that she was not interested and the man didn't stand a chance.

She was used to having men hit on her, especially when they were intoxicated in the middle of the night. She told him, "I'm flattered, but yes, I'm seeing someone."

He continued to explain all of the things he could do to her to make her feel good during the next few minutes, until they reached his home. As he was about to get out of her vehicle, he said, "Well, you have my number. When you break up with your boyfriend, call me."

She said, "Okay." This kind of situation wasn't uncommon for her, so she went on about her night, forgetting about the man and his advances.

When he exited the vehicle, I was overwhelmed with curiosity on why she didn't respond to his advances. The way he was talking to her seemed consistent with the men I'd known her to be interested in. He was obviously the right ethnicity.

I asked, "So, you didn't want to see what kinds of things he could do to you?"

She replied, "No. Just no." I could picture her shaking her head, with her nose scrunched up in disgust.

With my curiosity still unsatisfied, I asked her, "What was wrong with him? He sounded like your type to me."

In a sharp tone she explained how both men were dressed, their behavior, and how she thought they were a couple. She added, "Besides, he didn't meet the height requirements."

Now the puzzle has been solved. She's a good friend of mine, but I did realize she is incredibly shallow. You would think she's almost six feet tall herself. Character doesn't really make a big difference. Nor does responsibility or even loyalty in her eyes. He just has to be taller than six feet and attractive to her. Yes, she is very shallow.

"But he did tell you that he can do things to you that you've never had done before. You're not the slightest bit curious?"

She responded with a sarcastic tone, "All guys say that."

It seemed like it might be best not to pick on her any more due to the heightened level of irritation she was displaying. Just in time to avoid the awkward silence, she had her next passenger climbing into her car. I got my next ride at that time, as well.

After a few more rides, she found a phone in her backseat. It's not uncommon for us to find things in our vehicles, as they fall out of pockets or people forget about them. Typically, we will receive a message or a phone call within fifteen minutes stating that the passenger believes they left something and can we please call them. Between us, we have found several phones, a couple of wallets, ATM cards, jewelry, lip gloss, eye lashes, lighters, cocaine, joints, matches, water bottles, glasses, and keys. She tossed the cellphone in her center console, figuring she'd hear from the owner soon. It was a busy night and she soon forgot about the phone. She didn't get home until after eight in the morning and went straight to sleep.

Just after noon, Alyssa's roommate woke her up. He asked, "Did you Rideshare last night?"

Wiping the sleepies from her eyes, she answered, "Yes. What's up?"

He said, "There's a guy at the door who says he left his phone in your car?" He watched her facial expression go from irritation to confusion to fear.

She threw on a dress and flip-flops, grabbed her keys, and made her way to the driveway in front of her house.

As she unlocked her car, the creepy adult film star opened the back door and reached into the exact spot where she found the phone. Alyssa opened the front door, grabbed the phone, and handed it to him. They locked eyes for a moment. He looked like a kid who had been caught with his hand in the cookie jar.

After a moment of awkward silence, he mumbled, "Thank you." He and his roommate left.

Alyssa returned inside, stopping by the roommate's bedroom. He was sitting by the window, where he had watched the entire interaction. He asked her, "What was that all about?"

She told him about the ride. He said, "Hmmm. I thought something seemed kind of weird. When I opened the door, he looked me up and down and stuttered, 'You must be Alyssa's husband.' I said, 'Okay, what do you want?' He said he left his phone in your car, so I came to get you." Alyssa found this humorous.

The man was met with the exact opposite of what he must have expected. Instead of an attractive woman, he got a tall, burly, half-naked man of great size opening the door. I'm sure his image of who she would be with did not match the roommate. He's a bald Caucasian man with a long, unkempt beard, covered in skull tattoos, and generally pretty scruffy looking. On top of that, he was agitated at being bothered on a

Sunday morning and probably came across like a grizzly bear that had been awakened early from his hibernation.

She thanked him. The guy thinking that her roommate was her husband was probably helpful. He used the GPS on his phone to track the device and showed up at her front door. The Rideshare company does have an option in the app to contact the driver. It disturbed her that the guy showed up at her door and never even tried to contact her.

She was slightly worried about him coming back, so she emailed Rideshare to let them know that she felt unsafe. She asked for his information to give to her family in case something happened to her. They refused, saying that they could not compromise his personal information and that went against their privacy policy. They told her that in the future she should drop off any electronic devices to their hub or the nearest police station rather than going home with them. She sleeps with a gun by her bedside, so hopefully the guy isn't that dumb.

For me, the night was great. Productive, lucrative, and I had a great two-hour session with Veronica in a hotel room that she paid for that had an amazing air conditioner. I really do enjoy sex with her. Those occasional interactions, when I can just let go and enjoy her flesh, helped get me through. I find it to be therapeutic. Though I'm sure spending over eight hours in ice cold air conditioning between my car and the hotel room helped quite a bit.

Honestly, I think I wanted to just enjoy the cold air and rest more than I wanted to have sex with her. Veronica was extremely accommodating to my schedule. The highest part of her maintenance was her excessive communication. She had no desire or need to go on dates or be romanced in any capacity. Since her husband is well off, she's not financially dependent either. I guess that's a must, since I was not financially stable and could hardly even pay my own bills. Now that I think about it, I'm sure those are the reasons that I was so tolerant of her desperate cries for attention and nagging.

For a moment I drifted off in my thoughts. I guess I was delaying just so I could enjoy the cool air for a few moments longer. After I left the hotel room, it instantly felt like I walked back into hell. Or at least my hell, that was days that were long, demanding, and full of heat. I had no idea when this torment would ever end.

CHAPTER 18

UNDER THE INFLUENCE

SATURDAY, JUNE 23, 2018 8:30 A.M.

Friday night was another busy night, as usual. I found myself at one of the luxury movie theaters in the Green Valley area of Henderson. Green Valley is one of the more desired areas of town to live in, with really nice homes, wonderful shopping, and a cost of living to match. Most of the people that I have picked up in areas like this are pleasant and quiet. Every now and then you'll get a little bit of conversation out of them.

I picked up a younger couple who had just seen the latest horror film. In my normal attempt to make small talk, I asked what movie they had seen, if they enjoyed it, and how their night was going. The young lady was talkative and seemed to have a lot of opinions about the horror film genre.

I told her, "I must admit that horror films are not my preferred genre; although, I am a big fan of Stephen King. His movies and stories and the events that take place in them have always fascinated me."

She excitedly said, "I agree!"

We went back and forth for a while about his old titles, including the newest version of *It*. The gentleman didn't say much, even though my conversation addressed both of them. I've been in these types of situations before and found it to be a good practice to address a couple together, as a single unit, so that it doesn't appear as though I am trying to talk to the woman. This is especially beneficial if the man is insecure.

When the ride was over, I dropped them off and wished them a good night. I thought that was the end of that ride, though I was sadly mistaken.

Roughly seven hours after the ride ended, I received three emails back to back referring to conduct issues that I displayed. This was towards the end of my night when I was already deliriously tired but felt a sense of accomplishment for a full night's work.

The first email said that I made rude, slanderous, or disrespectful comments to a passenger. The second one stated that I appeared to be under the influence of drugs, narcotics, or some type of controlled substance. The third email reported that I had drugs, alcohol, and controlled substances in my car during a ride.

I utilize two different apps for my driving. I only did three rides on that platform that night, so I revisited each of the rides to figure out which one it was. Even though Rideshare will tell me I messed up, they won't tell me which ride I supposedly messed up on. They claim it's to protect the privacy of the passengers, but I think it's just to mess with me and confuse me even further.

I was wracking my brain trying to figure out what could have possibly happened. I drifted into the line of thought that maybe I did say something rude and didn't even remember saying it. It was beyond frustrating. How was I supposed to defend myself when I didn't even know the details of the situation? I thought, I need to stop this. I need to get in front of this. I was depending on being able to drive over the next few weeks, so I had to figure out which ride this was.

Ughhh. The aggravation was setting in. I remembered each of the rides, but none stood out in my mind. Okay. I decided to just take a few deep breaths and take this step by step. The first step was to eliminate all of the rides that didn't have any conversation. I think it's nearly impossible to offend someone without saying anything to them.

Just then, the next notification came in. The action that Rideshare took was to suspend my driving privileges. I was totally blown away by these emails. I had no idea where they came from, or why someone would make these kinds of comments about me. I am very careful to avoid all of these things when I'm driving.

I responded to the emails expeditiously, letting Rideshare know that the only substance I ever have during a ride is water or coffee. I asked where I could go take a drug and alcohol test because I never drive under the influence. I don't even participate in recreational drug use and very rarely drink. I can't afford it; though I left that part out. I also told them that I always do my best to carry myself in the most respectful manner. I asked what I could do to help resolve the issue.

My mind and all of my insecurities were racing out of control. What if I was banned from Rideshare permanently? How could I be banned so easily? Did I even get to defend myself? Does anything happen to passengers if they file frivolous complaints? Don't they understand they are messing with my livelihood? This took away every sense of progress or security I had been able to muster up. I needed this money to get out of the hole I'd sunk into, and even more now than ever since I had taken on an additional vehicle loan and higher insurance premium.

I also asked what was it that I said that was supposedly offensive in my response email. My response emails and questions were not being answered. It looked like the only thing I could do was sit around for the next three days - my earning days - and hope that they wouldn't boot me off of the platform permanently.

In trying to come up with solutions to my bigger problems - my finances - I figured I could sell the vehicle and get a second full-time job. That would cut into my time with my children severely, which was what I had been trying to avoid. I was trying to figure out what opportunities I may have to make some extra money that weekend, as I was banking on Rideshare.

I replayed all of my rides from the night. My first ride was a man who snored the entire time across town. How could I be rude to a sleeping man? Unless he felt that I was disrespectful by disrupting his sleep when we arrived at his destination. Or possibly the bumps in the road made it difficult for him to get completely comfortable?

The second ride was a man who was on his way to the church service first thing in the morning. He didn't even speak English. I'm not sure how I could offend a man I couldn't even communicate with.

I figured it had to have been the couple from the movie theatre. The man must have thought I was being flirtatious with his girlfriend, and then became spiteful, angry, and vindictive. All I was trying to do was provide a pleasant Rideshare experience. I had no interest in his girl. She wasn't even my type!

CHAPTER 19

HOLD MY CALLS, PLEASE

MONDAY, JUNE 25, 2018 10:00 P.M.

I had an incredibly long day, trying to stay focused on getting some work done at the store, along with spending time with my kids. It was summertime, so they were excited for the extra attention from me. I arranged a game night with Alyssa, since I couldn't drive, and the kids liked hanging out with her.

My phone was going off non-stop. And it was just one person, Veronica. Back to back text messages, along with back to back calls. It was just getting ridiculous.

How does one person have this much energy? Let alone this much time? I figured I would just turn my phone off, but I realized I couldn't turn it off because I was expecting a few calls. I figured I would just put it on mute, so at least I wouldn't have to hear it. It was ringing and buzzing inside of my head like an alarm in the near distance that wouldn't stop. I hoped she would give up before I got those calls.

The nice thing is that my Bluetooth does vibrate each time I get a call. The bad thing was that I still had to glance at my phone each time it rang because I didn't know if it was her or the calls I was expecting. I felt like I was being beaten into submission because I just wanted to pull all of my hair out and scream, even though I'm shaved bald so there's no hair to pull.

Ten minutes feels like ten hours when you are constantly being poked at. We got home and I told the kids to head upstairs and play for a bit. I figured I could gather my composure and put a few snacks together before Alyssa arrived.

Finally! One of the calls I had been waiting for came in. I answered the phone, thinking that at least I wouldn't be bothered with having to look down at my phone every few seconds. But it was worse. I was hearing the continuous beep letting me know that I was getting a phone call on my other line, which I kept ignoring. That was more annoying than constantly looking at my phone. I couldn't even focus on what was being said. I excused myself from the phone call so that I could answer Veronica's call and see if I could reason with her.

I didn't answer the phone in any way that could possibly appear to be rational. I answered, "What the fuck do you want? If I didn't answer your fucking call the first hundred times, what makes you think I'm going to answer it now?"

There was a slight pause where all I heard was dead silence. Immediately after, she hung up.

Ugh. I don't get it. What was the point of all of that?

She went through all that trouble to get me on the phone, then just fucking hung up? It was ridiculous.

As if on cue, there was a lengthy text message that came through explaining that she apologized for hanging up, but she didn't expect me to answer and wasn't ready.

Then the phone rang again. I answered.

Before I could even say anything, she asked, "Can we just talk? Please?"

I said, "Veronica, I don't get the point of this. I don't want to talk to you. I don't have anything to say to you. Can't you just leave me the fuck alone?"

She said, "I understand. But can we just talk so we can end this?"

"Fine. What do you have to say?"

"You don't get it. I *really* fuckin' love you," she said.

"Okay. What else do you have to say?"

She repeated, "Okay? That's all you have to say? I just told you that I really fuckin' love you."

With great agitation, I said, "This is pointless. There is no purpose behind this. What do you want?"

She said, "I know you don't want to deal with me. Let's just talk through this so we can end this and go our separate ways. I know I get erratic, and I know that I can be a lot to deal with, but you're not always easy to deal with either."

"Doesn't that mean that it's best for us to just end this? Since I'm so hard to fuckin' deal with, so we can just go our separate ways?"

"Why are you doing this? Why won't you just talk to me? Why are you turning so cold?" she pleaded.

"Cold? I don't get it. If I want nothing to do with you, am I supposed to be warm about it? You just won't leave me alone," I said, exasperated. "You text and call me so frequently that it's worthless. The constant beeps and rings are so frequent that I can't even have a decent conversation."

In a real sharp tone, she asked, "Well who were you talking to?"

"None of your damn business. Is this what you wanted to talk about?"

"You just don't get it. I really, *really* love you. There are hundreds of guys that would do anything to be with me. But you act like I'm nothing, a piece of trash that you can just throw away."

"Then go be with them. Obviously, that's a better situation for you, so go. LEAVE ME ALONE."

"No," she pleaded. "Why are you doing this? Quit acting like this. You don't know how badly this hurts me."

"You're repeating yourself. What is it that you want to discuss? I'm going to give you another five minutes, and then I'm done with this conversation."

"You don't know how lucky you are to have a girl like me in your life."

"Well then just let me be unlucky by myself and just leave me alone then."

"Would you please just stop. I'm trying to make a point here, and you just keep telling me to leave you alone."

"Okay, then what are you trying to say? Continue, please."

She went on a long tangent letting me know that I didn't appreciate her, I treated her poorly, and it was a privilege for her to want to be with me. A few minutes in, I tried to cut her off to tell her that I'd already heard all of this before.

She continued to speak, even louder, just to drown out my words. I was really confused. I did not understand what her goal was, or what the purpose was, or what she was seeking in the conversation. More specifically, I didn't understand what it was that she wanted, besides the obvious. At least what was obvious to me is that we continue riding this roller coaster that she calls a relationship. I didn't sign up for this.

After she repeated herself for the fifth time, I told her, "You've already said this."

"No, wait. Will you please just let me finish?"

I told her, "Then say something that I haven't heard a thousand times through your phone calls and text messages. Share with me an original thought. Or for God's sake just tell me what it is that you want to get out of this conversation. Having good sex every once in a while just isn't worth this."

She responded as though I said, "Please start from the beginning." She started again about how she loves me and I'm lucky to have her and began her whole rant all over again.

She said, "It was a mistake for us to get together in the first place."

I asked, "So how are we correcting that mistake by continuing to talk?"

"Will you please stop doing that?"

"Doing what?" I am clearly missing something here.

"I'm just trying to talk to you. Can we please just talk?"

I looked down at my phone and then told her, "We've been supposedly 'talking' for thirty minutes now. And you have not said one thing that is relevant or new."

"Well, can we just see each other? I think if we can just talk in person we can get it over with."

"No! I don't want to fuckin' see you. I don't want anything to do with you. I'm only entertaining this conversation so you can supposedly get it out of your system and move on."

"Well that's what I want. I want to move on."

"Okay, so how can I help you move on? Right now, it doesn't seem like you want me to participate in that, other than to sit here and listen to you think." I felt like I was talking to a brick wall.

"I don't want you to listen to me think. I want you to talk to me."

I repeated, "And as I've told you multiple times, I have nothing to say." I am truly not a fan of repeating myself.

"Are you acting like this because you want to get back together?"

"No! That is not what I want at all. I don't even get how you could put that together." I swear she had to be punking me. How does that even make sense? "You know what, I'm done talking. Just say whatever it is that you have to say. I'll listen to whatever it is that you need to say. You get it off of your chest, and then I never want to have contact with you ever again."

The next words out of her mouth were, "I just really love you. Why are you treating me like this?"

I put the phone on speaker phone and muted it, set it down, and walked away. I didn't have the time, patience, or energy for that. I thought about throwing my phone against a brick wall so that I would never have to hear from her or deal with her again. But, then, that would probably only result in her training carrier pigeons to send messages to me. It really was just utterly ridiculous. I felt like I was on the verge of being involved in some sort of fatal attraction.

Breaking my line of thought, I heard my name being called out multiple times. I walked back to the phone and unmuted it to say, "Please continue."

The rant started all over again. It was like she was stuck on repeat like the most annoying parrot to ever learn to mimic human language. Alyssa walked in and heard the phone in the background. She looked at me with a puzzled look. I asked her, "Isn't this a ridiculous situation that I have going on?"

She said, "What's ridiculous about it?"

I gave her a brief, general overview of the situation.

She said, "There's no way," and looked at me with disbelief.

I just moved the phone closer so she could hear everything. Within a few minutes, Veronica was calling out my name repeatedly, again. I unmuted it and said, "I'm still here. What's the problem?"

"Well, Scott, I can't hear you."

"I didn't say anything," I said curtly.

"Well, I can't hear you breathing." I looked over and Alyssa was looking at me with a surprised, yet amused, look.

"I'd rather not be. I don't want to be on the phone with you. This conversation is killing me slowly. I don't want to be with you. I don't want to talk to you. I don't want to hear from you."

"I just can't believe that you're treating me like this."

I said, "You don't fuckin' get it. How do you treat someone that you don't want to deal with? Someone that you just want to leave you alone? You don't want them to call you. You don't want them to text you. You don't want them to contact you."

"How can you say that to me? I can tell by the way that you looked at me and the things that you did that you care. But now you're just trying to act like I'm just a piece of garbage that you can throw away any time you choose."

Once again, I muted the phone and put it down. She continued talking.

I looked over at Alyssa. She shook her head and said, "Wow."

I said, "What? You thought I was exaggerating? This has been one of the most ridiculous situations that I have ever seen or heard of."

She agreed. "Yeah, that's kind of hard to believe. It's one of those things you kind of have to see or hear for yourself to believe," and broke into fits of laughter.

"Yeah, I do agree." I sighed.

"Did I really hear that correctly? Did she just say that she couldn't hear you breathe?" Alyssa asked.

"Yep. That's what it sounded like to me."

"Wow. What did you do to her? Did you tell her that you love her?"

"Absolutely not. How can I love someone who's already married?"

Alyssa said, "She's really married? And she has the time to do all of this?" I shared some of our encounters before, so she knew a little bit about our situation.

"Sometimes I wonder the same thing. The fact that she is married was one of the selling points of me dealing with her in the first place. I do not want the attachment, and I figured if she was married, she wouldn't have the free time like this. But, obviously, I was wrong."

I spent the next forty-five minutes or so socializing with Alyssa and forgot that I was still on the phone with Veronica. I went to retrieve my phone to look something up to see that the call had ended. I figured she must have hung up a long time ago because I wasn't saying anything and had her muted. I looked at the call log to see that the phone call was an hour and forty-five minutes long. All I could do was shake my head in disbelief as I realized how sad and pathetic it was. Veronica was able to conduct an almost two-hour phone call with very limited interaction or involvement on my behalf. What had I gotten myself into?

The kids joined us for a couple of rounds of their

favorite board games before Alyssa left to get to work herself. I was able to have an incredibly peaceful night since I forgot that I had put my phone on silent. It really wouldn't have mattered since the battery died sometime in the night anyway.

Three days later my driving privileges were reinstated. I didn't even receive an email with any kind of explanation. I even wrote back to them again and asked what measures they took to resolve the situation. I received no answer to that question either. Now I was wondering what would happen if the next person decided to complain? Should I just be silent and drive like a robot? How was I supposed to know what offends someone? Apparently a simple, friendly conversation about movies can offend someone.

CHAPTER 20

ACTING BRAND NEW

SATURDAY, JUNE 30, 2018 2:45 A.M.

It had been a busy Friday night on the strip with all of the summer bunnies and the guys that they attract. There were tons of college kids, young adults, bachelor parties, and girls' trips that were bringing large crowds to the desert heat to drink alcohol and party all day by the pools, and all night at the clubs.

I picked up a couple from Drai's nightclub at the Cromwell. The female was white, with a British accent. The guy was black, with a southern accent. They were all over each other, grabbing, kissing, and touching. It was quite apparent that they enjoyed the club and had at least a few cocktails.

They climbed into the backseat and I confirmed their destination, The Spearmint Rhino, one of our more popular strip clubs. As we got going on our short journey, I dismissed my normal small talk because they were talking among themselves. The conversation seemed a bit heated and I did not desire to interject into this couple's issues.

She said, "But you were out there talking to all of them girls. And ignoring me."

He said, "How? I'm the one who brought you into our area and was giving you drinks."

"So? You weren't really paying attention to me. You kept talking to other girls."

They continued to argue about her insecurities because he was talking to other women, while his defense was that he brought her into the VIP area. Halfway to the club I realized there was some road construction, accidents, and closures. I had to go all the way around. That meant the seven-minute ride turned into a twenty minute ride of torture with the arguing couple. They were both insecure from what I could tell, and he was trying to compensate or impress her with status or money or whatever he thought he had.

They took a break from their ridiculous argument and asked me for my opinion. By that point I realized that she was from London and he was from Miami. I asked a simple question. "Are y'all trying to be together? Or what is the goal that you have?"

She said, "Well, no. I fly back home to London tomorrow."

He said, "I'm going back to Miami on Monday."

I asked, "Then what the hell are y'all arguing for? It's pretty simple from what I can see. Enjoy tonight together. If you aren't trying to have a relationship or keep in touch, what's the point in arguing about all of this? It's not going to matter in twenty-four hours."

They agreed. Then started making out. I didn't understand what the point of any of that discussion was. They were simply two grown people who wanted to enjoy each other's company for the night. I guess some people have to act brand new like that because they can't handle the truth of a simple one night stand. You don't need to know each other's names, life stories, phone numbers, or any of that to enjoy a one night stand. They were wasting their time and creating an argument over things that didn't matter, instead of capitalizing on the little bit of time that they did have.

At least I got a nice little kickback from the strip club for dropping them off. That extra money comes in handy, especially since I had to play sex therapist. With the therapy and extra time, I still felt like I came up a little short.

I really have a newfound appreciation for strip clubs. I now get paid to take people to the strip clubs, instead of paying to go and spending unnecessary money and time that I don't have.

Adam recently mentioned that he added a new baby lobster to his tank. It was a beautiful little blue crustacean that added a new personality to his tranquil aquatic escape. I had wanted to add another fish to my tank for quite some time. I decided that I'd use my stripclub bonus money to treat myself to a new fish.

I kept thinking about that lovely swordfish that I saw the first time Adam took me to the Trop Aquarium. I decided that I was going to do it. I was going to go get me a new fish.

The next morning, I raced over to Trop Aquarium. I looked around, but nothing really caught my eye. The swordfish that I had been dreaming about was gone. One of the employees mentioned another location that I could look at since their selection was quite low at the time.

The other store is on the other side of town. I don't mind the drive, though, so I headed over to take a look.

I didn't even make it ten feet inside the door when it caught my eye. I saw the most beautiful stingray. I didn't even know that you could have a stingray as a pet. I thought they only lived in the middle of the ocean.

As I approached the stingray I started to think that they are saltwater fish, but my tank is fresh water. My heart sank, but I was still drawn to the stingray.

The man who worked at the store walked up to me and asked, "He's beautiful, isn't he?"

My eyes were wide open as I watched him flow through the water from side to side. I said, "Yes. But, he's saltwater, isn't he?"

The man responded, "Stingrays can actually survive in both."

"Really? But are they aggressive?"

The man answered, "No, they're not. But other fish don't mess with them either."

"Are you sure?"

He said, "Yes. They use their tail to defend themselves against any fish that messes with them. It electrocutes them. Besides, they spend most of their time on the bottom of the tank, so the other fish don't really bother with them."

Adam had advised me to inform the people of what type of fish I already have when I go to add new fish to my tank. Remembering that advice, I told the man, "My pacu is very aggressive."

He asked, "How big is your pacu?"

I held up my hand. "He's about as big as my hand." The area I showed him spanned about eight inches.

He let out a "Psssshhhhh. The stingray will be fine."

I glanced at the price. My heart was broken, yet again. The stingray was one hundred and eighty dollars. I planned on spending no more than one hundred dollars, which was a little bit more than the bonus money I received from the stripclub. I asked, "Is that the correct price?"

He said, "Yes. Stingrays, especially of this size, are not that easy to come by."

I let out a sigh. "I don't think I can do it."

The man said, "For our club members we offer a ten percent discount. What if I can take ten percent off, without you even having to join the club?"

That was still over one hundred and sixty dollars. I really couldn't afford that, but I really wanted that fish. I thought it would be a really cool addition to my tank. I went back and forth in my head and decided to go ahead and do it. I worked hard and rarely ever did anything for myself, I justified to myself.

My new addition and I headed home. I added him to the tank. So far, so good, I thought. The pacu didn't bother him and all seemed to be going well.

When I got home from work that night, I must have stared at the stingray going back and forth for over an hour. I was in a trance.

The next morning was when the trouble began. I realized the pacu was not swimming right. It seemed that he was having trouble swimming straight and his body wasn't even upright. I looked at him and asked, "Did you mess with the stingray?"

He stared at me, and then moved his mouth as though he were answering me. When he finished saying his piece, he swam off in a crooked manner again. He must have had his first run in with the stinger. That put some of my nerves at ease. I was wondering if the stingray would be okay in there. Now I was wondering if I needed to worry about the pacu. I told myself, he's a fighter, he'll be okay. And maybe this will teach him a lesson.

When I returned home that evening, I checked to make sure each fish was okay. So far, so good. Just as I was about to turn off the light, the pacu swam toward the stingray. I told him, "No! Leave him alone. He's going to shock you."

Then I got to watch it firsthand. It was so quick, it might have been a bee sting. He began to swim in a squiggly line and appeared to be quite disoriented. All I could do was grin. I told him, "That's what you get. I told you to leave him alone."

Over the next couple of days, I really worried about whether or not the pacu was going to make it. I woke up one morning and something seemed off. I couldn't quite figure out what it was. The pacu was floating in the middle of the tank staring at me. The stingray wasn't moving. I was trying to examine the stingray, but I couldn't figure out what was wrong. Until I finally noticed that he was missing his tail.

The fucking pacu bit the one-hundred-and-sixty-dollar stingray's tail off! I really wanted to go by the fish store to ask the salesman what I could do about this. I didn't have time to go by on that day. Hopefully I can get by there tomorrow, I thought.

Tomorrow was too late. I came home to find my tailless stingray floating upside down at the top of the tank. I was so angry that my one-hundred-and-sixty-dollar fish was just killed by a free fish. I didn't have the one hundred and sixty dollars to spare to spend on the fish in the first place, but this made it even worse because now I didn't even have the fish to enjoy. I was so angry I wanted to grab the pacu and throw him across the room. But what good would that do? Then I'd just have two dead fish.

How fucking stupid and irresponsible could I be? I really needed that money to pay off some of these bills, not treat myself to a fish. This was not my fault at all. It was the store salesman's fault. All he wanted was my money. Some fucking nerve he had, acting like he was doing me a favor, when all along he knew that the stingray was not going to survive in my tank. I told him my pacu was aggressive. With that cocky, smug look on his face when he said, "Oh, he'll be fine." I thought I should march into that store and make him pay for this; I should rip his limbs off like the pacu did the stingray's tail and tell him that he'll be okay. That was the only way to fix this. He had to pay. I went to bed that night full of anger and rage.

CHAPTER 21
STRIP CLUB WIENERS
SUNDAY, JULY 1, 2018 2:00 A.M.

I was on the phone with Alyssa when she got a hit to pick up at a strip club behind Circus Circus. It was a large ride (XL), which meant she would be getting paid a little bit nicer for her time. Ironically, we actually have the same car. She commented that she'd love to get a large ride to the strip clubs to get some of that kickback money, but at least she was making more than a normal ride.

The first guy came up and asked her to wait for a few minutes for all of his friends. I could hear them laughing and slurring and must admit, I was a bit jealous. I still hadn't gotten to go out and enjoy a night with alcohol and naked women and no commitments.

The first guy got in the front seat. They started the small talk. He told her, "We're here for a bachelor party, but one of the guys is getting food from that food truck. They're all drunk and broke now." He laughed.

She was a good sport and giggled with him. I'm sure

her tips are better than mine because she can just use her giggle and boobs to solicit more. We have actually compared our tip percentages, and she beats me out every week consistently by at least five percent. I wouldn't consider myself much of a hater, but I'm definitely jealous that I don't have boobs sometimes.

Two of the guys, who happened to be the biggest of the crew, crawled into her third row, which is not so comfortable for larger adults. They began to complain about how cramped their quarters were. As the next two guys climbed into the middle row, she addressed all of them.

"Y'all have temperature controls up here. I put the AC on full blast since I know it's a little warm back there with all that body heat."

One of the guys in the middle seat made a joke about how the body heat better not be rising since it's all dudes back there.

The final guy, the one who got food, got into the car while finishing his food. He said, "I'm sorry. I'm drunk and need food. I promise I won't spill."

Because they seemed to have a good-natured vibe about them, she decided to be a little more blunt in her playfulness. She told him, "No worries, if you spill or puke it'll be very expensive for your friend here. I don't know if he'll still like you tomorrow."

The guys talked among themselves for a few minutes about possibly changing the destination from their hotel, the Hard Rock, to another strip club. Her ears perked up, since that would be more money in her pocket. She even offered to take the ones who wanted to go sleep back to the hotel, and then take the others to the other strip club. She is the kind of driver who would do that even without the kickbacks. They decided to all just go back to their rooms. I know that must have been disappointing for her. It would have been for me. That's one of the cruelest teasers to get in this line of work, like dangling a freshly baked chocolate cake in front of a famished, dieting woman with PMS.

She addressed the guy with the food. "Wait a minute. You're telling me that you went to the strip club and came outside to *pay* for a *wiener*?"

All of the guys erupted in laughter, except the one with the wiener. He started to try to defend himself, but had a mouthful of wiener, which made them laugh even more.

She cut him off. "Didn't anyone teach you that it's rude to talk with a mouthful of wiener? Geesh, I'm sure you've even told someone that on at least one occasion." This made the rest of the guys laugh even harder. One of them was snorting. If I'm honest, I was laughing too.

He must have finished his bite. He told her, "I've never had a Rideshare driver roast me like this before. You're brutal." He didn't really sound offended though. More impressed than anything, but trying to hide it.

She said, "Wait, who's paying for the ride? I have to make sure I get a good tip." They all laughed again. A line like that would never work for me.

As the guys started talking among themselves, she

let it go. A few minutes later the other guys started roasting their friend about the wieners. The entire ride was a humorous wiener fest from the sounds of it. They just took turns messing with the guy, but he seemed to be a good sport about it.

As he was getting out of the car, he told her, "I guess I deserved this. I'm usually the one who gets all of them. Thanks for the fun ride. Hopefully you don't get any more unsolicited wieners in your car tonight."

That was one of those rare, humorous rides that remind us of the more enjoyable aspects of driving. Almost every conversation we were able to have for the rest of the night came back to wieners. It was certainly entertaining.

Our calls surprisingly didn't get cut off too much tonight. She was telling me more about the new guy she was seeing. He was living with his children and their mother, though he was telling her that he was done with her and it was just convenient and financially responsible at the moment. He said he'd move out when their lease was up.

She was somewhat hopeful that what he was telling her was true; although, she had to know that it wasn't. Apparently, they started seeing each other a few weeks earlier. It began as casual friends, as they'd known each other for about a year or so. They actually started talking and realized they have a lot in common. She thinks more like a guy when it comes to sex, and isn't afraid to say she's just fucking someone, but she was a little smitten with this one.

She had been telling me how this guy wanted her to

be all his, yet he was still living with his children's mother, but she was sure they were just "roommates." I just listened. Who was I to tell her that he was full of shit? Besides, I think she knew it. She danced around it, but she wanted to be optimistic.

They'd been spending a lot of time together. I think she was starting to come up short on her weekly goals. They were planning a trip to Florida at the end of the month. What the hell was she thinking? Had she lost her mind? How could she even think about taking a trip when her phone almost got cut off last month and she was trying to figure out how to pay her rent this week.

I couldn't really say that to her though, as her friend, because what kind of friend would that make me? She seemed so excited talking about it. Who was I to kill her enthusiasm? I didn't think I'd be able to take a trip for about ten years in my current situation.

To continue going along with the conversation, I just asked, "Really? Are you excited?" I tried to match her enthusiasm.

"Yeah, things are going pretty good right now. He's got a little bit of work stuff to do, but I've never really taken a vacation like this. He said he's going to cover everything and show me around. I think the time will be good for us. I mean, if he's serious about wanting to actually go further together."

Are you fucking kidding me? Was she even listening to herself? I mean, obviously dude is a clown. He was only messing with her to have his cake and eat it too. It's mighty convenient that he wanted to spend a whole week with her...on the other side of the country, where no one knows either one of them. I guess that's one way that you don't have to worry about getting caught.

I pushed all of those thoughts aside and told her, through my gritted teeth, "Sounds exciting. I'm really happy for you."

She's not new to this game, so there's nothing for me to really tell her. She said the sex is good and she enjoys their banter and conversations. She was going on and on, I think trying to convince herself.

I told her I had a passenger getting in. I wasn't sure if she didn't hear me, or if she chose to ignore it. My passengers were a young couple. I picked them up from downtown. They told me that they just got married. Of course, I said, "Congratulations! That's awesome."

Alyssa, in my ear, said, "Thank you! I knew you'd really be happy for me!"

I whispered into my Bluetooth, "I have a passenger."

As I tried to talk to my passengers, asking how long they've been together and where they met, Alyssa is still going a hundred miles a minute, saying, "That was clever! I know you really meant that for me!" She continued talking in circles and listing all of the reasons why she thought this guy was "the one" and they'd work out, even though she'd been through this exact situation a few times before. She was trying to convince herself, but she sounded like a broken record. I was having a hard time focusing on the couple over her rambling in my earbud. This sounds like a headache, I thought. All I heard is "Womp, womp, womp."

The couple was over the moon in love and super sappy to the point that it was nearly making me nauseous. You know, the over-the-top couple that just keeps finishing each other's thoughts, making kissy noises, calling each other "babe" or "honey" after every word? They were as mushy as a thirteen-year-old on Valentine's Day with her first crush. I literally felt sick to my stomach from all of the sugary sweetness. All of this, mixed in with Alyssa's rant about how great her triangle guy was and how it was going to be the best thing ever, was a bit too much for me to take in.

As I dropped the couple off at Circus Circus, my next passenger was right there waiting for me, which was great for my pockets. I tried to explain to Alyssa during the thirty second window that I had a passenger, but she wouldn't even let me get a word in. We did this every night and were respectful of the conversations with passengers since that is our money, but tonight she was not getting it. Was she really that blinded by her new love interest? Was it really that serious? I was trying to put food in my kids' mouths, and she was that inconsiderate and selfish?

My next passenger was a middle-aged man. He was one of the emotional drunks. The kind who believes the world is out to get them. He began to talk and sounded like the cliché old country songs. His wife left him for his brother, his dog died, and his old Chevy wouldn't start anymore. At that point, I had him in my car trying to drown his sorrows, just needing a friend's shoulder to cry on, and Alyssa was stuck on repeat about how great the new guy was, how he was different from the guys before, how much fun they were going to have in Florida, how she really thought she might be in love, and on and on.

I dropped the passenger off at a small, local bar on East Charleston and told him, "Well, I really hope things work out for you." He looked like he was about to cry as he turned toward the bar.

In my ear, Alyssa said, "Thank you, Scott! You're always so sweet; I knew you'd be happy for me. I can't talk about this with most people."

I thought, why not? Because they all tell you to grow up and get a clue? You know this guy is going to be just like the others. If, by some miracle, he actually leaves his old lady, he'll do the same thing to you! You know this. We've talked about it plenty of times.

I couldn't even cut her off since she wouldn't let me speak at all. I just let her keep talking. As I drove to pick up my next passenger a few minutes away, it clicked that she hadn't had a ride this whole time. Was she even working? How was she planning this trip when her bills were behind, and she wasn't trying to earn more money? I knew she wasn't my child, but I couldn't help but wonder where her head was at?

I tuned her out as the next passenger got in my car. I didn't want to be rude to her, because I don't believe that's what a friend does, but I couldn't take any more of that. I can only bite my tongue so much, and I actually did have to work. I didn't have a boyfriend with a wife who would pay for a trip for me. This whole thing is just absurd. How did she not see it?

The phone cut off. She must have gotten another phone call or something. I didn't even care to call her back because I couldn't take it anymore. I just drove the rest of the night without the Bluetooth in my ear. The obnoxious banter in my head was pushing me to my threshold of tolerance.

CHAPTER 22
WARRIOR STATUS
FRIDAY, JULY 6, 2018 12:30 A.M.

The night had been refreshingly busy and I was well on my way to making my goal. The Delano was my next stop. I was picking up at this hotel and casino, which is on the backside of the Mandalay Bay Casino and Resort on the south end of the main strip. The group consisted of four girls and one guy from Utah. They were in town to party for the weekend. Compared to Utah, Vegas is *the* extreme place to go hang out and party, so we get several visitors down for the weekend because it's only a few hours to drive. Utah has much stricter regulations on alcohol and isn't well-known for their nightlife. As a matter of fact, they aren't well-known for much.

The group was young and excited. I think they were all in their early twenties. They were going over to Drai's nightclub, which prides itself on being the "official" after-hours club in Vegas. The way that the group was talking and acting, I believe that they were a little bit high and already drunk, which is not uncommon. They were very respectful, high-spirited, energetic, and extremely pleasant.

The trip would be really quick, as we were only seven or eight minutes away. The young women were very attractive. Half-way through the ride, one of them, in the most calm and casual voice, said, "Sir? Driver?"

I responded, "Yes?"

She said, "You have a really nice car, and I really don't want to ruin your car, so do you think that there may be a chance that you could pull over?"

I asked, "What? How would you ruin the car?"

She explained, "Well, I have to throw up. So if you could pull over when it's convenient, I would appreciate it."

I thought to myself, this has to be some kind of a joke. Her behavior, posture, and her overwhelming calmness did not fit what I normally run into when a person has to throw up. Being respectful, I asked, "Are you sure?"

She replied, "Yes. If I throw up, then I'll be fine. It'll just take a moment."

At the next driveway that I could pull in, I turned in and pulled over. With no sense of urgency, she climbed out of the vehicle and began to throw up. I thought I was in something like the *Twilight Zone* because I had never seen anything like that. As the young lady was throwing up, the gentleman got out of the car and began to pee on a nearby bush. I just waited for Ashton Kutcher to jump out, saying that I was being punked.

No one jumped out of the bushes. They both concluded their business and got back in the vehicle. You would have never thought that anything unusual had just happened. I asked, "Are you good now?"

She answered, "Yeah. I'm ready to go."

I asked her, "Should I head back to the hotel?"

She said, "No! We're going to go party at Drai's."

"Are you sure?"

She said, "Yeah, I'm good," in a very nonchalant, normal tone.

I told her, "*You* are a warrior! I've watched many people throw up in my life. Most of the time we *think* that it's going to make us better, but I've never seen anybody throw up and completely reset themselves and be ready to keep going. If you were twenty years older, I would propose right now." She smiled. In my mind, I was hoping that the gentleman was not her boyfriend, but I really didn't care because that was exactly what I was thinking, straight warrior. She had definitely earned my respect.

I thought it would be nice to offer her a mint, so at least if she found herself kissing somebody later they wouldn't get the remnants of her throw up. I wished all of the partygoers a great time and hope they enjoy the rest of their weekend as I dropped them off at their destination. That young lady will always have a place in my heart, and definitely my utmost respect in terms of alcoholism.

CHAPTER 23

GIRL PROBLEMS

SATURDAY, JULY 14, 2018 11:25 P.M.

I picked up a guy dressed in all black with a grunge, rock look to him at the Silver Sevens casino on Flamingo and Paradise. This is a smaller property, more of a local's spot. I went through my regular small talk routine and he just opened up like a flood gate. I find that I'm more of a therapist than driver in many of these rides. We should be able to add a surcharge for counseling. Perhaps we can call it Rideshare Therapy.

He told me, "I'm here with a girl. I've really liked her for the past few years, but I'm not sure if she's into me like that, you know?"

I said, "Well, she did come on this trip with you."

"Right. But, I think it might be like friends. I just don't know."

"What don't you know?" I asked.

He went on to explain more of their history. They had known each other for a few years. There was a point when he told her that he was interested in more with her, and she told him that she wasn't. They stopped talking for a while. Then they recently came into contact with each other again and decided to just be friends. He won these concert tickets to a festival featuring a band they both enjoy and invited her to come to Vegas with him. They were sharing a hotel room, but they came under the guise of being friends.

He said, "Well, I don't know if she likes me like that. I'm getting weird vibes. Like, you know, when a girl is into you, you usually get a vibe like it's okay to make a move. I haven't made a move yet, because I'm so unsure of what she wants. And I think I might have blown my chance to make a move. Like, when we were at the concert last night, we kind of leaned in together and I put my arm around her and she put her arm around me, too. But then, after a couple of seconds, she moved away from me. So, I don't know if that was, like, more like a friend thing, or like a girl and guy thing."

I was sure that was not his first encounter with a female, at least I'd like to believe it wasn't. He mentioned that he was thirty-eight years old. How the hell could he not see that she wanted to come on the trip for the music, not to be his girl? He was actually going out by himself at that moment because she asked for some space. To me, it was clear as day, but I suppose this gentleman didn't want to see that she's not into him like that. The entire twenty-minute ride to North Las Vegas consisted of this man talking about how he didn't know if the girl was into him or not, and wanting me to validate that she was or she wasn't. He was talking in circles. It truly made me dizzy. I tried to be polite, but in my head all I could think of was how are you almost forty years old and can't figure out this girl doesn't like you like that?

I tried to give him a little bit of hope. "You could always just talk to her. Let her know that you still have feelings and would like to explore more with her. Or you can try to make a move tonight when you get back to the room."

"I can't do that. What if she says she isn't interested? Or if I try but she isn't into it? It'll be the longest, most awkward ride back to Phoenix tomorrow."

I told him, "If you don't want to try, you can always just torment yourself and wonder forever too."

I realized that I might need a break from these passengers. I didn't want to be so up front or rude, but this guy was torturing himself. I think he knew the truth, but he didn't want to see it. He had the nerve to get upset with me because of my comment. Why were you asking for my opinion if you don't really want to hear it? That almost reminded me of my conversation with Alyssa a couple of weeks ago. You want me to validate the bullshit that you know is bullshit because you're trying to convince yourself? Yeah, I needed a coffee break. Spiked would be better.

CHAPTER 24
SHARED CONFUSION
SUNDAY, JULY 15, 2018 1:20 A.M.

I picked up a young lady near Paradise and Harmon at one of the smaller hotels. She was going deep into Henderson, almost as far east as Henderson goes. The name on the ride was Benjamin. She clearly didn't look like a Benjamin, but people order rides for their friends or family all the time, so I didn't question it.

This was a shared ride. She wanted to be dropped off somewhere other than where the app was directing me. On shared rides, we are not able to alter the route or change the destination. I explained to her that if her desired destination was close to where the app was directing me, and we did not have another passenger, I would go ahead and take her. Just as I finished saying that, I got the notification that another passenger had been added to the ride.

We picked up a young man around the same age as her. I believe they were both somewhere between nineteen and twenty-two. When the young man got in, the two of them started having a conversation about where they were from, what they like to do, and what they were into, so I just let them talk.

In my mind, I was kind of laughing to myself, thinking maybe I had the Rideshare love connection going. I might be able to market this into some kind of game show or reality show, like Rideshare for Singles or something. I wondered if there are actual couples that have met in a Rideshare. Probably. These millennials are a little bit different than how I remember growing up. We didn't have technology and apps and things of that nature. We had to actually meet people in person, see them, and talk to them. Imagine that...a relationship where you have to communicate and spend time together to make it work.

We ended up dropping her off first, at the location in the app. Before she got out of the vehicle, they exchanged phone numbers. I wasn't trying to be nosey or be in their business, but I think they might have been making out a little bit.

I closed out the ride, verified his address, and went on my way. He must have noticed the name Benjamin on my phone when she was getting out.

He said, "Excuse me, but what was her name?"

I told him, "I'm not sure, but the ride was under the name Benjamin."

He said, "Her hands were really big and rough. Do you think *she* was Benjamin?"

I just started laughing. I couldn't even hold it in or pretend or give this young man hope. I wasn't sure if the girl was born a female, or if she was just transitioning or wanting to be a girl. We did have a really good laugh over the next three minutes, until we got to his place. He did mention that she was already texting him. That made me laugh even harder. The young man seemed incredibly confused. I guess, at the end of the day, we were both confused. Except I hadn't kissed or touched her...or him?

On another note, all three of my older kids are coming to visit this week. We'd be celebrating my second oldest son's birthday. I would have loved to let them entertain the little ones so I could get some extra driving time in, but I really did miss them. I realized that they are probably the only thing keeping me sane at this point. I had been able to maintain and get a couple of the bills almost current, but I was nowhere near where I needed to be. My life seemed to resemble a pointless hamster wheel, where I was chasing money to barely survive, nearly killing myself working over eighty hours per week and still not moving forward. I hadn't even been able to do anything this summer with my kids yet. Maybe I'd bite the bullet and take them all to a water park. I'd have to see which bill wasn't about to be shut off this week and shuffle it around.

The water was current, which to me meant it wasn't over thirty days past due and wasn't in immediate danger of being disconnected. I didn't have to worry about that one. They only threaten to turn that off after about five or six months.

The gas was about three months behind. I might be able to push that another week or so. I'd have to check the shutoff date. Actually, I could get at least another two weeks out of that one. It was only ninety-five dollars. That wasn't that big of a deal.

The power was about a month behind, but that was on a payment plan already. I could probably call and beg them to rearrange the payment plan and buy myself another few weeks.

The internet and cable was almost two months behind, but I could set up a future payment, and then change it if I needed to. Yeah, I'd be able to swing it. No problem. Plus, over the next few weeks of summer visitors, I'd be able to make it up. No worries. I got this. Problem solved.

CHAPTER 25

CUCUMBER WHORES

FRIDAY, JULY 20, 2018 10:30 P.M.

My younger kids were with their grandparents, and my older kids were hanging out together downtown on Fremont Street. They seemed like they kind of wanted to do their own thing, so I decided to get a few rides in. I figured I'd shut down early so I could get up and cook them breakfast and see what we could get into in the morning.

I picked up a man about my age, maybe a few years older, from a well-kept, older home in North Las Vegas. The gentleman had a way about him. He carried himself like any other hardworking, upstanding citizen in a friendly, good-natured way; though there was something about his tone that made me think he may have been an old school pimp or player who had just been domesticated. We were heading to the airport for him to go back to Indiana, where he was from, to take care of some family business. He mentioned that he had been in Vegas for quite some time.

"What do you do?" I asked, keeping with the small talk and friendly conversation.

"I'm the produce manager at a grocery store," he said.

"Oh," I replied. "Are you going to be back home in time for the first of the month rush?" My only association with the grocery store is how much I hate going during the first few days of the month. It seems as bad as Black Friday or Christmas Eve shopping. I just don't have the patience for it.

"Mmmhhmmm." He looked at me and shook his head. "I hate that time of the month. The cucumber whores get on my nerves."

I happen to be a fan of cucumbers and didn't quite know how to take that comment. Dumbfounded, I had to ask, "What exactly is a cucumber whore?"

He said, "Mmmhhmmm. You know. Those whores that come for the cucumbers." I wondered if maybe the "mmmhhmmm" was like a nervous tic or something. Either way, it made me think of Cleveland Brown from the *Family Guy* and *The Cleveland Show* cartoons. I didn't get much free time to enjoy TV, but those programs made me laugh when I could sneak in an episode.

There was a long silence. I realized that he may have assumed that I knew what he meant. Since I didn't, I broke the silence. "I'm sorry, I still don't follow. What about the cucumbers?"

"Ya see, at the first of the month, they get their money on them EBT cards," he explained with a slight grin. "You would think whores were spending a hundred dollars on them cucumbers the way they demand them to be firm and hard. And they damn near fight over each other to grab them. And they all want to complain to me about how they're not firm enough or hard enough, while they're waving them around like a bat that they want to slug me over the head with. They are the most demanding and ridiculous customers I have in all of the produce section. Mmmhhmmm."

I said, "I enjoy cucumbers just as much as the next. But I didn't think the people who use EBT eat cucumbers like that."

He gave that "mmmhhmmm," then said, "Them whores ain't eatin' the cucumbers. They can't use EBT for them there dildos and they're too cheap to spend their cash on them."

My stomach turned at the thought of one of my favorite vegetables being put inside of these nasty whores, even though I still didn't really know who they were or what made them nasty. "You have to be joking. You cannot possibly be serious. Plus, there's no way you could actually know." I was halfway asking and halfway stating.

He responded by telling me that he had been in the grocery business for more than thirty years. He said he can take one glance at a person's cart and tell you how they live their life. "And when these whores come to my section and the only produce they're grabbing is cucumbers, with a cart full of junk food, them whores ain't eatin' them cucumbers. And if they were, they wouldn't be worried about getting the firmest ones. Mmmhhmmm."

I said, "I guess you have a point. I don't think I'll ever look at cucumbers the same after this. I'd think there would be a fruit or vegetable that would be better suited for the job?"

He said, "I tell them whores the same thing, but they're too damn cheap. Why would you buy the Chinese eggplant for three dollars when you can buy cucumbers two for a dollar?"

All I could think was wow. Who would have ever thought about going to the produce section for a dildo? After thinking about it for a few minutes, I asked, "What about carrots? They're cheaper and way firmer than cucumbers."

He said, "These hoes need girth, and a little itty-bitty carrot ain't gettin' them off. Mmmhhmmm."

He really thought this all the way through. I thought he's got way too much time on his hands, and he was way too worried about what is in these hoes' carts. As if he was reading my mind, he kindly extended the invitation for me to come in there and join him on the first of the month to check out his cucumber whores firsthand.

"I'm grateful for the invitation, but that doesn't seem like my type of environment. It seems like you enjoy being harassed by the cucumber whores, so I wouldn't want to take away from your thunder."

As we pulled into the airport, I took the time for a brief reflection on the ride. This one seemed a lot less like work, and a lot more like I was giving a ride to an old friend. Why couldn't they all be like this? Oh well, on to the next one we go.

CHAPTER 26
THE "A WORD"
FRIDAY, JULY 21, 2018 2:15 A.M.

I was entering the Flamingo and Cromwell driveway. It had been an incredibly busy night. The cars were backed up and we were moving at the pace of a slow crawl. I wasn't quite to my passenger and the battery light started blinking on the dash of my car.

Immediately, I began to panic. What in the hell could this be? I knew it was too good to be true. I was having a really good day. I wasn't too stressed about anything. I knew I'd get to hang out with my older kids later. And then this. What would I do if it just shuts off? What was I going to do, get out and push it? Push it to where? As many cars and traffic as there were, I don't even think a tow truck would be able to get in there. It wasn't like I could really afford a tow truck anyway.

Maybe I should just cancel this ride, I thought. What difference would it make if I cancel it or not? It would take the same amount of time for me to pick up the passenger as it would for me to turn around and get out of there. I was still trying to sort out what I was going to do and the A/C shut off. I figured that meant that my vehicle was about to die. Unless the air conditioning just miraculously went out, the power going to the A/C had been cut to try to keep the vehicle running.

Maybe I should turn off the radio, too, just to save any little bit of power that I have left, my mind raced. This could easily turn into a long, awkward ride, especially in silence with no radio. It would be really bad to break down on the side of the road with a passenger in my car. What was I going to do, ask them to help me push? I hoped they wouldn't complain about the heat. I was already starting to sweat. Maybe it would cool off when I got to driving a little bit faster, I figured.

I finally picked up the passenger. I greeted her as usual and apologized for the A/C not working because I knew it was a little bit warm.

It was a really nice older lady. She told me, "No problem. The fresh air is nice."

All of the sudden, the destination changed. It was a shared ride. At that point I thought I may have just made the biggest mistake of my life. A shared ride on the Las Vegas strip on a Friday night that should take five minutes can take five hours. And it's not like I could skip picking up the second passenger because I didn't even know where the nice woman was going.

The second passenger was next door, at Harrah's. I thought it shouldn't be too hard to get in and out of there. I was already committed to the ride, so I figured I might as well go get the other passenger. The bright light on my dash was just stabbing me in the eye.

I attempted to turn my attention to the passenger, my children, or anything else to distract me. But all I could manage was to plot out all of the worst case scenarios in my head. I hadn't even come up with a plan for what I was going to do after I got these passengers out of my vehicle.

I picked up the second passenger. I was somewhat relieved to see that the first destination was across the street, at the Bellagio. On the flip side, my anxiety was at an all-time high. Because I figured it was highly likely that we'd end up taking on another passenger at the Bellagio and I had no idea how long I might have before my car just gave out all the way. Maybe that's where I should direct my thoughts. What am I going to do to fix this problem? Besides just curl up in a ball and cry like a little baby.

After the drop off at the Bellagio, my next destination was eighteen minutes away, heading southwest. Oh great. A long ride, and possibly getting stranded in the middle of nowhere. On this hot summer night.

I tried to engage in some lighthearted conversation with the woman I first picked up. She began to tell me about her situation. She was a widow. It sounded like she was incredibly lonely and didn't have many people to talk to. Her husband was everything to her, and she was trying to regain a grasp on life after losing him. Listening to the woman share her story, I remembered that there is a twenty-four-hour AutoZone in the direction that we were heading.

I figured that I could stop in there and have them tell me whether it was my battery or alternator that was the problem. As I started to feel a slight bit of relief, another situation began to arise. Something that I ate, or maybe the stress, had my stomach turning and twisting in knots, and I really needed to take a shit.

Bathrooms that are clean, and available, are a challenge when driving, especially at this time of the night. The casinos off the strip are a great option, but I wasn't sure if I turned the car off that it would turn back on. Though that would be a better way to relieve myself, I couldn't afford to do that and get stuck on that side of town, especially with my children in town to visit me. They would be calling any minute saying they were done hanging out downtown.

I thought the priority was getting to AutoZone, and I'd deal with the stomach issue later. I dropped off the passenger and turned my app off. I was only a few minutes from the auto parts store when I started sweating profusely, hoping and praying that I'd make it there in time. My butt cheeks were clenched and I was just hoping that I could make it there without shitting on myself.

As I approached the intersection, I noticed a bar off to the right. Should I go to the bar and take my chances? No. I parked at the AutoZone since it was only across the street. I flew into a parking spot and jumped out of my car in a dead sprint trying to get across the busy intersection to the bar.

I entered the bar to see only three people inside, including the bartender. I was hoping to sneak in, use the restroom, and sneak out undetected. Clearly that was not going to happen. I told the bartender, "I'm not actually here to drink. I really need to use the restroom. If it's required, I'll go ahead and pay for a drink."

He just waved me on to go ahead and use the facilities.

I barely made it in time. I was just grateful as I was relieving myself that I didn't have an accident because I don't know what I would have done in that situation. Being very appreciative for the use of the facilities, I exited the bar after leaving a five-dollar tip for the bartender, and made my way back over to AutoZone, where I left my vehicle.

Little did I know that I was about to enter into one of the worst nights of my life. If it didn't happen to me, I probably wouldn't even believe it.

I went inside of AutoZone and it was very busy. Instead of walking to the counter and cutting, I just waited patiently behind the other people who were waiting for service. The gentleman behind the counter seemed to have a lot more conversation with his fellow employee than with the customer standing in front of him that he was being paid to help.

I figured this is probably the best service one could expect in the middle of the night, so I did my best to not let myself be bothered; although, ringing up one person seemed to be a ten minute fiasco. Nine of those ten minutes were spent discussing weekend plans with his co-worker.

The next customer walked up to his counter and he lit up and had a long, personal conversation with that person. I thought to myself, maybe they're just good friends. The customer asked him to look up a part and got the price, then walked out without even purchasing anything. I would have imagined that process should have taken about three minutes, not thirty.

My turn finally came up. I walked up to the counter and asked the young man if he would be able to come outside with me to test my battery.

He said, "Okay, hold on a minute. I have to help the rest of the line because I'm the only one working." I cut my eyes over at the other person working and looked back at him. He said, "Oh, that's the manager. I'm the only one ringing up customers."

I simply said, "Okay," and stepped to the side.

Another half hour passed by as he slowly helped the rest of the customers in the store. The next customer walked in, just as he was about to be freed up to go outside and check my battery. She happened to be a very attractive young woman. He put the meter down and returned to his post. I think he spent more time flirting with her than anything else.

Halfway through his flirtatious conversation, he said, "Look, it's really busy. It would be a lot easier and faster if you just bring the battery in."

After checking the time and realizing I had several other things I could have been doing, I asked him if I could borrow the tools to take it out. Especially considering the steady flow of customers, I realized I could be there all night.

I had already gotten a text from my kids that they were on their way home from Fremont. Alyssa has been calling to check on me. Each time she realized that I was still there, she remarked it shouldn't take that long, and then she'd get a ride, so we'd hang up.

The gentleman asked, "What tools do you need to borrow?"

I said, "I'm not exactly mechanically inclined, so I'm not completely sure. Do you have any suggestions?"

He exhaled sharply and stomped over to what I guessed was their tool storage area. He came back and handed me a set of pliers. I assumed that he was a professional and had done this multiple times, so I took the pliers and walked outside.

After popping the hood and trying to figure out how to use the pliers on two sides of the bolt and nut, I just stood there for a moment perplexed, not knowing what to do. Then I watched him walk outside, with the same young lady following closely behind him. I got my hopes up, thinking that he was coming to assist me.

That hope quickly dried up when he stopped at the vehicle a space over from mine and instructed the young lady to pop her hood. I looked over, waiting for a few minutes to see if there would even be a visual acknowledgement of me being there, such as a slight nod or glance or something. I wondered what happened to him not being able to step outside. What? He could only step outside to help someone if they have tits and ass? It was thoroughly ridiculous.

After another five minutes of standing there, realizing that there was no adequate way of removing my battery with pliers, I went back inside to see if I could seek other assistance. The other employee that he referred to as the manager was now on the register. What an interesting turn of events. I thought the whole reason he couldn't step out to help me was because she couldn't ring up customers.

Once again, I patiently waited in line, waiting for my turn. I guessed one good thing was that she was actually helping the customers at a faster pace since she wasn't socializing like the gentleman was, but there was a long line again.

When I finally made my way to the front of the line, I asked the young lady if there was another person who could help me remove my battery or at least come test it. She told me that the only person who could do that was outside helping another customer and I'd have to wait my turn.

This was about the time that the kids texted me saying they arrived at the house and we could have a game night if I wanted to head home, as well. One of my favorite activities with them is our game nights. We play very competitively, but we also talk, joke, and learn each other as well as strengthen math skills and thinking on our feet. I texted them back letting them know that I'd be home as soon as possible, but I had ran into a bit of a delay.

Alyssa was back in my ear at that point, on the phone. She heard the entire conversation. I think she was getting worked up enough for the both of us. She said, "Didn't you already wait in line? Didn't you already wait your turn? What the fuck does she mean?"

I quietly told her, "I'm just trying to get this situation resolved. Me getting worked up about it isn't going to get it handled any sooner."

She sighed and said, "You obviously have far more patience than I do."

I told her, "I'm just trying to get through it."

Alyssa continued to tell me, "It's not getting handled, because you are still waiting."

Under my breath, I told her, "What could I possibly do? Yell, cuss, and scream? How much faster will that get this situation taken care of? How much more likely will they be to help me with that kind of behavior?"

I stepped to the side to let her finish helping the people that were in line behind me. A few moments after the manager worked through the line, she looked over and started to speak. She said, "Oh. I'm sure he'll be with you in just a moment," referring to the same gentleman I was trying to get help from in the first place.

A few more minutes went by with me patiently waiting, and then the gentleman came back in. I looked at the time and calculated that if we could get this resolved quickly, I would still have a couple of hours for game night, even though quite a bit of time had already elapsed.

I was strategically positioned so that the gentleman had to pretty much walk through me to get back to his terminal. Even though I was twice his size, you would have thought that I was invisible. He walked right by me without making any contact. He didn't even glance in my direction.

The manager and the gentleman engaged in a conversation that seemed to be very personal. I was thinking, what the fuck is going on? This is ridiculous. Just as I gathered the mental strength to ask for assistance, again, three more customers walked in. They were all greeted by both the manager and the gentleman. What made this even more bothersome was that both employees had to look past me to see and greet the new customers. Clearly, I must have been invisible.

I thought, you've got to be kidding me; this is completely absurd. To make it more ridiculous, I got back in the line, behind the new customers. Maybe I was standing in the wrong line this whole time. Even though there was only one line. What else could it be?

Alyssa heard the conversations going on and asked me if they were finally getting around to helping me.

"Nope. They have new customers, so I got back in line."

She spouted off. You would have thought she was the one in my place. "You're fucking joking, right?"

"Nope."

In disbelief, she said, "There is no way this is really happening."

I finally took a second to stop and think about what this might seem like on her end of the phone. I realized that I was being very short with my answers to her, but that was all that I could do to try to contain my agitation.

They helped two of the three customers in the line when the manager finally looked at me and acknowledged my presence. "Sir, you don't have to stand in line again."

I thought, how the fuck else can I get some attention in here? Instead, I responded with, "I didn't want the other customers to think that I was cutting in line."

The manager sighed heavily and directed her attention to the man, "Ugh. Will you please go outside and help this gentleman with his battery?" Clearly, I must have been delusional. It appeared as though she was irritated like she was the one waiting for service this whole time.

Through gritted teeth I said, "Thank you." Obviously, I was causing these people a great inconvenience.

With an extreme and exaggerated amount of disgust and discontent he followed me outside. When we got to my car, he asked me for the tools. I handed him the same pair of pliers he had handed me.

He looked at me like I was stupid. "We can't get the battery out with this."

I guess I should have been relieved. That meant that there was nothing wrong with me; although, that seemed pretty obvious when he handed it to me in the first place.

He walked slowly back into the store. I was hoping he was going to retrieve the proper tools.

After another ten minutes had passed, I decided to go in to see if he got lost. I saw him standing there with a tool in his hand. He was talking to yet another customer. With an incredibly relaxed posture, he half-heartedly assured me that he was just on his way back out.

I nodded and headed back outside, continuing to remind myself that the ordeal was almost over.

He joined me a couple of minutes later. He disconnected my battery swiftly and effortlessly then headed back inside like the job had been completed.

I shook my head, confused. I did the only thing that made sense to me. I picked up the battery and took it with me as I made my way back inside. As if Murphy's Law was my personal assistant and that old cliché saying, "if something can go wrong, it will," it did. I felt like I was in an old slap-knee comedy and I was the butt of all the jokes. There was another long line. Both the manager and the ever-so-helpful gentleman were assisting customers.

I did the only reasonable thing I could think of to do. I got back in line, holding my battery.

After about ten minutes, the manager noticed that I was standing there holding the increasingly heavy battery. She said, "Sir, you don't have to stand there holding the battery."

Completely confused, I was trying to future out what she meant. Was I supposed to go back outside with the battery and wait there? The gentleman didn't give me any further instructions, so I was completely clueless. Maybe he snapped his fingers like a fucking genie after disconnecting the battery and all of my issues were resolved? But I still didn't have a functional car.

I pushed the trail of unproductive thoughts to the side. I said, "Ma'am, I wasn't sure what I was supposed to do next. I originally came to get my battery tested to see if I needed to purchase a new battery. The gentleman was kind enough to disconnect my battery but then he walked away. I wasn't sure what to do next."

She looked at him and rolled her eyes at him. She instructed me to set the battery on the empty spot on the counter.

I believe she was trying to speak to him under her breath, but I heard her clearly. She said, "You wasn't gonna test the battery?" Perhaps her escalating irritation would yield speedier and more favorable results since she was the manager. I could only hope.

Another fifteen minutes passed by with the battery sitting on the counter and me standing off to the side of the line. I was angry, frustrated, and confused all at the same time. She finally noticed that I was still standing there and instructed him to test my battery.

He retrieved a cart to haul my battery to the back of the store for him to test it. Apparently, the battery was light enough for me to stand there for half an hour holding it, but too heavy for him to simply carry it twenty feet to the back of the store.

My frustration continued to escalate. I was hot and sweaty, and it felt like my blood was literally boiling beneath my skin. He was in the back with my battery for another ten minutes or so. He came back to the front and told me, "Your battery is no good." Then stared at me with a blank look.

I said, "Okay? Do you have a battery that I can purchase to replace that battery?"

He simply responded, "Yeah," and continued to just stare at me. I must be speaking a foreign language. The responses that I was getting didn't seem to line up with what I was requesting or asking.

I spoke a little bit slower. "How much is the battery?"

He sighed with frustration and started typing slowly with loud, exaggerated pushes of the buttons. He pulled up the list of batteries that would fit my car. He scrolled past the first four options quickly and told me "It'll be one hundred and ninety-nine dollars."

I hadn't purchased a battery in quite some time, but I didn't figure inflation had taken that much of a turn. I asked him, "What was wrong with the other batteries you scrolled past? It looked like there was one for sixty-nine dollars."

He shook his head quickly and said, "You don't want that one."

I asked, "Why not?"

He simply stated, "It's just not a good battery."

Due to my finances and this being an unexpected expense, I really needed that sixty-nine-dollar option to work. I asked him, "Is it compatible with my vehicle?"

He hesitated. "Well, yeah."

"Okay. Can I purchase that battery then?"

He clicked his tongue, disgusted. He said, "Let me see if I have one," and leisurely walked away.

When he returned a few minutes later he told me, "There's one here." He didn't have a battery in his hands and just stood there looking at me, yet again.

I asked, "What do I need to do? Do you want to point me in the direction for me to go get the battery? Or what is the next step?"

"You just have to pay for it." He just stared at me.

I waited for a few moments, trying to figure out what I was missing. I asked, "Can we do that?"

This entire transaction seemed completely unusual to me; however, it appeared to be just another normal day for him based on the way he was conducting himself.

He asked me for some of my information, charged me for the battery, and then brought it out to me. And stared at me. Again.

I found myself in the position once again to need the tools to do the job at hand, although I was also holding a heavy battery. This seemed like double déjà vu. I asked for the tools.

He said, "Oh, yeah. I guess you might need those." He kind of chuckled, then retrieved them and gave them to me.

I dared not ask for his assistance this time. After watching him remove the old battery I felt fairly confident that I could install the new battery on my own, with much less frustration than it would take me to ask for his assistance.

I spent the next fifteen or twenty minutes trying to do the opposite of what I saw him do when he removed the original battery. When I tried to connect one of the posts to the battery it didn't seem like it fit. It wouldn't go all the way down.

I didn't know what to do. I was just done. I couldn't take any more. It was completely out of hand.

Standing there with my back against the wall, no other viable options in sight, I dropped my head and humbly walked back inside to ask for further assistance. Of course, the gentleman was busy, yet again. Busy smiling, flirting, and *possibly* selling something to another attractive woman.

I patiently waited for him to complete his transaction. When he was free, I told him that I was having a difficult time installing the battery.

With a sly smirk, he replied, "I told you that battery was no good."

In an incredibly sharp tone, I rebutted, "You told me that it would fit, but maybe I'm putting it in wrong. I would deeply appreciate it if you would give me a hand so that I could get out of the way." I wanted to add, clearly, I'm interrupting your social hour so the least I could do is politely get out of your way.

He let out a gasp. "Alright. I'll come help in a minute."

At that point, I was so annoyed just being in his presence that I chose to wait outside, even though I had good reason to believe that would make his return to assist me take even longer.

In my ear, Alyssa asked me if there was anything that I needed. I really don't like to impose on anyone, but it had been quite some time since I had some water. She wasn't too far away, so she offered to bring me some and offer some support. I really didn't like thinking that this mess was going to cause both of us to miss out on some earnings, but I could really use the support of a good friend. I honestly believed that a part of her motivation was curiosity. I didn't think it was easy to believe this situation was real, so it might have seemed like I was playing some sort of a joke on her.

The gentleman was clearly in no rush to help me resolve my situation because Alyssa pulled up as we were finally making it out to my vehicle. She was a life saver. She came bearing gifts. Along with the water, she had a coffee. The timing was perfect.

The man approached my vehicle with an arrogance that is really hard to describe with all of the words I have at my disposal. He looked as though walking up to my vehicle was truly beneath him. It must have been because I am not an attractive woman because his approach was completely different than it was with the woman he helped roughly an hour ago.

Nonetheless, I pushed those thoughts out of my mind because I just wanted to get this taken care of to get back to my kids. When he noticed Alyssa, he suddenly became incredibly helpful. His whole disposition changed. I just looked at her and shook my head in disgust. If her presence was going to get me the help I needed, I'd be incredibly grateful for it. I should have asked her to come an hour ago.

As a matter of fact, she should have been the one with this issue. It's not like her back is against the wall. She didn't have anything better to do tonight. Plus, she could have just flirted her way into some quick assistance and it wouldn't have even affected her night. I actually had real problems.

I turned my attention back to my issues as I gulped down some of the ice cold water she gave me. I was just hoping that he would get the battery done so that I could leave, but another part of me was hoping he ran into some sort of resistance so that I didn't feel completely handicapped for not being able to do it myself.

He swiftly worked under the hood of my vehicle and smiled. "See, it fits right on. No problem." After a closer inspection, I noticed that he started with the opposite post than I did. I hung my head low and just hoped he could finish quickly so I could leave.

"Huh." He seemed perplexed. I looked over at him. "There seems to be a problem." He looked genuinely confused.

"Oh, really?" I inquired. "What seems to be the problem?"

"It doesn't fit."

Are you fucking kidding me? That's what I told him two hours ago! Some of the arrogance escaped him like the used up hot air being expelled from his lungs. I think he was coming out to prove that it was not that hard to put a battery in and was coming out just to try to make me look stupid.

"Yeah, that's what I told you when I went inside."

"They must have this battery listed wrong in the computer because this obviously doesn't fit your car."

"Okay. Can we get the correct battery?"

"Yeah. Just bring it back inside." He walked away

before he even completed the sentence.

I disconnected the post and lifted the battery out of the vehicle. For the first time all night, when I walked in, I was the only customer in the store. I walked up to the counter and he began to promptly help me.

He informed me, "The battery you need is forty dollars more."

I sighed. "Whatever we need to do to get this done." At that point, I think my agitation with the fact that I was spending money that I didn't have was greater than with the gentleman. It was still less than I would've paid for a tow truck, though. I mean, it was just a battery. It wasn't supposed to be this complicated.

He rang up the battery and asked, "Do you need my help this time or do you think you can figure it out since you have the correct battery?"

I snatched the battery off the counter and didn't even dare ask for his assistance. I headed back outside.

I repeated the same process, only to find that the new battery didn't fit either. You've got to be fucking kidding me; there is no way this is happening, I thought. I didn't want to go back inside and ask him anything else.

I walked back in carrying the battery. He looked at me and in the snarkiest tone possible said, "What, you couldn't figure it out?"

I humbly replied, "This one doesn't fit either."

He said, "If that didn't fit, you've got to be doing something wrong. That's the right battery."

I told him, "I believe that is the situation, and that is

why I am asking for your help." Reluctantly, he followed me outside once again.

He repeated the same steps that I just did and came to the conclusion that it must require the third battery, which was the most expensive. "You must need the one I first told you to get."

I started off buying a battery that cost sixty-nine dollars, and now we're at the point of him saying I need a two-hundred-dollar battery. Who the hell has two hundred dollars lying around for a battery? I certainly don't. But if I didn't spend the two hundred dollars, I wouldn't have the ability to make more money. I told him, "Fine. Let's just get this done."

I always thought that batteries were more universal. This vehicle is newer than any other vehicle I had ever owned before. I just wanted to get out of there. I went ahead and paid the difference for the most expensive battery on the list.

We went outside, yet again. This time, he tried to connect the terminals in the opposite way. Maybe that was his good luck quirk to connect the battery and get it to work. When he attempted to connect the post that had not been connecting for us, the car began to scream. All the lights and honking and siren were going off nonstop.

I thought, something is definitely not right. The car is not supposed to make that kind of sound. Yet the gentleman was persistent in trying to force the connection, despite all the noise. In a desperate attempt to prevent any further damage, I asked him, "Do you think we're possibly connecting it backwards?"

He said, "I know what I'm doing. I've done this a thousand times. I just have to go get another tool, and then I can get this battery done."

Ten minutes later he came walking out with a mallet. I don't have the vastest experience in auto mechanics, but I don't believe I've ever seen someone use a mallet to change a car battery. He began to beat the cable onto the battery terminal.

After forty-five minutes of beating, and subsequently disfiguring the battery cable completely, he said, "There we go. All done."

I looked at the mangled job that he did, and the amount of time that had elapsed, and thought, I'll just deal with this tomorrow, as long as I can get my car running.

I went to start the car, and nothing happened. Well, nothing except the loud noise of horns, sirens, and flashing lights. I looked over at the gentleman.

He put his hands on his head and said, "In all of my years of mechanical experience, I've never had a problem like this before." He couldn't have been more than twenty-two or twenty-three years old, so I couldn't help but think how much experience could he possibly have? The only thing that I could see that he had verifiable experience in is making a big mess out of a situation, and he had successfully wasted four hours of my night at that point.

He then pulled out his cell phone and resorted to searching Google for an answer. As he was looking at his phone, the manager came out to figure out what was taking so long. When she looked at the mess that he made with the battery terminals, she looked at him and said, "Did you get it?"

I didn't hear exactly what he said, but she left rather rapidly. I peered over and took a closer look at the connections that he made and noticed that they were connected backwards. He had the positive cable connected to the negative post, and vice versa. I guessed that was why it didn't fit.

As I pointed this out to the gentleman, he said, "No. The red goes to the positive." There was a portion of the cable that was red, making it appear as though it should be a positive connection, though it was clearly marked with the negative sign. A look of embarrassment came over his face, though he didn't say anything. He quickly removed the cables and switched them around. It was too late for that though, as the battery was dead.

He said, "That must have killed this battery. Let's go get you another battery."

Alyssa has been observing this situation the whole time and stuck around like a good friend, or curious spectator. I had carefully tuned out anything she was saying because her frustration was growing rapidly, which was only contributing to mine.

When he went inside to get me another battery, I turned to Alyssa, figuring that I could at least pay her some attention since she had been patiently waiting with me over the last couple of hours.

She said, "So, he was trying to put the battery in backwards?"

I said, "Yep. And that may have just fucked up my

car. We'll know as soon as this new battery comes out." I did a little bit of my own research on Google while he mangled my car.

The gentleman returned a few minutes later and said, "That was the last of those batteries. If you'd like, you can go pick up another one at the other twenty-four-hour store because they have some in stock."

I said, "I can't go to the other store because my car won't start."

He looked down and said, "Well, that's all that I can really do for you."

I took a deep breath. I felt like he just wanted to get rid of me. I said, "Since the problem was the battery going on backwards, maybe one of the cheaper batteries will fit. I'll just take the less expensive battery, like the first one I picked out."

He said, "I won't be able to do a refund until the manager comes in tomorrow morning."

I looked at him with a sense of confusion and disgust. I said, "How does that work, when you just did it twice?"

He said, "When you're buying a more expensive product, that works. But we are not able to give refunds and cash back."

I was speaking to him with my response, but I was looking at the manager. "So, you're telling me that I have to buy a second battery to put in my car tonight and to take this broken battery with me, to come all the way back here tomorrow to get a refund for this broken battery that was broken while *you* were installing it?"

The manager put her head down, and then rapidly

found something that needed her immediate attention in the back of the store. The gentlemen said, "Yes."

I said, "You've got to fucking be kidding me. You know this is completely ridiculous, right?"

He said, "It's store policy."

I said, "Go ahead and give me the battery that I need so we can put this in so I can get out of your hair."

He fumbled around with his computer trying to process the transaction for the next thirty minutes. When I originally bought my first battery, I forgot to get my twenty percent discount for being a Rideshare driver. Trying to focus on the positives, I made sure that I did get the discount this time around. That may be what took so long that time.

In a great fit of frustration toward the end of the transaction, he ended up doing a refund on the original transaction to complete the new one. That should have pleased me, but it just irritated me further. "That's what I fuckin' told you to do in the first place."

He said, "It wouldn't take it the other way, so I had to do it this way." He seemed more disturbed than me.

How did he have the nerve to act like he was bothered at all? He was working, so he was being paid the whole time to "babysit" me, if that's how he wanted to see it, yet this was costing me money. Damn near the whole time I had been there, I had been spoken to as if I were a child, irrelevant, and not capable of basic functions. He, and his manager, had both used extremely condescending tones, and just treated me like a pure piece of shit. Yet both of *them* were irritated? I wanted to just get this done so I could fucking go.

Once again, the gentleman came outside to install the battery. All I was thinking was that I just couldn't wait to drive away. I never wanted to see that place or those people again, *ever* in my life. The mangled battery cable wouldn't even tighten down over the battery post. Just fucking great. My whole night was shot, and now I couldn't even get my car home. What was I going to do now?

At that point, Alyssa had become silent. I looked over at her and realized that I had ruined the rest of her night as well. That made things even worse. To make things even worse than that, I was going to have to ask her for a ride home, which is way out of her way. I didn't even have enough left on my card to order a Rideshare to get home. I told her, "I'd really hate to ask you this, but is there any way you can give me a ride home? I'm going to have to figure out what to do tomorrow."

Without any hesitation, she said, "Sure. No problem."

The whole ride home, she bombarded me with questions. What are you going to do? What do you think is wrong? Did he really mess your car up? I fumbled my way through the questions, but each time she asked my rage flared. I was sure he was getting off of work right about that time. My thoughts drifted to how nice it would be to wait for him in his car and just strangle him. He killed my time, so I should kill him. I was fairly certain that he destroyed my car. Without my car, I would be without my earnings. Without that, my children and I will be homeless for sure.

We pulled up to my house and I thanked her and said goodnight. It was all that I could do to maintain a somewhat positive outlook. I decided the best thing I could do at that point was to get some sleep so I could be clear-headed in the morning to figure out what to do next, and be able to make breakfast for the kids. I couldn't really afford to take them out, especially now.

CHAPTER 27
TWO FOR ONE
THURSDAY, JULY 26, 2018 9:45 P.M.

I hadn't been able to work all week since the whole battery thing ended up frying my battery, alternator, and some other stuff. I had to have the car towed to a shop. About a thousand dollars and four days later, I had my car back. The older kids were all back home and I was back on my regular schedule. I think I would have completely lost my mind if they weren't there to distract me a bit, even though it kind of added to my financial stress.

I picked up a large group of drunk, tired people at the small Best Western tucked away on the strip. I had driven by it so many times without realizing it was even there. I think there were seven people who climbed in the car - way too many. We were going into a neighborhood a few miles away off of Spring Mountain and Rainbow that their company rented for them to do some work out here.

The group made me extremely uncomfortable. I'm

not even sure of why. I sensed some kind of anxiety or impatience, or something. In short, clipped conversation they shared that they were in town for the weekend for work and had more co-workers/friends coming into town in the morning. They decided to take advantage of the evening by spending their first few hours in town walking around the strip and challenging each other to drink. They had loaded all of their equipment in the morning, drove five hours from California, unloaded their equipment at the house, and then hit the streets.

We were a couple of miles away from their rental house when the guy in the front seat started asking, "How much longer until we're there?"

After the third time that he asked in less than five minutes, I asked him, "Are you okay? Do you need me to pull over?"

"Yes, please. I get car sick, and I think this is just too much." I pulled over, into a parking lot. I've never seen anyone get car sick in the front seat in less than fifteen minutes. The rest of the group was laughing and joking and talking among themselves, mostly in Spanish.

He was standing between a couple of trees off to the side of the parking lot throwing up. One of the guys in the back got out and walked toward him. I assumed he was over there checking on his friend. Nope. I was wrong. Now there were two men standing about three feet apart, throwing up into the same puddle. I didn't know if I was more amused or disturbed.

The entire car erupted into hysterical laughter.

After a few minutes of weird teamwork of the duo

creating a vomit puddle, they got back into the vehicle. As disgusted as I was, I took a little bit of satisfaction knowing that their friends weren't likely to let them live that experience down.

One of them asked, "Is this is a first for you, or does this happen often?"

I shook my head. "I've had a few throw up, but this is my first two-for-one."

They all exploded in hysterics again, except for the two who couldn't hold their liquor.

I was sure I must be setting some kind of throwupper record. I have heard of other drivers having issues, but my percentage seemed pretty high. Alyssa has only had a couple, and she drives way more than I do.

I don't really make any money when I'm just sitting in my car waiting for them to finish throwing up. I didn't want to rush them either. Then they might not have gotten it all out. I really didn't think I could handle them throwing up in my car on a money night when I was coming off of a week of no revenue and a large mechanic bill. I didn't think I had the patience for that at the moment. I knew I didn't have the time or funds to get it cleaned up. And I was certain that I could not possibly have handled it if someone got some of their puke on me. I think I would have lost it. Getting arrested for committing murder would make things in my life even worse.

These people were here for work, yet they went out to be completely irresponsible and not adhere to their limits. Why do people think this behavior is okay?

What the fuck is wrong with them? How is it okay, as an adult, to completely disregard responsibility and self-accountability and drink oneself to complete oblivion to the point that it causes you to not be able to control your bodily functions? I had not cleaned up after my own children for years at this point, so the thought of or need to clean up after other grown people completely baffles me and makes me cringe.

Thankfully, they didn't throw up in my car. I was able to let those thoughts escape me and move on to other paying passengers.

CHAPTER 28

BOOKSTORE EDUCATION, OR NOT

SATURDAY, JULY 28, 2018 1:30 A.M.

To this day, I'd had very interesting and exciting experiences when it comes to the Rideshare platform. Up until this point, I really didn't have too much I could complain about, as far as my rides and passengers go. I'd become rather numb and didn't get shocked very easily, until this ride.

I picked up the gentleman - and I use that term *very* loosely - at the Grand Vacations place, just off of the strip. He got in just as any other passenger and sat up front where he believed he would be most comfortable. I went through the typical formalities; how are you doing, how was your night, etc.

He explained that he's a performer and an entertainer, but he was speaking in fast forward. I'm no expert, but I would say that he was influenced by cocaine, or maybe molly. He began to tell me about how all these guys were just all over him, he'd had all these wonderful encounters, and men couldn't keep their hands off of him.

Once I realized that he was one of the aggressive homosexuals, I took a different approach. I ignored certain comments that he made that I believed to be fishing comments and I attempted to change the subject to a more light-hearted topic.

His destination was the Orleans Casino, which was only ten minutes from his pick-up location. As soon as we got to the first red light, he began to ask, "Do you know of any good adult bookstores around here?"

I told him, "There's one on the way that's not too far from where you're going."

His hands were moving quite erratically, as though he was making an effort to try to brush against me or make contact with me. That made me *incredibly* uncomfortable.

He asked, "Does the bookstore have glory holes? Because I just need to get my dick sucked."

I answered, "I only know where the bookstore is. I'm not sure what they offer inside."

In a more aggressive tone, he repeated, "Well, I just need to get my dick sucked."

I ignored what seemed to be his urge to request for me to do that once again.

He asked, "I don't look like the type of guy that should have to go to an adult bookstore, do I?"

I ignored the question as though I didn't even hear it. He reached over to touch my arm, as though he was trying to get my attention.

I looked at him and in a very stern voice said, “Yes? What can I do for you? And please do not touch me.”

I thought that my tone would let him know that I was not interested in the kind of conversation that he was persistent on having, yet he took a more aggressive posture.

He repeated his question. “I asked, do I look like the type of person that needs to go to a bookstore and pay to get his dick sucked? As handsome as I am, I should be able to get that done with no problem. I'm a performer. People throw themselves at me anyways.”

I said, “How you see yourself is what's most important. My opinion is not relevant.”

He said, “Well, sometimes I just want to get my dick sucked.”

By that point I was sick, disgusted, upset, and ready to be out of this ride. The thoughts going through my head were what if he touches me? If I hurt him, will I be able to continue to drive? What if he grabs me by the back of the head trying to force my head down to give him head? Does he not get the hint, I am *not* a homosexual! Would it be best if I just pulled over and forced him out of the car?

I was running red lights and exceeding the speed limit in some of the most heavily policed parts of the city, just in an effort to get this ride over with. Finally, we arrived at the bookstore. Really? I have to drive all the way around to the back to get this freak out of my car? We pulled around to the back and up to the door.

I asked, “Is this a good spot for you?”

He said, “Keep the meter going. I'm going to run in

really fast and make sure that they have what I'm looking for." He winked at me and added, "I'll be right back out."

I'm not sure why, but I did wait for just a few minutes. He came right back out with a devilish grin and told me, "I'm good here. You're still welcome to join me."

My stomach turned inside out. It took everything in my power not to throw up. I felt nasty, dirty, violated, and thoroughly disgusted. All I wanted to do was turn my app off and go home, take a shower, and go to bed. It was still early, only about two in the morning. It was way too early to stop working on a busy Friday night, especially since I didn't get to work all weekend last week due to my kids being in town and the battery episode.

I took a moment to breathe, try to clear my thoughts, and remove that whole experience from my mind. The impact that seven and a half minutes can have on a person - me, specifically - is amazing. And disturbing. I struggled through the rest of the night trying to drown out that whole experience. I wasn't sure if I could really take this. I needed this gig, but these episodes were going to give me a stroke or a heart attack!

CHAPTER 29
TAKING SOME GOOD GOOD
WEDNESDAY, AUGUST 1, 2018 11:40 P.M.

I had a long morning but was able to get everything situated. A call came across from the 323 area code that I didn't recognize. I believed it was a California area code. Being that my boys are in California, I answered.

"Hello?"

A familiar voice responded, "Hi Scott. How are you?"

"I'm well. How are you?"

"Are you surprised to hear from me?"

That's when it registered who I was talking to. It was Veronica. "I'm just wondering why you're calling me. I believe the last thing you said to me is that I'd never hear from you again, and goodbye."

She said, "I know that's what I said. But you don't understand; I was really mad at you, but I miss you."

"Okay? So what do I owe the pleasure of this call

to?"

"Well, do you miss me at all? I said I miss you."

I said, "No." Although, there were certain aspects of her that I did miss.

She said, "You didn't miss me at all? You didn't think about me, not one time?"

"Well, sure I thought about you." I didn't see a reason to lie.

"But you didn't miss me?" she insisted.

"No. What would I miss? The lovely things you always had to say to me? The constant phone calls? The nonstop text messages? Or what about the constant evolution of what you wanted to call a relationship? Is that what you're wondering if I missed?"

She said, "Well, I don't want to talk about that. I understand that I was hard to deal with. And I understand that I put you through a lot. But that's not what I want. Can we just be friends?"

I was honest, as always. "I don't believe that you can handle being just friends."

"I'm friends with all of my exes, so I don't understand why this would be difficult."

"I think we have two very different definitions of friendship. What are we going to do as friends? Go on double dates? Can you handle seeing me, or even thinking about me being with another woman? Besides, my friends don't give me a hard time about me not being able to talk to them when I'm busy working or with my kids. The entire time that I have dealt with you, you have been disrespectful of my time and the things that I have going on, even when it comes to my time with my children."

She responded, "I know that I haven't treated you right. I know that I haven't done right by you. I realize that now, and that's not what I want. Wasn't there anything that you actually enjoyed about being with me or dealing with me?" She was nearly begging.

"Sure there was," I told her.

She said, "Really? Like what?"

"I enjoyed some of our conversations when it wasn't all about relationships. I find you to be very intelligent. The things you shared regarding theory and science are fascinating."

She said, "Really? Tell me more."

I said, "You can be very gentle and nurturing, when you're not caught up in trying to be insecure. When we sit around or lay around, just enjoying each other's company, I found it to be very relaxing. I drew a considerable amount of joy and pleasure from it."

She said, "Oh. You're talking about sex."

I said, "No, it's nothing that crude."

"So...what? You don't enjoy having sex with me?"

"I do. I believe that we are incredibly compatible. But I enjoy more than just physical stimulation. Some of the things that you talk about and research, they stimulate me, mentally. When you show a heightened level of independence, and you don't display an overwhelming need for attention and reassurance, those are the parts that I enjoyed about you."

"That's who I am. That's who I've been trying to show you. But you don't give me the chance. And I don't know what it is about dealing with you, but I get crazy. I'm not normally like this. If you give me the chance, I can show you that I'm different than what you think."

"I'm not interested in riding this roller coaster anymore."

"It's not a roller coaster. Just, please, give me a chance."

"I'll see. But right now I have to go. I'll talk to you later."

"Oh," she hesitated. Then, "Okay, bye."

I thought to myself, maybe she is different. That was the easiest time I've ever had with trying to get off of the phone with her. Nah, I'm sure she'll call back any minute now.

Hours went by and I hadn't even heard from her, which was highly unusual, and I didn't even do it on purpose. The day had been incredibly hot and long. I had a lot going on, as usual. To top it off, I was incredibly sexually frustrated. Maybe that's why I spent so much time thinking about her. It was getting late. It was nice to have the opportunity to drive a little bit after work, since Alyssa had the kids for a sleepover.

I was hoping to take advantage of the surprise free night to make a little bit of extra money, but I found myself getting sleepy. I figured I should head home and try to get an early start the following day. As I started in the direction of my house, I received a text message.

"Didn't want to bother you, just wanted to say goodnight. I hope to hear from you soon."

Was Veronica watching me? How did she time this so perfectly?

I guess I did imply that I was going to call her back. I was on my way home, so what would it hurt to follow through? After all, keeping my word is of high importance to me.

She sounded incredibly excited when she answered the phone, "Hello!"

"Hello. Are you busy? Is this a good time?"

She said, "I'm just laying here. I'm not busy. Why are you calling?"

I told her, "I did say that I would call you back. And I wanted to keep my word."

"Aww, you're so sweet and thoughtful. I didn't plan to hear from you."

"Well, if you didn't want to hear from me, I can let you go." I barely got the sentence out.

"No, no, no, no! Please, stay on the phone. I haven't seen you in a long time. It's nice to hear your voice."

I took advantage of that one. "Would you like to see me?"

She said, "What? Are you serious?"

"Never mind. You're already in bed, and it's late."

She said, "No, I didn't mean it like that. I can get up. I can get up and come."

I said, "Well, I'm on my way home. And I'll be home alone. So you're welcome to come see me if you'd like."

"Okay. Well, how long before you'll be home?"

"I'm about fifteen minutes away. I'm going to jump in the shower. If you're not there when I get there, I'll leave the door unlocked for you."

"Okay, bye." She hung up abruptly.

The front door opened shortly after I got out of the shower, as I was just sitting on the couch. She came closer. I said, "You're welcome to sit down if you'd like."

She sat down on the edge of the couch, a great distance from me. She told me, "When I showed up, I didn't know what to expect."

I said, "Then why did you come?"

"Because I really just wanted to see you. You're on my mind, always. It's really hard for me to concentrate at work or just to get through my day because you are constantly in my thoughts."

"Is there anything that I can do to help with that? I don't want to be a distraction or disrupt anything that you have to do."

She said, "Just don't turn cold on me."

"How did I turn cold? You told me that you never wanted to hear from me again, and I respected your wishes."

She said, "Wow. So if I wouldn't have called you, you would have never called me?"

I said, "Correct. I would have respected your wishes."

"That's incredible. And we just never would have seen each other again?"

I repeated, "Yes. Why would I call someone who doesn't want to hear from me?"

She stood up and took off her coat. After setting her jacket down, she came and sat down right next to me.

She carefully examined my face, as though I were an exhibit at a masterpiece art show. She proceeded to tell me how much she really missed me, and how handsome I am.

It had been a while since I'd felt the gentle touch of a woman. It was actually very relaxing. I work all the time and almost felt selfish for indulging and enjoying her company. Then I started to reminisce on how good it felt to be inside of her. And I just let go.

I told her, "I find you very attractive, as well."

She slowly came in for a kiss. I didn't even fight it. The feeling of our lips touching was almost electric. She drew away from the first kiss, and then she aggressively came in for more. Soon we were grabbing, holding, pulling, and kissing as though we were one. In that moment I remembered, clearly, one of the highlights of dealing with her and riding that roller coaster that she comes with. As erratic as her conversation and emotions were, she compensated greatly with the amount of love, passion, and tenderness that she shared during sex.

The thought occurred to me that I should push her away and end it immediately, but I felt like I was getting high off of a drug and I couldn't seem to stop myself. She stopped to catch her breath, and said, "Why don't we go upstairs?"

I hopped up like a kid on Christmas and proceeded to follow her up the stairs.

CHAPTER 30

BUILDING A SNOWMAN IN LAS VEGAS

SUNDAY, AUGUST 5, 2018 2:30 A.M.

It was just an average Saturday night. After all of the weird rides in my lifetime, I finally came across one that I truly enjoyed. There's a really neat bar on the far west side of town that typically gets a fairly large crowd, just on the outskirts of Summerlin. I went to grab a pair of folks from there, though I wasn’t sure if they were a couple, together, roommates, or otherwise; but it was a man and a woman.

When they got in the car they were both in a high-spirited mood. I'm guessing that they had spent the last few hours drinking, having fun, laughing, and possibly meeting up with other friends. My mind often wanders when it comes to my passengers and creates multiple scenarios about the people.

The guy, who may not have been all the way heterosexual, was controlling most of the conversation.

Outside of confirming the name for the ride, I didn't get the opportunity to get many words in. I didn't want to be rude, and I didn't want to overstep my bounds. If they wanted a private conversation to themselves, I would respect that and just be the robotic driver that I am sometimes.

There was a stale moment in their conversation when the gentlemen mentioned Milan and several other Disney movies, all in a positive tone. I took advantage of the fact that I have the Frozen soundtrack on one of my playlists, thanks to having an eight-year-old daughter. In a leap of faith, I switched the music over to one of the more popular songs from the movie, which is "Do You Want to Build a Snowman?"

I didn't say anything and didn't offer any forewarning. It took about three versus before they realized what had taken place, and then the girl began to hum.

The guy asked, "What is this?"

I responded in a smart-ass manner, "If you have to ask, then you truly are not a Disney fan, being that this is probably one of the biggest songs from Disney of all time."

After my comment, the gentleman joined in to prove that he knew the song. It's a good thing that all of the windows were up because it would have probably appeared to be really strange that three grown people were driving down the street at two in the morning, singing "Do You Want to Build a Snowman?"

Yes, there were only two passengers, so I was the third one joining in. I'm certain that I knew the words better than they did, being that my kids and I listen to it on a regular basis. What kind of father can let his kids listen to the soundtrack of a movie for the hundredth time and not encourage them to sing by joining in with him? Of course, we belted out "Let It Go" as well.

As we got closer to their apartment they said that they wished we could circle around the block a few hundred times so we could continue our sing along because that was far better than the karaoke night that they had at the bar I picked him up from. I replied, "I would love to, but duty calls. There are more folks that I'm going to introduce to the Frozen soundtrack this evening!"

CHAPTER 31

HE NEEDS A HUG

THURSDAY, AUGUST 16, 2018 1:30 P.M.

Sometimes driving Rideshare can be a *very* challenging experience with all of the different personalities that you come across due to a great sense of entitlement that most people carry around. So let me tell you about this gentleman that I picked up who got very, *very* upset and aggressive when I simply wouldn't do as he instructed me to do.

Shared ride passengers are my favorite by far because they somehow think that they get more out of their ride than a person who pays full price for the ride. Please note the sarcasm here.

I picked this gentleman up on the east side of town, really close to Sam's Town, in the Suites. The gentleman seemed to be having a pretty decent evening, as he came across up spirited and in a pleasant mood. We didn't get even two minutes away from his pick-up location when he received a phone call.

He appeared to be speaking to a young lady. The young lady informed him that she was at the Cosmopolitan and he told her, "Okay. I'll meet you there."

The issue was that his destination was the MGM Grand. This wouldn't be a problem if he was driving himself, or if he had ordered a regular ride. Since he ordered a shared ride, changing the destination is not something that is permitted.

As soon as he got off the phone, he instructed me to take him to the Cosmo instead of his destination.

I told him, "With the shared rides I cannot change the destination."

He said, "Come on, man. It's just a block away. It shouldn't be that big of a deal. What? Are you new to this?"

I told him, "If there's not another passenger on the way or anyone else for us to pick up, I'll see what I can do." No sooner than I finished that statement, they added another rider. From where I picked him up at, it would typically be a straight shot down Flamingo to get to the destination that he desired to go to.

When he noticed the navigation was instructing me to get on the freeway, he got very agitated. He asked me, "Why in the fuck are you getting on the freeway? Why the fuck don't you just go down the fucking road?"

I kept my voice calm and even as I told him, "We've had another passenger added."

He abruptly interrupted me, telling me, "This doesn't make any fucking sense. It's right down the street. I don't understand why we'd get on the fuckin' freeway."

I told him, "I have to follow the navigation."

He said, "That's just dumb. This is fucking dumb. Where is that person going?"

"Sir, I don't have his destination until after I pick him up."

"That doesn't make any fucking sense. Is he getting dropped off first, or am I?"

He continued to be aggressive and vulgar, and insisted that I didn't know what I was doing. I had enough of that. It was way too much to deal with, especially for just a few dollars. I really don't understand the nerve this motherfucker had. He ordered the cheapest ride he could. He took forever to get in, which held me up. Now he wanted to act like a big shot and try to tell me what to do? Was he accustomed to bullying people or bossing people around?

In a very calm manner, I abruptly stopped the vehicle in the middle of the street and let him know his options. "You can get out and cancel this ride and then order a new ride to go to the destination that you desire, or you can continue to your original destination."

He screamed. "What the fuck is wrong with you? Putting me out in the fucking middle of the fucking road? I'm not getting out of your fucking car."

I began to continue on my drive, although by that point I was getting extremely agitated myself. All I could think of is how much I wanted to hurt this guy.

I was much larger than him. I was also much younger than him, and I'd bet I was a lot stronger than him. He had some balls to be talking to me like I'm a fucking child, and it was not *my* fault that *he* ordered a ride that doesn't give him the option to change his destination, or did he pick the wrong destination in the first place? Why didn't he call the girl *before* he got in the car, or before he ordered the ride?

I continued on to pick up the second passenger. There were several more little comments the gentleman made under his breath, such as threats of a bad rating or making it so that I couldn't drive anymore. I think I was just waiting for that one comment where he actually threatened physical violence so that I could say that he threatened me, and then I could brutally attack this man. It was a lot to take in for a ride that he may be contributing seven dollars to. I was trying to stay focused on the fact that this income was essential to maintaining the balance in my life and taking care of my kids, but the frustration was taking over.

I changed the music playing in the background to some very calming smooth jazz, hoping that maybe it would deescalate the situation, even though the gentleman was even more frustrated because we were going away from his destination. It was all about *his* ride and *his* destination, even though he was in a shared ride. He stopped muttering his negative comments as the new passenger got in.

We had a relatively calm ride for the rest of the way to the first drop-off, which was the first passenger's destination, the MGM Grand. He watched as I approached the hotel, though I don't think that he realized it was his destination.

When I pulled up to the front valet, I said, "Sir, we have arrived."

He looked around and then muttered, "I told you I'm going to the Cosmo, not MGM."

I ignored his comment. He turned to the other passenger and asked, "Where are you going?"

Andre, the other passenger, responded by calmly saying, "I'm not going to tell you where I'm going."

Out of frustration, the passenger began to explain himself. He said, "I'm trying to get to The Cosmopolitan and this idiot driver won't take me there, so if your destination is there, or close to there, I just want to get dropped off, bro."

Andre responded, "We all have our own destinations. If you wanted to change it, you have to pick a regular ride, not a shared ride. But I'm going the other way, so that's not even close or in the direction that I'm headed."

The man got really upset and turned back to me and demanded, "You're really not going to fucking take me to the Cosmo? So stupid. I'm going to fucking give you a one-star rating."

My only response for him at this point was, "Have a good evening."

As he was getting out of the vehicle, he turned to Andre and said, "Well fuck you too, Andre." He slammed the door shut and stormed off. I was incredibly relieved that there wasn't a confrontation because he was very rude and disrespectful towards me and the other passenger; although, I would have liked to see Andre go ahead and whoop his ass. That would have made my day. I was concerned about how this would reflect upon me because I get rated by both passengers and somehow, I thought that this was all going to be my fault.

I immediately turned to Andre. "I do apologize for that. Before you got in the car, the other passenger was very aggressive and upset about the fact that we weren't going straight to his desired destination, which was not where he ordered the ride to go."

Andre took the whole situation very well. He told me, "Don't worry about it. I drive, too, so I know how that goes."

This was a great relief. I'm hoping that he'll actually understand and then I won't have any repercussions from the rating. Andre and I had about twenty minutes to his destination, so we were able to talk about quite a bit. He actually shared with me, "If I had known that you wouldn't have reported me, I would have smacked the hell out of that guy."

I said, "Only if you knew how it went before you got in the vehicle. I actually stopped in the middle of the street trying to put him out."

By the time we got to Andre's stop, the mood was completely different. I was relieved. I sometimes wonder how people like that first passenger managed to get through their days when they're so angry all of the time. I was starting to think my good rides were just a fluke and now I was going to have a slew of difficult rides, but Andre helped turn it around for me. He gave me a little bit of hope to keep going with this Rideshare stuff.

CHAPTER 32

IT'S A SMALL WORLD

SATURDAY, AUGUST 18, 2018 12:00 A.M.

I picked up a man in his late thirties or early forties from the Venetian. He ordered a shared ride. He was very friendly, and we began talking about a number of things almost immediately. He had just gotten off of work and was heading home. He managed a restaurant there, which is why he moved his family to Vegas from the east coast a few months earlier. So far, they seemed to be settling in okay, even though they missed their last home.

It took a while to navigate through the Friday night/Saturday morning strip traffic, but we finally pulled out onto Las Vegas Boulevard, only to get a ping to go grab another passenger from Drai's. We continued talking. He was telling me about his three children, and we began swapping fatherhood stories. I was enjoying the conversation quite a bit, as it was different than what I'm accustomed to during my Rideshare hours. Especially late on weekend nights by the strip.

We pulled up to retrieve a couple. Before he could jump out to move to the front seat, the other man put his girl in the front with me and got into the back behind her. I guess in this case I was seen as the lesser of two evils. I'm certainly not used to that.

After quick pleasantries, we started to head to the couple's hotel on West Tropicana and Decatur. They wanted to stay for the featured performer but were tired after experiencing the Vegas nightlife for the past three nights. They were visiting from Texas.

The first man received a phone call. He began talking in his native tongue, which he had earlier informed me he was from west Africa. All of the sudden, the second gentleman turned to the first, stared at him for a moment, then grinned and started speaking to him in a language I was entirely unfamiliar with.

The first gentleman ended his call and they had a rapid conversation in that language. The woman looked at me and said, "I don't even know what language they're speaking. He speaks at least five or six different ones." She shrugged, with a smile on her face. She was excited for her man being so excited. It was nice to see.

Somewhere in the midst of their excitement, they decided to clue us in. I think we must have both looked slightly curious as to what was going on in the backseat. They explained that they were both from the same small region in Senegal, Africa. They went right back to their conversation.

After we dropped off the couple, the first gentleman told me they were speaking Wolof. He was on cloud nine the rest of the way to his home in Mountain's Edge, a community in the far southwest part of town.

The ride made me appreciate that as big as our world is, it's still pretty small. People and the connections that we share and create are unmatched by any other species that I'm aware of. I guess I believe in the ripple effect, as I can see how something I may do in an interaction with someone can have an impact on multiple other people down the line, particularly if the impact is negative. I'm just happy that there are some positive people who look forward to connecting, rather than rides like the last one I shared.

It was steady, but not really busy, which gave Alyssa and I some time to catch up in between rides. More importantly, we got to meet up for a much desired coffee break, and it gave us time for her to fill me in on how she's been; nothing new was really going on with me.

She just got back from her trip with Triangle (my nickname for her guy) and seemed to be really happy. She told me about how much fun they had hanging out all night and she just relaxed during the day while he was working. She got to visit a couple of different cities while they were there. She told me that she's never really been on a vacation like that and wanted to start traveling more.

Maybe I was wrong. Maybe dude really is about to make some moves so they could be together. She showed me some of their pictures. They looked like any other happy couple vacationing. He bought her a ring and they're talking about moving out of state together if his job transfers him. Maybe I'm just pessimistic.

As she was talking, I started daydreaming about what it would be like to be able to walk away from my responsibilities and let someone else take care of me for a while. Of course, I could never do that. For one thing, I couldn't leave my kids. Who would take care of them? I thought, I'm all they really have, and that's not really saying much; besides, they are the only bit of bright light in this sea of darkness that I call my life.

My phone pinged with another ride and pulled me back into my reality, where I would more than likely have to hustle and grind for the rest of my life to barely get by.

CHAPTER 33
AN INDECENT PROPOSAL
SATURDAY, AUGUST 25, 2018 2:00 A.M.

Driving had many advantages and had shown me many things about my city (the city I thought I knew well). I pulled up to a strange looking building. At first glance, it appeared to be a very large house, which would make sense since it is in a residential neighborhood. Upon a second glance, I noticed several things that implied that the place is not a house, or at least not a typical house.

There was an excessive amount of neon around the windows. I noticed several cars in the front, which were positioned more like a business parking lot than a home. A couple approached my vehicle, after they seemed to appear out of thin air.

"Good evening. How are y'all doing this evening?" I asked.

"Eh. We'rre ok," she replied.

"Just ok?" I asked.

"Yeah, it was not what we expected," he said.

"Did you spend some time at a friend's house, and things didn't go well?" I asked.

"Not exactly," she said with hesitation.

He asked, "Do you know what that place is?"

"I can't say that I do," was my honest reply.

She offered, "It's a swingers club."

Oh wow, there really are swinger clubs? I had heard of them, but didn't realize it was something that was still around. I had heard of two from many years ago in Vegas. What type of person would *want* to watch someone else have sex with their wife, husband, or committed partner? While lost in my thoughts, I realized that there was an awkward silence.

They were watching me to see my reaction to them telling me that it was a swingers club, and probably watching to see if I was going to judge them. I didn't completely understand their way of life, but I did understand that this income is important to mine, and I could really use a good tip, so I wanted to make them feel comfortable.

I asked, "Was there an issue with some of the other participants?"

She spoke up and said, "There was one gentleman that was just completely disrespectful. He kept trying to interact with us, after I let him know that I was not interested."

I said, "Did you make it clear? You should also keep in mind you are a very attractive woman, and that might inspire a person to be a little bit more pushy than usual."

She said, "Yes. We made it very clear, but he just

wasn't getting it."

I replied, "Well, that would make for a very unpleasant experience, I suppose."

Then they asked, "Do you swing?"

Oh my, how was I supposed to answer that question? I'd never been in that position before. I didn't want to offend them, and I wanted to make sure that the rest of the ride went well. I guessed maybe I should just be honest - to a certain extent.

I said, "I haven't partaken in the lifestyle, but I do find it incredibly fascinating. The facts behind swinging, to my knowledge, give it great support in my mind. I think that being incredibly open about sexual desires and physical needs makes it so that a couple won't have to hide anything from each other. Secrets and lies are what destroy relationships, in my opinion."

They both agreed and said, "Totally! That's why we have such a healthy relationship."

The gentleman began to speak. "Sometimes I just want to see a big black guy fuck my wife, and sometimes it just turns me on watching her suck somebody else's cock. And today, we came up short because she didn't get to suck as much cock as she wanted to."

I wasn't sure if this was an actual invitation, or a test to see if I was going to harass them sexually. What type of man wouldn't jump at the opportunity to have sex with an attractive woman without doing any work? I didn't have to come up with some BS conversation to try to get the woman's attention. I also didn't have to become some type of charming individual to hope to get to second base because they're just blatantly putting it out there. It was unfamiliar territory to me and I had to be mindful that I was still working.

The best response I came up with was, "That's terrible! A woman shouldn't have to come up short of what she truly wants."

He responded, "If that creep in there wouldn't have run us up out of there, my wife would have gotten plenty of cock for the evening. Now I'm not sure what we're going to do. As her husband, I feel like I've let her down because it was my job to help her get all the cock she can handle."

My mind began to race in all different directions. I began to picture a vivid scene of her sucking on my dick and then riding me rough and hard in their hotel room. In this image, I glanced over and he was sitting in the corner, just watching and drooling. The thought of a complete stranger sitting in a room, watching me have my way with his wife, made me feel a little uncomfortable, but slightly turned me on as well.

I asked myself, would I be able to do this? Is this real life? Is this really happening right now? Or am I in the *Twilight Zone*? Then, the dark thought seeped in - what if he tried to participate? Could I handle him accidentally brushing his cock against me? What if his idea of me fucking his wife entitled him to fuck me?

I began to pay more attention to my thoughts than the road. I quickly adjusted because I was drifting into the curb. Immediately, I apologized, "I'm sorry. I was paying more attention to our conversation than the road, and that is not the best idea."

He chuckled and said, "Yes, please be careful. We have precious cargo in the back here with us." Then, too quickly to be a complete afterthought, he asked, "How late are you working tonight?"

Between the subject matter of the conversation and my thoughts wandering, I was going well below the speed limit. I really didn't see any rush to get them to their destination because I was trying to figure out whether or not I should attempt to go to their room with them.

I replied to his question. "I don't have a set time. I typically work until I'm tired, although I've already put in quite a few hours tonight. I always have the option to take part in better opportunities."

She responded by asking, "Do better opportunities present themselves frequently?"

I answered, "Not the ones that I would actually look forward to." I looked at them in the rearview mirror while I was talking to them, with a slight grin on my face.

The gentleman took control of the conversation again. "We had to call it an early night, so she wasn't able to get her fill of cock for the night. We are still a bit wound up, so maybe you'd like to have a drink with us?"

That was exactly what I was thinking, but wasn't sure if I should be that forward. I said, "I don't want to impose, but I do believe that the conversation is going quite well."

As we pulled up to the Hard Rock, realizing that the

ride was coming to an end, I added, "Well, if it wouldn't be too much trouble and I'm not going to disturb you guys, I'd love to join."

He said, "We can meet you downstairs at the bar, because I'm guessing you're going to have to park."

I said, "Just give me a moment and I'll be right in."

The gentleman turned to his wife and said, "Be careful getting out of the car, honey." He looked at me and reminded me, "We are carrying precious cargo, so we will be cautious."

I stared at her silhouette as she got out of the vehicle and immediately got aroused. When the door closed, I started to pull around to park in the back parking lot. Rational thinking stepped in. I asked myself, is this okay? Better yet, is this even safe?

With that, the negotiations began. What is the worst that can happen? What if they try to drug me? What if I wake up in the bathtub without a kidney? Or worse, what if they tie me up and rape me? But she *is* attractive. And this just seems too good to be true. I've never been in a situation where I've met someone and had to do no work as far as courting them, and they're just telling me to come upstairs and have sex with them. What if there is something that I'm missing? What if there's something that they make reference to that refers to a certain etiquette or expectation that they have of me and my posture gave consent? Is it really worth the risk? I mean, really? Could he *really* sit there and get off on watching me fuck his wife and not touch me?

Even with these internal negotiations going on I

must have already made my decision, because I did not hesitate to pull around to the garage. Nor did I hesitate to get out of the car and head inside.

As I approached the bar, all of the thoughts of inadequacies due to my insecurities still did not deter me. I began to wonder if it was too dark in the car, so maybe they didn't get a good look at me. Maybe I'm not what they're expecting, or maybe I don't look like what they thought? What if they change their mind and I get let down, yet again?

Still, I proceeded to the table to have a seat next to them. My palms were sweaty, and I was incredibly nervous. I wasn't even sure what I was going to say. Focus, just focus, I told myself; I'm just going to be casual and cool, and I'll figure out my way through this. After all, nothing is guaranteed to happen. It's just a drink. That was the final thought that I had before I sat down.

Without even a second thought, I blurted out, "You're far more stunning in the light than what I imagined from the glimpse I got in the car." Wait a second, did I just compliment this man's wife right in front of him? What if I upset him? Is this even appropriate? These questions raced through my mind.

He responded immediately. "Yes, she is the most gorgeous woman on the face of this Earth. A goddess by nature. Definitely one deserving of our worship."

Even though I thought his response was a bit extreme, it did give me a great sense of relief because I realized that I was a little more free to speak my mind. Although I was still wondering what kind of person would actually enjoy or even partake in this type of a situation. Were they just nasty like that? I was still thinking that it was far too good to be true, and she is a very attractive woman, so the temptation was great.

We continued on with small talk. They shared that they were visiting from Arizona and being out of town gave them a great opportunity to let their hair down because they do have children. It did help to hear this, being that I'm a father myself, because I am optimistic about the decency that parents must possess. I briefly shared vague details about my children, as well.

Through the conversation, I was cautious not to seem too anxious or come across as just a pure horn dog. I tried to keep the conversation more relaxed so that we were actually getting to know each other. I also kept reminding myself that nothing was guaranteed, besides this drink, which I drank very slowly. As much as I thought that the liquor would help relax me, I was still slightly worried about waking up in a bathtub missing my kidney.

After finishing a couple of more drinks, they asked if I'd like to join them upstairs in the room to "relax."

I didn't even hesitate. I responded, "I'd love to." I couldn't even believe how much time had already passed. I felt like we'd known each other for quite some time already.

She smiled and leaned over to whisper to him, "I like this guy."

As we walked through the casino towards the room, you would have thought that she was my wife because she was closer to me, very friendly, and affectionate.

She led me by the hand and gently stroked my arm as though she was petting me.

I don't know why I expected them to open their hotel room door and reveal chains and swings dangling from the ceiling, with all kinds of leather outfits scattered around the room. Still unsure of what exactly to do or say to get the party started or even gesture consent, I walked in and sat on the couch. It was just a regular hotel suite, with no trace of the bondage fantasy that invaded my mind.

Before I could even settle into the couch all the way, she grabbed me by the hand and said, "Come back here. The best seat in the place is over this way." She guided me to the bedroom. She patted the edge of the bed and said, "Please take a seat and relax. I'm just going to change into something more comfortable."

Blinded by desire and lust, I lost track of where her husband had gone off to. I didn't even let my thoughts wander in that direction for long. With great anticipation of what was going to come next, I removed my shoes and sat back, awaiting her return.

She came out of the bathroom wearing only a see through nightie, with a look of burning desire in her eyes.

My first thought was to compliment her. Just as soon as I got out, "Wow," she pushed me onto my back.

In an aggressive tone, she scolded me, "I told you to get comfortable." She ripped my pants off and began to suck my dick.

I lost every ounce of control and awareness that I

possessed when I walked into that room. The warm, relaxed sensation that I began to feel had me blinded to my surroundings or anything else that was going on. I no longer resisted or even tried to think about what I was doing.

I grabbed her by the back of her head and guided her along, as she continued to suck on my dick. With my free hand, I reached around and explored the other parts of her body. As we began to move in synchronicity, I noticed her husband sitting in the corner as a lustful observer.

He began to whisper suggestions for our interactions. At first, they were directed at her. It was strange in the beginning because up until then the only man's voice that I ever heard during sexual encounters was the one in my head. I imagined that he was picturing himself in my place, and that's where he contrived his joy from.

My focus quickly returned to what I had going on with her. I began interacting with her in cautious and gentle motions, which rapidly became more aggressive. I went from gently caressing the back of her head to grabbing a handful of hair and moving her at the pace that I desired. What started as a gentle touch, exploring her body became an aggressive and abrasive hold that I had on her, as though I was restricting her from moving away from me.

I was fully aroused and ready to progress from foreplay to copulation, so I pulled her off of me, spun her around, and began to take her from behind.

Then I heard the whisper in the background,

"Smack her ass." I followed the instruction, with the intention of punishing her. I smacked her with the objective of leaving my handprint as a permanent reminder that I was there.

She let out a scream that teetered the line between pleasure and pain. I didn't even bother to ask if she was okay, I was so aroused and turned on that I began to thrust uncontrollably harder.

Her husband began to say, "Yes, just like that." His comment broke my concentration for a moment. I looked back just to make sure that he wasn't approaching. He had adjusted himself to a position that allowed him to masturbate, while watching me have my way with his wife. The least I could do to pay him back for him allowing me to penetrate his wife was to provide a great show. I began to picture myself as a porn star performing before a live studio audience.

With a giant thrust and the yanking of her hair, I felt a tremor between her legs and an explosion from deep within her pussy. I paused for a brief moment to allow her to regain her composure. As she began to relax on the bed and curl up, I grabbed her legs, threw them over my shoulders and began to stimulate her clitoris with my tongue. She attempted to push me away and say "No," yet at the same time she grabbed and pulled me in closer and cringed up.

I went with the struggle and gave her the impression that she was actually putting up a good fight. There were no longer any chants or taunts coming from the corner of the room where her husband was sitting; instead, he began to handle himself in a far more rapid and aggressive pace, while breathing heavily.

Right when I felt her next orgasm, I jumped to my feet and began thrusting again, without giving her any break or time to recover. She began to claw at the bed to pull herself away, and I felt her legs tremble multiple times, back to back. In a feeble voice she whispered, "I can't, I can't take any more. Please finish."

With an adamant tone, I said, "Let go of yourself. Let me feel you have a massive orgasm, and then I'll cum."

In a very faint voice, she pleaded, "I can't cum anymore. I have nothing left."

I said, "See, you're still holding back. Let go. Let your body release. Give in." All the while, I was pounding her in the way that I now know she can't get enough of.

At that moment, she gave out one final moan and a waterfall came dripping down my leg. When I felt the moisture reach my knee, I lost all control of myself. I quickly pulled out and shot my load all across her face. Every muscle in my body relaxed, as I melted into the bed.

All I could say is, "That was amazing." I felt completely vulnerable to anything that could have happened to me next.

There were a few moments of silence, as we all got our breathing under control. The husband broke the silence, saying, "That was spectacular."

I couldn't believe how I went from being nervous, unsure, and skeptical about this whole experience to being this relaxed and comfortable in a situation that I had no control over. I don't know why I thought that there would be more interaction after the fact, but they graciously thanked me and told me it was a pleasure to spend the time with me, as they insinuated that it was time for me to leave.

We did not exchange information or imply that we'd see each other ever again. But I'm forever left with a lasting memory of this experience. I abruptly exited the room, still covered in rapidly drying juices, so I thought it to be a good idea to stop by one of the bathrooms downstairs. I quickly took a bird bath and made my way back to my vehicle.

I reached to push the start button, as an unfamiliar feeling fell upon me. So I sat back in the chair before starting the vehicle to try to understand what it was. Maybe I was feeling used and cheap? Was I the one who actually performed, or was I just a local entertainer or puppet, here only to amuse them? Did I actually fuck her, or was I merely a toy that they pulled out of the street to play with for a moment only to be discarded rapidly? When I walked in the room, I felt like it was an incredible opportunity that was too good to be true, when maybe it was the opposite. I thought about the pride that I entered the room with, and wondered if I took it back with me when I left?

I didn't like this. I was finding it to be incredibly disturbing because I was starting to think that maybe I was just a cheap whore who didn't even get paid. Through this whole event, I was so consumed with what type of couple or individual would partake in such an activity, that I never looked at the other side of that. What type of individual would allow himself to be used for the entertainment of a couple? Do they allow everyone to go raw? Could she have given me something? Ahhh. Maybe I should have just stayed working. Saved by the bell, again, my phone alerted me that I had my next ping for another ride.

CHAPTER 34

THE LETTER

TUESDAY, AUGUST 28, 2018 1:00 P.M.

It is amazing the type of people that you come across in Rideshare. You get all different walks of life, from all different backgrounds, from all different parts of the world. Driving for Rideshare has really tainted my view on the privileged and wealthy. I have yet to meet anybody who seems to come from a privileged background, or who is well off, who seems to be grounded or have a realistic sense of reality.

You get the entitled young people who believe that they are the Kardashians. They can tell you everything that you're doing wrong and you need to cater to every minute of their ride, in addition to their unrealistic expectations.

You get the older crowd who believes that you should kiss their ass the entire ride. They want to critique every moment in the vehicle, from the bumps on the road to the temperature being a degree too hot or too cold, and my personal favorite, why is this drive taking so long.

When these folks are in your car, you just want to pull your hair out and scream, "I HAVE NO CONTROL OVER THESE VARIABLES THAT YOU'RE COMPLAINING ABOUT!" I don't control the street lights, so I'm not forcing you to sit at this light for two and a half minutes. I am not able to read your mind to know the exact temperature that you are comfortable at, even though I let them know that they can change the temperature when they get in the vehicle because I point out that controls are directly above them. I have no previous experience in the field of road development, maintenance, or paving, so I did not have anything to do with that bump in the road that I attempted to slow down going over for your comfort that was not good enough for you.

On the upside, these passengers typically only represent about ten percent of my rides. On this particular afternoon, I found myself in the heart of Summerlin, an affluent neighborhood in the west. Things were not going all that well for me financially. I had a couple days before my power was going to be disconnected. The previous weekend did not yield the type of money that I was expecting from either of my jobs, in addition to the fact that groceries were low at the house. I didn't know what else I could sacrifice.

I've lived a very humble lifestyle to the point that my socks have holes in them, and I only get rid of them if the holes become incredibly visible to others. I've worn my plain t-shirts until I can stick my finger through the holes created from the wear and tear of washing and drying them. I don't know what a designer shoe looks like in my size, and cannot remember the last time I bought myself something that I just truly enjoyed.

I rarely go out anywhere for myself. It's always for the benefit of my children, and I had limited that to a reasonable amount because I didn't want them to see how bad we were struggling. I'd been creative enough that they didn't even realize how little we spent on our outings because we frequented the parks, libraries, and other cost-effective locations more than anything else.

After thirty minutes, a ride request came in. I was starting to panic. The navigation took me up to a golf course neighborhood, a really nice one at that. It was a gated golf course, so I had to call the passenger to see if he wanted me to wait at the gate or provide the code to get in. I know what type of person that I usually picked up from these types of places and I just was not in the mood, but I also didn't have the luxury of turning down any rides.

When I pulled up to the front, the gentleman walked out with a great stride of confidence. I rolled down the window to verify his name.

As he threw a letter in the vehicle, he said, "You're going to take this over to the destination. Thank you," he mumbled as he walked away.

I was completely baffled and feeling very belittled in this situation due to the manner in which he barked his orders at me. Was I able to give a ride to a letter? I couldn't see why not. It wouldn't be any different than a passenger, but I'm no delivery boy. Did he even ask me, or did he give me a command? I guess it really didn't matter, because his request was to take a ride. I got paid whether he was in the vehicle or not if I completed the ride, so off we went. Me and the letter.

To try to calm my nerves, I put the seat belt around the letter. I thought it would lighten up the situation, since safety is important and that was my passenger. I looked at the bright side - I didn't have to worry about the conditions of the vehicle, weather conditions, or what music was playing. I began my journey across town.

The drive was a little bit over twenty minutes and curiosity set in. What was in this letter? Was it really *that* important that he was willing to pay this kind of money to take it across town? How much money would you have to have to justify thirty dollars for someone to drive your letter across town? This is ridiculous, and completely absurd. You couldn't step away from your round of golf to take this letter where it needed to go? Or you just have *that* much money that you can command people to carry out your will and everybody's beneath your feet?

That was the conversation that I was having with the letter. What did that say for me? With all of the struggles going on in my life, was that the first sign of my sanity fleeting away from me? I honestly sat there and looked at the letter, waiting for a response. I'm sure that to no one's surprise, there was none. But the letter still needed to travel the rest of the distance to its destination, so I figured we'd make the best out of it.

The other instruction that the gentleman had given

me was to make sure that I handed it specifically to Adam. As I arrived, I guess I was surprised that somebody wasn't standing outside waiting for this letter to arrive. Did I really have to get out of the vehicle and walk up to the door like a delivery boy? Regardless of the answer, the faster that I got this ride over with, the sooner I could get back to earning more money.

I knocked on the door, though I wasn’t sure if it was heard because the music inside was so loud that I could hear every word in the lyrics clearly outside. I rang the doorbell, and still no response. I knocked a second time, even louder, with no response again.

I began to text the gentleman who ordered the ride, just as the door began to open. A young man answered the door and didn't have the decency to turn down the music. He extended his arm, as if trying to snatch the letter out of my hand.

I asked, “Are you Adam?” so that I could verify that he was the one who was supposed to receive the letter.

He didn't even acknowledge my question or respond, as he reached even further in order to grab the letter. I repeated my question, “Are you Adam? I have to verify that Adam receives his letter.”

In a very hostile tone, he said, “Yes. Give it here now!”

My first notion was to get upset and make a rude or hostile comment, but I could only remind myself that I really needed to maintain this second job, so I should not do anything that could jeopardize that.

“Hand me the letter,” he demanded. He quickly

snatched it out of my hand and slammed the door in my face.

I felt incredibly low and extremely disrespected. Not only was he half of my age, his conduct was completely inappropriate. People think that because they have money that they don't have to have manners and worry about how they treat others. I was starting to despise rich people. What was the difference between them and me? What made him better than me? Just money? A number on a piece of paper issued by the bank? The square footage of his home or where he lived?

I was getting frustrated even thinking about it. I went out of my way to do him a favor by taking a letter that he could have clearly taken across town himself. Instead of being their delivery boy, what if I came back and took all of their stuff? If that letter was so important to him, what about the rest of the stuff that they have in their home? I did have their home addresses now. I would have loved to see the look on their faces if they came home to an empty house that was recently broken into.

My thought process was broken up by the chime of the new request coming in, so it was time to go pick up my next passenger and leave these thoughts behind me.

CHAPTER 35

A STRANGE ENCOUNTER

FRIDAY, AUGUST 31, 2018 10:15 P.M.

Over the years, I've learned that things are not always what they seem. Life can throw you some real curveballs. I picked up these two ladies in the area of Mojave and Flamingo. When I arrived at the complex, it was pitch black. There were no streetlights and very few lights in front of the doors.

I was looking around for my passengers, though I couldn't see much of anything. Apartments typically pose issues in finding passengers because the app will direct me to the leasing office or the center of the complex. That's not always helpful in large complexes. The name was really strange, or at least it had a unique spelling. I believe the name was pronounced Tanja.

After a few moments, the two ladies approached the vehicle and got in. One of them sat in the front and the other sat in the back as I verified the name. Something was really different about this pair, but I couldn't quite place my finger on it, so I continued with my normal conversation.

"It looks like your destination is the Las Vegas Lounge?"

The one in the front seat said, "Yes, it is."

I said, "That sounds familiar. Is it a nice place?"

They both giggled and the one in the front said, "It may not be the kind of place for you."

This sent my mind racing in a few different directions. The first thing I wondered was, am I not good enough to go to this kind of place? Were they judging me as being low class? I tried not to show a reaction.

Instead, I asked, "Do they have a strict dress code?" I was trying to be optimistic about their reaction. Maybe it was because I had on my casual attire of basketball shorts and a t-shirt?

The woman in the front said, "Well, it's a different kind of lounge."

I still wasn't sure what they were referring to, or what they were trying to say. My confidence was really shaken at that point. So, I asked, "What type of crowd do they get in there?"

The one in the back spoke for the first time. She explained, "It's a special place, and not all men feel welcome there." After hearing the tone of the voice from the back seat, I realized that these two ladies in the vehicle with me were not born females. The voice had that edge and sharpness to it that is distinctly a man's voice. The one in the front may have had alterations done to the Adam's apple, or just proper voice training, so it was hard to tell.

I'd never been that close to transsexuals in the past, or at least I've never been aware of it. Once I realized what was in the car, I had this chill go up my spine. I immediately became concerned with what might happen next. I attempted to keep the conversation going without showing any kind of reaction.

I asked very generic and bland questions for the remainder of the ride. Then I almost passed the destination, as it's tucked behind Commercial Center (a large plaza on Sahara) in a really small part of the parking lot so that you wouldn't even notice it if you weren't looking for it specifically. This was awfully coincidental, due to the nature of the guests that the bar attracted. Ironically enough, there was another establishment in that center that I had heard of, but I didn't think was still around. The Green Door was one of the most well-known swinger clubs in Vegas. I found this to be coincidental due to my recent transgression. Maybe that's why I noticed it in the first place.

The two ladies, as we'll call them, were very respectful as they got out and went inside to take care of their business. As I was pulling away from dropping them off, I would have thought that I should feel disgusted and dirty from the involvement that I just had with two transexuals, yet curiosity was the number one thing that was going through me. What if I just walked inside? Would people know that I was not taking part in that lifestyle? Would I even fit in there, in that environment? Oh my, what if somebody actually recognized me and thought that I like them?

I drove away as quickly as I could. Ironically, over the next few days many of my rides took me to that same area. Since I now know what's over in that area, I kept looking around and noticing a lot of homosexuals and transsexuals around there.

I mentioned to Alyssa about the night that I had dropping of the ladies at the Las Vegas Lounge and she told me that the headquarters for the lesbian, gay, and transsexual community is in that plaza. I thought at first that she was going to express disgust and tell me how nasty that whole situation was, but it ended up being a nonchalant conversation that she and I had, just like any other. Maybe I misjudged the whole situation. Maybe these different sexual orientations and lifestyles were more widely accepted than I realized.

CHAPTER 36
A COOL MORNING ON THE BOULEVARD
SUNDAY, SEPTEMBER 2, 2018 5:00 A.M.

I've had so many weird and negative interactions lately that I figured it's time for me to share a good one. I only share the things that I think are truly out of the ordinary, and this morning was no different.

Las Vegas is a city unlike anywhere else. We have celebrities, locals, and multitudes of visitors every single week. There is always something going on, from concerts, to special engagements, to conventions, to sporting events, and so on. I've seen some crazy things as I've driven around this city, things that you could only see here. Some of these things would seem abnormal elsewhere but is almost commonplace here.

For example, I've seen Mickey and Minnie Mouse twerking on Las Vegas Boulevard in front of the famous Bellagio fountains. I've seen the police swarm a Lamborghini at the stop light on Las Vegas

Boulevard and Flamingo, dragging the shirtless guy out and putting him in handcuffs. There were police cars surrounding the car from every possible angle. I've seen countless people throwing up in trash cans, bushes, and in the gutters. I saw a girl pop a squat and pee on the sidewalk in the median of Tropicana Avenue just east of Las Vegas Boulevard, between the MGM and the Tropicana.

Of course, you're bound to see an Elvis or two, even the one who drives around town in his pink Caddy. There are Vegas showgirls with the huge, old school headdresses up and down Las Vegas Boulevard and on Fremont.

Leaving the strip alone, I've seen a man in an electric scooter going down a residential street in Henderson holding a fifty-five-inch TV. There was another man pushing a hand dolly down Charleston with a full-sized roll of carpet on it. I've also seen some very interesting things around downtown, including the area heavily populated by the homeless on Main Street. There was a woman with her shorts down around her ankles leaning her naked bum against a brick wall, hitting herself mercilessly. I found some of it to be fascinating, disturbing, entertaining, or sad, and sometimes a combination of these things.

None of that had prepared me for what I would see this morning. It was like the deepest, freshest breath of air I'd ever experienced while driving around Sin City.

I had been working all night and was getting delirious, so I decided to head home. If I got another airport run, I'd take it, but I was heading home. I had just dropped off a couple at Encore and made a left to head south on Las Vegas Boulevard. As I made the turn, I saw a young man float by me on a skateboard - actually on the street. At first, I was a bit taken aback. What on earth would possess someone to carelessly ride a skateboard down one of the busiest streets in the country? He could easily get hit and hurt, or even killed! Didn't he know how many distracted, drunk, sleepy drivers are out here?

As I sat at the next red light and watched him glide by, clearing the large intersection with ease, I realized that he must feel completely free. I was envious of him at that moment. He looked so at peace, just enjoying the sunrise, perfect weather, and lighter than normal traffic conditions. I wondered what it would feel like to be him? I mean, I'm not exactly in the best shape and hadn't been on a skateboard in years, but I could imagine the feeling. I closed my eyes and wished I was him for a minute, feeling the cool air on my face and being completely free.

I watched him navigate through the intersections, skating through the red lights, without slowing down too much and without stopping at all. He was moving at a decent pace, though I got to catch up when the lights would turn green for me. This went on all the way down to Harmon when he made a wide left and disappeared east of the strip.

I was happy I got to witness those few minutes. It made me smile and appreciate some of the small stuff that I typically take for granted. I made it home and lay down to rest with a smile on my face. Dreams of freedom visited me during the four hours of sleep that I could barely afford.

CHAPTER 37

A CRAZY KIND OF LOVE

MONDAY, SEPTEMBER 10, 2018 11:00 A.M.

I picked up a couple from a dealership in Henderson heading deep into North Las Vegas. The couple seemed oddly paired and I wasn't certain that they were actually a couple. They definitely didn't appear to be related, though. She was a fair complexion, really well kept, and resembled what I would imagine a valley girl to look like, though I've admittedly never been to the valley. The "gentleman," and I use that term very loosely, seemed to be fresh out a low-budget rap video that never quite made it to air. He appeared to have a grungy look to him; although, his clothes were definitely well-pressed. He didn't look like he lived a day in the streets in his real life. I assumed that during the ride I would be able to determine their relationship.

Once I confirmed the destination, I smiled because this would be a lucrative ride. After my usual small talk introductions, I let my mind wander since they didn't seem to be interested in a conversation with me. I had a fairly profitable weekend and was trying to figure out which of my bills needed the most immediate attention. Most of the children's school supplies and clothes had been handled, so I could get back to working down my piling debt.

My thoughts were interrupted by their conversation. Her tone seemed dangerous to me, even though it wasn't directed at me. She was trying to speak quietly but was so agitated that she didn't realize how loud she was. "Do you thinking I'm fucking stupid, Jaevon?" I rolled my eyes before I could catch myself, thankful that they were too distracted to see.

"Naw, bae, it ain't even like that," he stammered through a ridiculous fake gold grill that was squared and clearly not custom fit to his mouth like a grill should be. He mumbled through the excess saliva that was built up in his mouth. Listening to him try to suck it up struck a nerve and disgusted me. To my knowledge, in current times grills were not a "thing" on the west coast. I was hoping he was at least from the south or wherever grills were still a thing. I hadn't seen one since high school and will grudgingly admit to having one myself in my younger days of trying to obtain a "cool" status with the young ladies. This man, however, appeared to be in his mid-thirties.

Their body language was still perplexing. Her tone, and the edge in her voice, seemed like she wanted to kill him, though she lay against him under his arm. I could tell by that point that they were a couple, though an odd one. His posture suggested that he trusted her with his life and didn't have a care in the world. I couldn't imagine myself in his position. All I could think was that he better sleep with one eye open.

"So you expect me to believe that you're NOT still fucking her? When she's clearly begging you to come fuck her right now? How does that work?" She was beyond mad. Big mad, as my teen would say. She sounded like she was going to blow. It made me think of the cartoons from my childhood where you could literally see the smoke coming out of someone's ears and hear their temperature rising, like a tea kettle.

"I told you, she wants me. But I haven't talked to her like that in months. And I told you that ain't my baby. The timeline don't even add up. Ask my little cousin, Pookie. He'll tell you." His words came across like what she was saying was completely ridiculous and an utter waste of his time. His tone was as cocky as I've ever heard, rivalling the arrogance of Donald Trump.

"Jaevon. Just stop. Please," she was almost begging. "I'm not these dumb little young girls you're used to messing with. You just showed me her messages to prove that you're not dealing with her, yet she's talking about things that are going on with you now. Today. Things that I didn't even know about. I told you we should just leave this whole thing alone. I told you it was okay when we were just fucking. But you keep insisting on trying to be together. I don't get it. Why do you think you have to lie and play games with me like this? I have too much going on in my own life to play these high school games with you."

Wow, was this real life? Was I being punked? They had to be joking. I mean, would a chick really handle something like this *that* well? And there's no way she'd still deal with him. Could this be real life? Or was I in some reality TV episode, like the broke Vegas edition of Love and Hip Hop? I began to think that I needed to pull over and get some popcorn to really get the full experience. Overall, I must say that she was handling this far better than I, or anyone else that I know, would. I mean, why even deal with him?

He was stuttering and tripping over his own words. "Bae, look at the messages. I didn't even respond about fucking her. I just asked about her sister. She was the one who would set up the deals for me to sell the weed to her sister. I don't want her. I haven't touched that girl in, whew-" he paused and motioned in a very exaggerated way, "ages." He had an extremely evil grin to go along with it.

"Jaevon, STOP calling me bae. That's your ghetto ass nickname for every bitch that you're fucking because you can't keep our names straight. I can't do this anymore. This isn't working for me. You're never there when you say you will be and there's always a million excuses. I'm tired of trying to understand. I'm tired of waiting. YOU wanted to take our situation to this 'serious' level and have seriously stepped down since then. I take relationships very seriously. And this is a joke." She turned to look out the window.

I started thinking this would be break up number two in my car. I wasn't even sure whose house we were headed to or what the plan was. We were only five minutes into a thirty-minute ride. During the awkward silence, I wondered if I should interject.

"Baby, it's not like that. I don't want that girl. I told you there's just been so much going on." He broke the silence before I came to a conclusion.

"Right. So much that you missed my birthday dinner. You never make it out when I invite you. You never show up on time. The only time you're really around is when you need me to do something for you."

"Oh, right." He snickered. "So when I had you tappin' out after two rounds, that was about me?" His cockiness was in full force.

You've gotta be fucking kidding me, I thought. There's no way she's buying this. What could she possibly see in this clown? Does he really just fuck her and that makes all of this go away? I spend all of my time alone and can't meet a decent person to be with, yet clowns like this pretty much have girls begging to be with them? What the fuck is wrong with me? Am I that horrible? Is this really what the world is coming to? What do my children have to look forward to when they grow up? All of this is just beyond frustrating.

She stared at him for a moment with her mouth wide open with disbelief. "Jaevon. Are you serious right now? Yes, we've had some good sex. But seriously, that does not outweigh you falling asleep all the time."

What the hell? He's even falling asleep on her? How good can it be? I really did want some popcorn. It was getting difficult to keep my eyes focused on the road with this circus act going on in the backseat. And if it wasn't the sex, what was this guy doing to have girls fall over him like this?

He giggled nervously. "What are you talking about?"

"Last night you fell asleep while going down on me." Her tone was so sharp, *I* felt uncomfortable. I was silently rooting for the young man to say something to redeem himself. Crickets.

She broke the silence with even more hostility and animosity in her voice. "I stopped bothering to try to wake you up. I just grabbed your head and held it where I needed it until I finished. That is not my idea of good sex. I'm really tired of this. What do you bring to the table?"

"What do you mean what do I bring to the table?" He really sounded like he was shocked at the audacity she had to even ask that question. "I bring *me* to the table, Jennifer. What do you bring?"

"Ha! What about *you* makes you something I should be trying this hard to hold onto?" I could almost feel her blood pressure rising. "I bring a lot. I have my own money. My own car. My own place. I am working toward things in life. I have goals and dreams and things I'm doing to get there. I cook. I clean. I help your mother. I'm honest with you and I don't play games. My kids are grown and I have absolutely no drama with their father at this point. That's what I bring."

Wow! This sounded like a dream girl. I was barely making ends meet. She had her own stuff *and* had the time to waste with someone like him? What was I doing wrong? I mean, Veronica was a time waster, not adding anything but drama to my life. I was constantly on the verge of losing my home or having a utility shut off and couldn't even fathom the idea of time to spend with a woman, and he couldn't even stay awake to have sex with her? Was I in the middle of the *Twilight Zone*? Maybe he had a time-consuming job or something distracting him?

"Calm down, sweetie. I just didn't understand what you really meant." I will say his tone never got too loud. He didn't seem to be the arguing type, really. But it seemed like every time he opened his mouth it just irritated her even more. He added, "I can't wait to get home. I need to lay down. I don't want to talk anymore."

"That's the problem, Jaevon. You never want to talk when it's something serious or if it's not about you getting something you want."

"I have a lot going on. You know that. I'm sorry that my people keep dying and my mama's sick and I'm struggling to see my kids."

She took a deep breath and shook her head, then just looked out of her window again. After about five minutes she broke the silence again. "Jaevon, you can't keep playing with people's emotions like this. You're lucky that I have a grasp on myself."

"What the hell does that mean?" he asked, truly confused.

"I mean I can totally understand why the women you've been with have tased you, ran you over, stabbed you, and shot you," she said, exasperated.

"What?" Oh shit, did I say that out loud? I guess I

got a little carried away listening to this drama-filled soap opera that I forgot to keep this in my head. I better figure out a way to clean this up. I quickly apologized. "My sincerest apologies. I didn't mean to intrude, but it has been somewhat difficult to ignore the conversation you've been having."

She took a deep breath and began to just let it all pour out. "This is utterly ridiculous. I've been nothing but good to him. I've done nothing but stand by his side. He went to jail and I took his phone calls. I ran his mama around town to get his paperwork, pay his ticket at one court, and pay his bail at the other one. She even listed me as his significant other and had them calling me when his silly ass wouldn't show up to his court date. He has several girls calling him all the time, including one who's about to give birth next month. He stands me up all of the time. In the beginning the sex was good and I didn't look at him as someone I could be serious with. Then *he* realized I could be with other guys and wanted to do the whole relationship thing. I agreed for some dumb reason. Then he fell off. He would act like he was coming, so I'd be home. He wouldn't come. I wasn't able to work as much because I was always waiting on him. Then he started falling asleep on me all the time because of his damn drugs. I can't do this anymore. And despite all of this, I'm nothing but a good woman to him. I stand by his side. And all I'm looking for is a little bit of respect, but I can't even get a decent conversation."

Wow. She unloaded an earful on me. And he just sat there, silent. We were only halfway through the ride. I didn't want to escalate the situation at all, but I did find it to be completely absurd, and intriguing.

In an attempt to lighten the mood without belittling the situation, I said, "All I was going to ask is did you really get tased, ran over, stabbed, *and* shot?"

He chuckled as though it was all one big joke and said, "Yeah." I've never been shot, stabbed, ran over, or even tased, but I'm fairly certain that if I had, I wouldn't find anything about it funny at all. I guess they could sense my puzzled state, or maybe he just enjoyed talking about it. After a few moments of silence, she encouraged him.

"Why don't you share, Jaevon?" I was honestly hoping that he would elaborate. This was the most entertaining ride of my morning, to say the least.

He chuckled with a very arrogant expression on his face. "The girl I was real cool with in high school hit me with a car just after high school, but she didn't really mean it. We got love for each other."

The woman cut in, "That's what I'm talking about. You still have love for the bitch, and that's why she's always on your phone, *still*!" She moved away from him a bit, out of embarrassment perhaps.

"Come on, shawty, miss me with that stuff. It's not like you're going anywhere anyway. Me and her are just cool."

If this is how he always acts, I can see why the girl ran him over. I was surprised Jennifer hadn't hurt him. I wondered if someone could get me mad enough to actually run them over. What would that take? I mean, that's just not normal.

I asked, "So, are you guys a couple? I don't mean that with any disrespect."

"Yeah, Jaevon, what are we? Why don't you tell him?" She sounded more aggressive and angrier as her voice was a higher pitch than before.

"Why is you trippin'? I tried to hang out with you so we could have a cool night, and this is what you do? If I knew this was gonna happen I would've just gone and did something else, with someone else. I told you that I stopped hanging out with these crazy girls like that because I thought you were cool. I thought you were different. I haven't hung out with anyone like that since that last one shot me."

The woman sat there with a blank look, like a deer in headlights. I didn't want this situation to get out of hand, so I thought maybe I could curb the situation.

I asked him, "You really got shot by a woman you were dealing with?"

"Yeah, last year. Twenty-three times. I'm like the Jordan of gunshot wounds," he answered. He laughed again, arrogantly.

"Jaevon, that's not funny. You don't understand how you make us feel and what you do to make a woman want to actually kill you. And her *mother*?"

"Come on, why is you trippin'? I'm the one who got shot anyways. I can feel however I want to feel about it. Besides, I'm like Superman. I can't die."

My mind began to wonder in a different direction. I wondered what it would feel like each time you pulled the trigger for someone you hate. A tingle came over my body. It must be one hell of a rush. Feeling the gun buck, hearing the explosion, and seeing the impact of the bullet just tear through the flesh and rip it to shreds. Wait - why was I thinking like this? What was wrong with me? This was wrong. You're not supposed to feel excited at the thought of shooting someone. I was so lost in my thoughts that I missed the last couple of exchanges between the pair.

I did catch that he had been shot more than once, so I asked, "You've been shot multiple times?"

Maybe I had a look of doubt, because the man started to pull his shirt up, saying, "I can show you the scars. I'm not making this up."

"That's not necessary," I reassured him as quickly as I could get the words out of my mouth. I had no desire to see this man's body, or any other man's body for that matter.

I think he liked the shocked responses he must be accustomed to getting because he continued. "The first time I got shot had nothing to do with a female. I was just in the wrong place at the wrong time. I actually think my cousin is the one who shot me though. It was dark and everyone was shooting." He shrugged, and then he added, "I guess it happens."

The woman shook her head in disgust. "No, Jaevon, it doesn't *just* happen. This is *not* normal."

This was getting more amusing by the minute. I found it to be incredibly fascinating, and disturbing, that this clown could get a woman like this and I couldn't seem to find a good woman anywhere. Even my kids' mothers were garbage. Did I have to be garbage to get someone decent? Or was there something very wrong with me?

"Wait a minute. Did you say that your wife and her mother shot you?" That little tidbit almost escaped me.

"Yeah," he sounded half excited, half disturbed. I think I would have serious issues if that were me. He continued, unprompted, "We were having some issues."

No shit, I thought.

"She took the kids and moved out a few weeks before. We hadn't seen each other or spoke. I went to church with this girl I was rockin' with and came home. I didn't know whose car was in the driveway. I told shawty to wait down the street and gave her my gun in case there were any issues."

"So you went to your wife's house with another woman? I'm surprised the girl didn't join in and shoot you, too!"

"I told her to go down the street and wait for me to call her, so she wasn't actually there when I went inside." He paused. I think he was getting a rush, like he's the star of his own movie and enjoying the shock value and entertainment it's bringing.

"When I went inside, I saw my wife on one couch, her mother across the room, and my cousin's girl on the other couch. I just tried to figure out what they were all doing there. They started yelling. I asked what was going on and why were they in my house. I saw her mother go in her bag and pull out something. I turned to leave, but the door was locked. I remember hearing pow, pow, pow. I kept telling myself to stay calm. Then I saw all the blood. I still can't drink red drinks because it makes me think of the blood."

I felt for the guy. I couldn't imagine what it would be like to know that someone I called my wife hated me so much that she literally tried to kill me. I mean, I've had some women hate me before and say they wanted to kill me. But to *actually* try to kill me? I stopped myself. I remembered that he took another woman to the house that he shared with his wife just weeks before. I can understand why she wanted to kill him.

He went back into his clown, gangsta-self living his own movie life. "I had to call the police myself. They wouldn't even dial 9-1-1. I told the paramedics what they needed to do. I told them I been shot before, so I know the drill. My lungs were punctured. I might have passed out after that, because the next thing I remember is waking up in the hospital with my whole squad around me and like twenty cops. They had to have me protected."

I actually believed most of his story. I think he added a bunch of rap lyrics and movie scenes to it, but the bones of the story rang true.

I'm guessing she had heard the story a few times because she seemed unfazed by it. I figured I should say something at that point. "Damn, I'm sorry to hear that. That sounds rough."

We were only a few minutes away from their drop off location. I figured I'd try to lighten the mood. "So I guess that means you should be able to be a rapper or something now, right? I mean, don't all the greats have bullet scars, too?"

He lit up and she groaned. "Exactly. That's why I be in the studio every day. And my doctor told me I need to write a book to share my story."

I told him, "I'm sure a lot of people would read your story." I couldn't help but wonder which section of the library it would be in, perhaps the fantasy section with all of the extras he wanted to put on it?

We pulled up to a nice condo in an affluent part of North Las Vegas. "Alright. I want to thank you guys for letting me drive you, and good luck with everything."

She said, "Would it be okay if I change my destination? I think I want to go home."

He started to say something, but she cut him off. "You need to rest, and I can do some laundry and stuff at home."

"That's fine." That meant even more money for me. I was even happier when my app updated and showed her destination was across town in Mountain's Edge, the far southwest corner of the city. This ride was going to fill up my gas tank and give me a few dollars on the water bill.

They said goodbye in an awkward exchange, and he disappeared inside.

She let out a huge sigh as I pulled off. She seemed to have the weight of the world on her shoulders.

"Can I ask you a question?" She began.

"Sure," I replied, wondering where this was going.

"Am I *that* bad? I mean, I know I have my issues. Maybe he isn't that bad. I don't know. I just feel like I'm really giving it a try but it's just time to move on. I can't even blame him. I'm just really upset with myself. I feel like a fool."

My natural instinct was to tell her that yes, she looked like a fool. But I somehow didn't think that would make anything better. Actually, it would have probably made it worse. I didn't have the best track record with women and didn't really want her sobbing in my backseat. That would have made me incredibly uncomfortable; instead, I offered, "I think you have to do what you feel is best. Love is never simple."

The dam broke, the tears started, and I was beginning to regret the extended trip. We still had another forty minutes to go. That's an eternity when you have a grown woman crying uncontrollably in your backseat, even if you're not the subject of her tears.

"That's the crazy part. I don't even think I love him. I mean, this probably sounds cruel, but what am I doing with him? He's not someone I can really take seriously. I mean, yes, I did fall for him. I do care about him. But I don't think I could ever actually count on him. I need something more in my life, especially with all of this going on. I've only been talking to him for about five months."

I didn't want to talk badly about another man. My initial thought was to agree with her and tell her to drop that clown, but I also realized that so many women say these things and cry it out and yell and scream, and then they go back. The more abusive and absurd the situation is, the more they seem to want it. "If that's how you feel, I think you should follow your heart." I don't even think she heard me. I don't even think we were actually having a conversation. I think she was talking to herself and I was just there, a captive audience if you will.

She was sobbing. "I just wanted to try something different. I thought maybe if I stepped outside of my comfort zone, I would get a different result. I have terrible taste in men and seem to always pick wrong. I have made a complete fool of myself with him. I mean, look at him! He's like a bad hood movie. I feel like I'm trapped in a never-ending cycle of foolishness. And I just keep on making it worse. I made a complete idiot of myself at my friend's dinner. I called Jaevon out on BS and made everyone uncomfortable. It was supposed to be a good time. A special event. There were kids and everything. I'm so embarrassed." She started crying so hard I thought she was about to hyperventilate.

I thought this woman needs a therapist, not a driver. The only thought that kept repeating in my mind was that this woman is completely ridiculous. I thought it would be best if I kept my comments to myself and just tried to get through the rest of the ride. After a few more comments I confirmed that she was just talking out loud to herself, so I stopped responding. Someone should just put her out of her misery. The rest of the ride was like a song stuck on repeat with her basically saying the same thing over and over again. Déjà vu set in because that felt like an uncomfortable Veronica conversation.

CHAPTER 38

AIN'T NO PARTY LIKE A VEGAS PARTY

SUNDAY, SEPTEMBER 16, 2018 3:00 A.M.

It was the middle of the night. I got a request in the area somewhere near Tropicana and Pecos. These are older homes, but still really nice, and the area is typically pretty calm. The navigation took me around a few corners as I entered a large neighborhood. I turned the last corner to see the street lit up like a Christmas tree.

There must have been five or six police cars, in addition to the ambulance and a fire truck, all of them with their blaring lights swirling. The first thought I had is, oh my God, what happened? What am I doing over here? To be honest, I'm not the biggest fan of law enforcement and don't aspire to be a getaway driver for an individual fleeing the crime scene.

I slowly approached because I had not yet arrived at the destination that the app was taking me to. It seemed to be three houses just past where the police and festivities were. With a sense of relief, I slowly tried to make my way through the maze of obstructions in the middle of the road. As I got closer, there was a row of what appeared to be teenagers sitting down on the pavement in handcuffs with a couple of the officers standing over them.

One of the officers saw me approaching, so I made sure all of my windows were down. I continued approaching, very slowly, until he signaled for me to stop. All I was thinking is I had my credentials saying that I was there to pick up somebody and I was just going to cooperate to the best of my ability.

As soon as the officer noticed the Rideshare emblem in my windshield, he turned to the group of young people who were handcuffed and demanded, "Who in the fuck ordered a Rideshare?"

All of the young people sat there very quietly, and he repeated his question, in a much louder and angrier tone. No one responded, so he just signaled for me to go ahead and pass on through, which I did very slowly.

Another young man was walking past my vehicle on the other side. I heard him ask the officers for medical attention for his friend who had been shot, who was in the back of another car. The officer responded with, "We'll get to him in a moment."

I was trying to wrap my head around everything that was going on because it was a lot to take in at three in the morning, especially after driving for the past five hours, tired and delirious. Instead of trying to understand everything, I just hoped that all of the festivities were done and there would be no more shooting because I definitely did not want to be involved.

As I crept just past the commotion, another young man came out of the shadows and jumped right in the back of the car, and then he slumped down. I stopped to verify that he was the correct passenger. He hastily tried to ask me to just keep driving. His destination was not very far, and I didn't want to be in this environment any longer, so I took a chance that he was the correct passenger and continued on to where he was going.

I attempted to make small talk. Trying to make light of the situation, I asked him, "So you just had a wild party?" He began to tell me that it got out of control pretty fast, and that was his friend who got shot, and many more details that I really did not want to know. Thankfully, the ride was over pretty fast. I was glad to put that whole incident behind me.

That night and the hectic events I found myself surrounded by is what I was learning to be a somewhat common occurrence during these Rideshare hours in Las Vegas. I really didn't need to be in the middle of a house party shooting and I really didn't have time for police questioning. I also didn't want to have to clean blood out of my car from an injured passenger. I didn't remember house parties like this from when I was younger. I don't know if I was more impressed with the young man's cognitive skills to get a Rideshare to leave the scene or disturbed that I may have played a part in aiding and abetting.

CHAPTER 39

JUST BE COOL

SATURDAY, SEPTEMBER 22, 2018 1:00 A.M.

I found myself in a residential area, which is always a nice break from the hustle and bustle of the strip on a late Friday or Saturday night. It was one of the nicer areas in town, which led me to believe that it would bring about a driving opportunity that would be far more pleasant than normal.

I've had my fair share of crazy rides and I've had my fair share of hectic individuals, but I don't think that I was ready for this one. The ride pinged me to go to a Shell gas station. I picked up two gentlemen, one was probably in his mid-thirties or early forties, and the other turned out to be his father.

They got in holding a case of beer and both of them had an open beer in their hands. The son asked me, "Is it cool to drink this?"

I said, "Well, if we get pulled over, I'm going to get a DUI."

The son respectfully offered to leave his beer or

throw it away. The father aggressively got in, and in a slurred voice told me, "Don't worry about it."

Because of the son's respectful posture, I told him, "Let me take a look and see how far you're going." When I started the ride, it said that it was less than five minutes. Being that we were in a better part of town, the chance of a DUI checkpoint was minimal, at best. I told him, "Go ahead, you're fine. If we get stopped, just kind of put it on the floor in between your feet and we'll just deal with it like that. I'll act as though I didn't see it."

That seemed to satisfy everyone in the car, so I headed toward their destination. When we got to the dot on the navigation, it was in the middle of the street with nothing within thirty feet other than a dirt lot. The lot was fenced in. We quickly put together that the address that they put in did not exist. When that happens, the navigation takes you to the middle of the street and tells you that you have arrived.

I asked him, "Which house is it?"

The son didn't reply, but was frantically touching his phone. The father looked back and slurred, "Junior, where we going? Where's your guy?"

I repeated my question in a louder tone, "Which house is it?"

The son said, "I'm trying to call him now to find out." Someone finally answered the number he had been dialing. There was a lot of background noise. I could hear it even though his phone was not on speaker phone. He asked the man on the phone, "So where you at, fool?" He asked him again, and still didn't get an answer. From what I could hear, the guy was trying to give him directions again.

I told him, "Just ask him what the house number is; it has to be close. We can find it if you just have the house number because the house number he gave is not correct."

The man on the other end of the phone finally offered a house number, which was the number the son put into the app, only the first two numbers were reversed.

We pulled up to the house and he was still on the phone with the guy. He said, "We're out front."

A gentleman came out, almost skipping to the car. They opened the back door and began to exchange words. During this time, another ride request came in and I accepted it, thinking that this ride was complete.

The son, who was sitting in the back, asked me, "Can you turn on the light?" I obliged.

I realized he wasn't trying to get out of the car. I said, "We've arrived, and I have another passenger to go get."

The father began to say, "Just be cool; just be cool."

Now my attention was on the interaction in the back. The gentleman that came out of the house was showing the son a variety of illegal drugs. They were in the process of making a transaction. When I looked back, I realized they aren't even fazed by me observing their transaction.

I said, "Come on, what are you doing?"

And once again, the father told me, "You're cool, just be cool."

I looked at him and said, "I'm not that damn cool."

He said, "Don't worry; don't worry. We're going to take care of you."

I asked, "How? You're going to put money on my books?"

He said, "No, no. No, it's cool."

I responded with, "It's *not* cool. I'm getting nothing out of this, besides the five dollars that you guys paid for this ride. You guys are getting high. This gentleman is making the money from the drugs that he's selling you. We're all going to get the same amount of time in jail. Somehow, this does not seem fair or balanced, and I don't want any part of it."

I took a deep breath and continued, "All you have to do is step out of the car. With them being *out* of the car, then I don't know what's going on and it's none of my business."

Them doing this transaction in the backseat with the light on made it pretty hard for me to sit there and say I had no idea what was going on because they weren't that far away from me.

The father once again told me, "We will take care of you."

I said, "You know what? Never mind. I have to go. I have another ride to go pick up, and they're waiting so that you guys can take care of *your* business. You can order another ride when you're done."

The father asked, "Will it be you that comes back to get us?"

I explained, "If I'm still in the area, they'll give me the ride." In my head, I thought, there's no way in hell.

The father then began to try to negotiate with me. "We'll give you a tip if you cancel that ride. You can't just leave us here."

I was thinking, you're good enough to come buy drugs here, but you're not good enough to be left here?

The father just asked me, "well can you just take us somewhere around the corner?"

I reluctantly agreed. I said, "I'll take you to the major street and leave you at a gas station or something of that sort, but it's going to have to be on the way to where I'm going to pick up my next ride."

He continued to negotiate, talk, or whatever the hell he thought he was doing, and I ignored everything else that he said. I was completely done with talking to him. It didn't help the fact that I could only understand one out of every four words that he said because he was *that* inebriated.

All night, the thought kept running through my head that I could have gotten two years locked up in jail for drugs that I was a part of buying, but I wasn't even going to get high off of and didn't want any part of. Then the gentleman offered me a five-dollar tip. I was insulted.

How would I be able to continue with Rideshare? Being that I had a five-year loan to pay on a vehicle that I cannot afford without Rideshare, I would have to figure it out. Hopefully I figured it out before I ended up incarcerated over something stupid like this.

CHAPTER 40
CLOSE ENCOUNTERS
THURSDAY, SEPTEMBER 27, 2018 1:00 A.M.

I found myself sitting in that same parking lot inside of commercial center after I had just dropped a couple off at the Green Door. The Green Door is a swinger's club that's really well known here in Las Vegas, and ironically is in the same parking lot as the Las Vegas Lounge and a few other establishments for those who are more sexually adventurous or live alternative lifestyles. Before these past few months, I thought that this area was a myth or long gone with the days of the mob running the city.

Normally, when I'm in this area, rides come in very fast. So, I typically just park and wait until the next ride request comes in. As I sat there in the middle of the night, I started looking around and noticed a high level of working girls walking to and from in the parking lot.

One saw me staring at her and started to walk closer, thinking that I somehow signaled for her to come to me. As she approached, I noticed that she was not born a woman. In a masculine tone she asked me, "Baby, are you looking for some company?"

Sitting there like a deer in the headlights, I just stared at her masculine features. I started to see the man underneath the feminine decor. The long fingers and broad shoulders were the most obvious giveaways. Then my attention drifted on to the feminine breasts and attire, complemented by the makeup and perfume.

With a shaky voice, I responded, "No, thank you."

She must have been able to pick up on the lack of confidence in my voice and blatant stare that she had captured. She asked again, "are you sure? Baby, we'll have a really good time together." She said with a sly smile.

Strange, or at least unfamiliar, thoughts started racing through my head and I began an internal negotiation with myself. I could almost see the little winged creatures that looked a lot like me on either shoulder. You know, the sensible self and the devil's advocate self.

The first thing I argued was, I can't. What would happen if everybody found out? The other side argued, but nobody would find out because it would be just the two of us.

I couldn't go to the Las Vegas Lounge because I didn't know what was inside, and there were probably too many people in there. I didn't know who I might see or run into, but in this situation, I didn't recognize her, and it would be behind closed doors - or in the privacy of my vehicle. My windows are tinted as dark as possible, and there are some dark corners in that parking lot.

No, no, NO! You are supposed to be with a woman. One who is born that way. How could you? Why would you?

Beep, beep. The sound of a ride request pinged, and I was saved by the bell. I said, "No, thank you. I have somebody to go pick up, but have a good night." I'm not sure why I felt the need to explain or justify.

The curiosity and thoughts surrounding the encounter plagued my mind all night. What if I would have just declined the ride request and turned off my app? I tried to convince myself that there was just nothing natural about that situation, and that I was not supposed to do things like that. Then other thoughts began to go in the direction of, what if I did? It's my life, so what's the problem with that? And then, before moving on to other topics, it ended up with a question of, why not? I guess this just left me with another unanswered question.

CHAPTER 41

RUN, FORREST, RUN!

SATURDAY, OCTOBER 6, 2018 10:45 P.M.

It was fight night in Sin City. We have plenty of them in Vegas. Both boxing and UFC draw large crowds, lots of money being thrown around, and an excessively drunk crowd. As with any event throughout the history of humanity that involves brutal violence, it really brings something out of people. The crowd gets riled up and the brute force and savage nature comes out of people. I'm not judging, but I do notice the brutality of these events and the pure barbaric nature that they incite.

I enjoy working on these nights, however, because we tend to get quite a bit of traffic. And sometimes, the drunk ones will flash and throw money around - including larger tips - either by mistake, or because they are trying to impress a female companion with how much of a baller they are or they're trying to one-up a friend.

I got pinged to a neighborhood in the north for a shared ride. It was one of the newer housing tracts that feature stucco homes that are fairly close together, small rock yards, and strict HOA regulations. I moved down the street slowly, trying to find the right address. There were a lot of cars on the street, along with people. I always get a little anxious, and maybe a little insecure, when I'm being watched. I can't tell who I'm there to pick up because everyone is looking at me like I don't belong. All of the focus being on me is just too overwhelming. I've never wanted to be the center of any attention. I was looking at them, trying to see who my passenger was, which is impossible since I only had a name and location. This goes on nightly, and even after six months I still do the same thing.

I figured out the pattern of the addresses on the street and stopped in front of the address on my app. I pulled up to a circus. The cars were lined up on both sides of the street, bumper to bumper. The garage was open, with people floating between the garage and the house, a few groups were gathered along the driveway, sitting in the back of a pickup, and on the sidewalk in front of the gravel lawn.

I used the app to send a text to my passenger, since no one seemed to be approaching my vehicle. I was watching them, and a few of them were watching me. Finally, a man appeared at my window. He motioned for me to roll my window down, and I obliged.

"Give me just a moment, please. We're trying to get my friend," he slurred.

I nodded, as if to agree to his request.

He walked back to the largest group of people standing at the end of the driveway, where a heated exchange was underway. I had rolled my window back up, so I could only hear muffled voices, but the body language and escalated volume seemed to indicate that the parties were not all in agreement about whatever the topic was.

I lost track of the time, as I was watching the people instead of the timer on my app. We are only supposed to wait for two minutes for shared rides, and then cancel the request to be available for other passengers.

Because I couldn't hear them, I started making up my own argument for the crowd. I was amusing myself, when a woman approached. She said, "My fiancé went back to get his friend. I'm sorry. We'll be ready in a second."

At this point, I was slightly confused. Shared rides only accommodate up to two people so that the other seats would be available to other passengers who may be picked up along the route. I decided to go ahead and wait a bit, since this was abnormal, even in North Vegas. I was entertained.

The woman disappeared into the middle of the crowd. A few minutes later, the man reappeared. He climbed into the passenger seat and sighed.

I asked, "Are we ready to go?"

He said, "No. We have to wait for them."

I had started the ride by this point because they had acknowledged me. At least I would be paid a few pennies for hanging out while they worked on getting it together.

When the woman reappeared, with another man, I explained to them that I couldn't take all of them in case there was another passenger added to the ride. I don't think that their comprehension levels were adequate to take in what I was saying.

The couple begged for me to just take their friend around the corner to his house. They were visiting from Wisconsin, but the friend lived here. I attempted to explain how the shared rides work, again. It was like I was trying to explain quantum physics to a class of toddlers.

Once I determined that it would take me about a week to explain it in a way that they would understand, I decided to just take a chance and go with it.

As they started to climb in the backseat, the friend suddenly jumped back out of the vehicle and took off toward the house, saying, "My TV!"

The man in the front seat started laughing uncontrollably. The woman said, "Oh, yeah. I'll go help him."

About five minutes later the man in the front went to find them, again. I was trying to figure out if we were ever actually going to get to leave this street.

He came back a couple of minutes later. He got in and said, "It's okay if you want to just leave them. We can go. I don't even care." He broke out into uncontrollable laughter again.

By now, I had figured out that the couple was newly engaged and had only been a couple for a few months.

This was their first trip together. The man had been friends with the local gentleman since high school. He acknowledged that there were always problems when the friend was intoxicated

I asked, "What about your fiancé?"

He shook his head and said, "It's okay; it was new. I can find another one."

I said, "That sounds fine right now, but you might feel differently tomorrow when you wake up."

Just then, the woman returned to the vehicle and asked me to open the back. A few minutes later, the friend came up carrying a sixty-inch TV. He practically threw it into the back of the vehicle, shut the back, and jumped into the backseat, yelling, "Let's go! Hurry!"

I didn't know if I should jump in and take off or give it a minute. I was wondering if he was stealing the TV or if it was really his. Could I be considered an accomplice for driving off right now if they did steal it

Although everyone was looking in our direction, no one appeared to be in a hurry to come our way, so I slowly drove off, skeptically.

The woman and the friend were in the backseat laughing. She was a petite woman, but had apparently gotten in between the friend and the owner of the house, who were supposedly friends of the friend. The trio came to watch the fight and brought the extra TV for the garage for the other partygoers paying for the Pay-Per-View event. There were drunk words exchanged, although none of the three could clearly articulate what the actual disagreement was, and the small woman threatened the other man, who was much larger than her. She thought it was funny that he backed down to her and insinuated that the crowd was under the impression that she was tied to the mob.

I was trying to take it all in, though my head was spinning. It was like listening to a group of high schoolers who were drunk and high for the first time, trying to make sense of their combined fantasies mixed in with some toddlers at story time.

We pulled up to the friend's house, which was only a few blocks away as they had promised. He got out to return the TV to his home, but he had no keys. He was walking around the perimeter of the house, trying the windows and doors.

I had to ask the couple, "Is this for sure his house?" I really didn't want to add a possible breaking and entering to the list of potential crimes I was involving myself with by remaining with this odd group.

They slurred that yes, they thought so. She got out to help the friend, who had disappeared. He came stumbling out of the house through the front door, and two small dogs escaped. He got the TV out of the back of my vehicle and went back in the house with it. He came back out and seemed to be locking the door.

I asked, "Are the dogs supposed to be outside?"

He started screaming profanities and ran down the street in the direction I told him they went. The woman retrieved one dog, which was only a few houses away. He had to go further down the street to get the other one. The dog wasn't having any of it, however. The man came out of his flip flops, continued chasing the dog barefoot, and then lunged for the animal. He missed. He did go into an expert roll that would have made any three-year-old jealous. In one swift motion, he got back to his feet to continue the chase. The only words that came to mind were, "run, Forrest, run!"

By this point, I was laughing hysterically with the gentleman in the front seat. The woman was standing at the front door, holding the captured pet, with her jaw hanging open. Somehow, the drunken fool managed to grab the dog and put them both back in the house. He went to retrieve his shoes and came back to my vehicle.

The friend and the woman climbed back into the backseat. I was a bit confused, as I thought we were taking him home. They asked if he could go with them to their hotel, The Plaza, which is downtown off of Fremont Street.

At this point, I didn't figure it could get any weirder and I was somewhat defeated. I agreed. The rest of the ride was fairly uneventful. After they climbed out of the vehicle and I began to pull off, I heard a phone ringing from the backseat. I stopped to fish out the phone and the friend came running up to me. He was ranting about his phone. I handed it to him and continued out of the driveway toward my next pick-up at the Golden Nugget.

As I came to a stop at the red light at the end of the driveway, I noticed a wallet in my front seat. I looked back to find the group, but they had disappeared into the crowd.

I think the entertainment value of that ride far exceeded the minimal payment. At least the guy in the front seat gave me a ten-dollar tip and an additional twenty when I returned the wallet to him the next morning.

In hindsight, I made pretty good money throughout the night. Fight nights are busy and there were plenty of surges. Almost the entire city was surging for a few hours throughout the night, especially around the strip and downtown.

It may have been more lucrative if I would have declined or ended that ride, but sometimes a laugh is necessary. I shared that experience with several of my other passengers throughout the night, keeping the comedic relief going for several people. I'm glad I took the ride instead of my initial thought to tell them to fuck off. Despite being an entertaining story for the rest of my passengers, it took my mind off of all of the other obstacles and struggles that one deals with when driving Rideshare.

CHAPTER 42
DOMESTIC ISSUES
SATURDAY, OCTOBER 13, 2018 1:50 A.M.

I'd like to believe that I was a fairly experienced Rideshare driver at this point. I had over six months and more than two thousand rides in. Of course, there are drivers who do this full time, or started before me, but overall I think I withstood the test of time. I heard a report that the average Rideshare driver lasts about three to four months. Maybe, just maybe, the self-doubt that I had experienced was more common than I wanted to think. I thought I had experienced a good variety of rides and that nothing would really catch me off-guard at this point. I was wrong.

It was just before two in the morning when I got pinged over to a nicer hotel on the outskirts of town. The JW Marriott in the Summerlin area is a nicer property that's far enough away from the hustle and bustle of the strip to seem like it's in a whole different city. It seemed to be a bit early for an airport run, but I do realize that some people, especially of a more affluent class, tend to be more punctual and plan ahead far better than I.

I pulled into the valet area to find an older gentleman in a full suit. He looked angry. He appeared to be in his late fifties or early sixties, about 5′4″, missing a couple of fingers, and as stern and grumpy as the Grinch.

I got out of my vehicle to open the back, since it's good customer service and the lever is hidden to the far right, instead of the center where everyone expects it to be. I greeted the man, though he seemed to completely ignore me. Before I could grab his stainless-steel suitcase, he picked it up, twisted his body around toward the back of him, and flung it into the cargo space. It appeared to take some serious effort and cause quite a bit of pain for him to get the luggage into my vehicle. I almost felt bad for him, but he didn't give me the opportunity to help him. Some men are proud like that, so I don't take too much offense.

I climbed back into the driver's seat and he settled into the front passenger seat while I confirmed his name and the destination. I was correct; it was too early for an airport run. We were headed to the Venetian. Switching hotels isn't terribly uncommon, though doing so in the middle of the night is. I attempted to lighten the mood and make conversation since the ride was going to be over twenty minutes long and conversation helps keep me alert.

"So, how's your night going?" I asked.

"It could be better," he said curtly.

"I see. Did you not like the Marriott here?"

He grunted with disgust. "I've had better nights."

We were circling around to exit the property when his phone rang. He said, "Excuse me," and took the call. He began yelling and demanding, "Where are you?"

I couldn't quite make out what the caller was saying, but it sounded like a hysterical woman. He didn't really talk or ask questions, but more like barked out demands. He said, "Give them the phone." A moment later, he told them, "Bring her to the valet area. I'll pick her up." He yelled the same phrase a few times, then hung up and turned to me. "Can we please go back? I'll make it worth your while."

I obliged. As we pulled back into the valet area, I informed him that there are two main doors to this property, as his agitation was increasing with every passing second that the woman wasn't at the door. He made another phone call and barked the orders and directions and what he saw. I attempted to give him the primary detail he needed - that we were at the spa entrance - but he couldn't hear me over his own voice.

After a few very uncomfortable minutes, a woman appeared with two large men who appeared to be members of the hotel's security team. She was stumbling and rolling her luggage, which matched his, behind her. She was in a sparkly evening gown, though her hair and makeup looked like they had seen a better hour. The woman was of Asian heritage and appeared to be in her early thirties.

I got out to open the back of the vehicle and put her luggage inside. He also got out. As I was hefting her luggage into the cargo area next to his, he grabbed her by the upper arm to guide her to the backseat.

She cowered away from him, into the side of the vehicle, and looked at me. She started pleading in broken English, "Please don't let him abuse me anymore. Please call cops if he hit me again."

I kind of nodded because I was unsure of what I should do in that circumstance. That was not my situation to get involved in. I'd seen far too many news stories and internet videos where the person who is trying to help actually gets attacked by both the man and the woman. I really couldn't afford the time to find myself injured or wasting countless hours giving statements to the police or attorneys. Or even worse, not being able to drive Rideshare anymore.

She got situated in the backseat, while the gentleman and I found ourselves back in the front of the vehicle where we started about ten minutes prior. As I started to drive, she made a phone call in the backseat.

She was speaking in another language for about ten minutes, crying hysterically and gasping for air. The man was frustrated and seemed to be trying to contain himself. He was breathing a little heavy but remained quiet and calm, except for the wringing of his hands that he didn't realize anyone was paying any attention to. I just drove in silence. I can't afford bad ratings, and I was hoping this man would tip me well for the inconvenience and awkwardness of the entire situation.

She started talking in broken English again. "The

police know he crazy man. His coworkers know too. They have statement saying he hit me. If he hit me again, they arrest him. He crazy. His coworkers say they never see him like this, but they all on my side."

He shook his head. He calmly said to her, "Just tell them to send you a plane ticket to go home. Please, just go home."

She yelled at him, "Fuck you, you coward. No one talking to you. You monster. You're crazy monster. Don't talk to me. Fuck you." Then she continued in another language on the phone. That sort of conversation between the phone call and yelling at him went on for more than ten minutes. It made for a very uncomfortable experience.

I'm not quite sure what happened between the pair earlier in the evening, but they both probably needed some time apart. It appeared that he was a wealthy businessman and she might be his trophy partner, but she was no longer behaving as such. I can't say whether or not he put his hands on her because I would think she would have gone to the airport instead of to another hotel with him. Who knows? They say battered women defend their abusers and go back all the time.

The car was as quiet as an abandoned tomb for the remaining fifteen minutes of the ride. I took their luggage out of the back of the vehicle and he handed me ten dollars. I can't lie, I was hoping for more. At any rate, I was grateful to get the extra.

Was it wrong for me to sit there silently? If he would have hit her, should I have intervened? The ride left me questioning my own morals and what I believe could reasonably be expected of a Rideshare driver. I mean, should I have reassured the woman? I suppose some might think it best to be chivalrous. On the other hand, I was more concerned with my income and my ratings. I mean, he had all the power in that situation, did he not? I actually think that in that situation, I had no clear "best" option. Maybe in the future I'll just put them both out. But then again, it was a fruitful ride. After all, I was doing this for income.

CHAPTER 43
THE GIRL ON THE COUCH
WEDNESDAY, OCTOBER 17, 2018 11:30 A.M.

It was a nice, beautiful day. I was enjoying my time doing Rideshare this morning. The weather was doing a good job of distracting me from all of the woes of my life. I got a request on the north side of town. The ride was in a man's name, but a young lady came bouncing outside. It didn't look like she was a day over fifteen.

I'm always hesitant when it appears to be a kid getting in my car without an adult. Especially females. They are the passengers that always make me the most nervous. Kids these days have no respect, and I'd hate to put myself in a situation where one of them says I did something inappropriate.

Technically, we're not supposed to take minors without an adult, but I'm not sure if we're supposed to profile and card these passengers? Some people just look young. Either way, that conversation isn't even a can of worms I'd really like to open.

Oh great, she was getting in the front seat. Just what

I needed.

At first, she was very quiet. It looked like she just rolled out of bed. She began to help herself to the mirror and started doing her makeup. The app said the ride would last nearly a half an hour. Twenty-six minutes of silence is not one of my favorite ways to spend my time.

I asked, “How’s your day?”

I received the short answer, “Good.”

“Are you on your way to work?” I asked.

She said, “No. I’m heading to a wedding.”

I said, “Really? That sounds nice. Do you know the bride or the groom?”

She said, “Both.” Then she went into the story about how she was the one who encouraged them to get together and they were all three friends in high school.

I said, “In high school? It looks like you’re still in high school.”

She told me, “No, I graduated...well I was supposed to graduate a few years back.”

I asked, “What happened?”

She walked through the details of the story of her parents divorcing and finding difficulties living with both and she ended up finding herself couch hopping.

“Couch hopping? I’ve never heard that term before.”

She explained, “Well I wasn’t house hopping because I wasn’t using the house. I was only using whatever couch was open to me at the moment.”

“I see. I agree, that does sound more accurate. Did that happen recently?”

She paused and said, "Well, I began couch hopping when I was fourteen."

As I started to process that, I was thinking that a young lady at fourteen hopping from couch to couch and place to place had to be rough.

I asked, "What's your relationship like with your parents now?"

She said, "You just picked me up from my mom's house. It's weird...but I speak to her."

I said, "At least you guys found a way to work through it. Do you still couch hop now?"

She said, "No. I have evolved."

I said, "Really? What do you do now?"

She said, "I'm originally from San Diego, so some nights it's great to just sleep on the beach. But I met a great group of people who actually hired me to work at one of the coffee shops out there, and the manager decided, since she was aware of my situation, that I could have the opening shift so that I could just sleep inside the shop."

I said, "That sounds like quite an adventure," trying to sound as optimistic as possible. "What are your plans in the long term?"

"I don't really plan long term. I like to go with the moment and see how I feel at that time." She continued, "I enjoy being a free spirit. Instead of trying to plan out the rest of my life and figure out what I want to do or what I'm supposed to do, I'd rather take it moment by moment and day by day. I believe that it truly gives me the option and opportunity to live in the moment and bask in the moment."

I took a moment to reflect on what she was saying. I pictured a bird soaring through the sky like there's not a care in the world. After thinking about all of the weight that I constantly carry on my shoulders, the way this young lady lived seemed like a little slice of heaven. I wouldn't even know what to do with myself in that situation. I don't know if I was more envious or experiencing a sense of greater admiration. Nonetheless, I couldn't do anything but respect this young lady. She went from being what most people would consider a victim, being left in the streets like a stray dog, to finding the greatest sense of peace and direction and freedom that any of us could hope to find.

I asked, "Do you ever plan - or see yourself - getting married?"

She said, "If there's a husband out there for me, I'm sure we'll find each other."

I just blurted out, "I must tell you that you sound at ease for a situation that most people would have hostility and anger over. You're not angry or mad at your parents?"

She said, "I was at first. But not anymore." The tone of her voice was as calming and alluring as the way they described the sirens in the old days.

I said, "That's just fantastic. I really appreciate you sharing your story and your situation with me. Because for some reason, after our conversation, my day seems to have just gotten a whole lot better."

She smiled and said, "Well you're the one who did all the work, because you're the one who gave me the ride."

We pulled up to her destination. Her friends were very excited to see her. They ran up to the car as we were still coming to a stop.

"I wish you well, and I hope that everything works out for your friends as well."

That ride set me up to head to the shop in very good spirits. That young lady's enthusiasm and joy were contagious. Why can't we all be like her? Why does the world have to be such a dark place when we can all be as free as that young lady was?

CHAPTER 44
COMPROMISING ENCOUNTERS
FRIDAY, OCTOBER 19, 2018 11:00 P.M.

Over the previous few weeks, indecent thoughts had begun to haunt my mind. Any man in my position should be thinking about all of the attractive women who I came into daily contact with; however, my mind kept getting invaded with the transsexual passengers and encounters I'd had. I'd had plenty of beautiful women, but as much as I tried to close the door and push them out, they kept racing back in. I had begun to try to position myself in different parts of the city, which I didn't believe would bring me back into the area of the Las Vegas Lounge. This had been a challenge, due to the fact that the community of homosexuals, lesbians, and transsexuals are spread throughout the entire city. I just avoided the areas that were heavily concentrated, or at least the ones that I was aware of.

And then it happened. I was pulling out of the hospital on Maryland Parkway and got a ride request to pick up at the Las Vegas Lounge. Every rational thought in my mind said to push the button "Deny" for the request. I have to be honest, I'm not sure if it was habit or curiosity that motivated me to push "Accept." Either way, that's what happened.

During the four-minute ride to pick up the passenger, my thoughts started racing and my imagination took off with them. I guess I was trying to tell myself what I wanted to hear. I was thinking that it was fairly early in the evening, so maybe I'd just be picking up somebody that went in there looking for a date, who was now coming out with the "walk of shame." There was a good chance that I wouldn't be picking up a transsexual that early in the evening, at least that's what I told myself.

I could pretend like I didn't know exactly where to pull up to pick somebody up from that location, but that's not the truth; besides, as soon as I hit the parking lot she came to the car. I verified the name and the address as usual, and we began heading toward the Budget Suites.

I started my small talk at the same pace as I normally would with, "How's your evening going?"

She responded with, "It's dead in there tonight, so I think I'm better off just taking the night off." I didn't think she was a bartender since it was early and she definitely didn't look like she was dressed for security, so I didn't know what she meant by taking the night off.

I asked, "Do you work there?" just like I would anyone else in any other situation.

She chuckled and said, "Pretty much, but I work anywhere that I can do well at."

I said, "What are the better spots to work at?"

She said, "Well, I travel a lot. When I'm in Vegas I typically do very well in the Las Vegas Lounge."

I asked, "Oh really? What type of work do you do?"

She said, "I'm an escort." Her tone made it sound as though she was expecting me to know that already.

I didn't even try to hide my surprise. I simply told her, "I didn't realize that escorts worked in there."

She said, "Oh honey, all the time! Nobody goes in there to bother us because most people are uncomfortable being around trannys."

I said, "I didn't know. Please forgive my ignorance."

She didn't hesitate with a question of her own. "Well, have you ever been with a tranny?"

I tried to hold my composure because I didn't want to act as though that was uncommon, since I was trying to be professional. I said, "I cannot say that I have had the pleasure."

"Oh honey, you have no idea what you're missing out on. You must be at least curious about it," she said, almost as if asking me.

I had no idea how to respond to that because if I was honest about my curiosity what did that make me? Yet, if I showed what I think everybody is supposed to show, which was disgust, then how am I being professional?

I stayed quiet for a moment, trying to think.

She said, "You don't have to say anything. It's like that in the beginning for everyone, and I completely understand."

I repeated, "Like that in the beginning for everyone? What do you mean?"

She said, "Men always want to fight their urges or their desires because they're worried about how people are going to judge them, or what their friends and family will think of them. That's what transsexuals go through in the process of exposing themselves to the world. It took that moment when I had to realize that I'm either going to be true to myself or pretend to be somebody else for the rest of my life. And I'm *tired* of pretending."

I asked, "Was it difficult to decide?" I guess I went from defensive to inquisitive in a very short period. She realized at that point that she was controlling the entire conversation because of her confidence, and the lack of mine. She was very kind to my feelings because she could have made me feel very uncomfortable, but she didn't.

She said, "It was hard in the beginning, but now it doesn't bother me at all."

I had about a million more questions that I wanted to ask, especially since she was being so generous with information and made it so comfortable to talk about it, but we had just pulled up to her destination.

She asked, "Would you like my number? You know, in case you want to talk in the future?"

As tempted as I was to accept, I still wasn't *that* comfortable. So I said, "I appreciate the offer, but no thank you."

She smiled as she exited the vehicle. As she walked away, she had a switch in her stuff that was hard not to stare at. I'm not sure if this was her normal walk, or if it was just for my benefit.

Just as I raised my eyes up from looking at her lower half, she looked back to catch me in a trance. She stopped and turned around and asked, "Are you enjoying the view?"

I didn't look in the mirror to see if I turned red with blush, but I'm certain that I did. I fumbled with words to try to clean up my stare.

She interrupted and said, "It's okay, I'm just giving you a hard time. It doesn't look like you're ready to leave."

I felt as though I was stuck in quicksand and for some reason, I was not ready to leave, but had no idea what to say or why I wanted to stay. I said, "I do apologize. I didn't mean to be rude, but I'm just… it's just... Well, I don't know what it is," as I hung my head with shame.

She approached the vehicle again. Gently patting my back, she said, "Look, I'm calling it an early night and I haven't made any plans. Would you like to come in and sit down and have a drink with me, just to help you relax a little?"

Without even thinking I blurted out, "I definitely would." I immediately parked, turned off the vehicle, and jumped out. I went offline because I couldn't even think straight, let alone try to navigate my way through another ride.

I felt anxious, like I was a kid waking up on Christmas morning, but yet had butterflies in my stomach like I had asked a girl out for the first time ever. The confusion running through my mind and body is hard to describe. The thoughts going through my head were how crazy am I? What the hell am I doing? Have I lost my fucking mind? and so on. Even with all these thoughts going through my head I didn't even break stride as I approached her front door.

She opened the front door and graciously invited me in. The dwelling was not anything magical or special; it was just your average, everyday room. I took a seat on the couch as she poured us both a drink. I was still wondering what I was doing there and what the hell was wrong with me, but I did not feel compelled to get up and leave.

She sat down on the couch next to me after handing me my drink and raised her glass to gesture for us to toast. I said, "This toast is to new experiences."

She replied with just a smile and we both sipped on our drinks. To break the ice, she said, "If you have any questions feel free to ask, and I promise to be gentle with my answers." After a playful pause she added, "Unless you'd like me to be rough."

I asked, "Is it wrong if I sit here and think about you in the same way that I think about a real woman?" Oh shit. "I mean no disrespect, not saying anything about you but…"

She interrupted my stammering and said, "It's fine. I understand what you're trying to say. It's not wrong, because in my mind I am a *real* woman. I think I was just born into the wrong body and how you see me on the outside is how I feel on the *inside*. And what was really wrong was me trying to live and pretend to be a man when I don't understand what that is, and it's not how I feel." She continued by asking, "Is it wrong for me to look at you in the same way that a woman would look at you, with the same desires that a woman has?"

I thought for a quick second and said, "Well no, I don't think so."

The conversation that she and I were having made a little bit too much sense. For some reason, I hadn't even thought about the fact that I was supposed to be working or that I was sitting on the couch with a transsexual.

I took the final gulp of my drink to get the nerve up to ask my next question. I said, "May I ask another question?"

She responded immediately and sweetly, "Yes baby, go ahead."

I asked, "Well, what's it like, you know, being together?"

"Do you mean physically?"

I nodded my head yes.

She said, "Better than what you could ever imagine. I have all the feelings, motions, and actions of a woman with the understanding of a man's desires."

As I thought about what she just said, my eyes opened up very wide.

She broke into my thoughts. "Can I fix you another drink, honey?"

I handed her my cup and said, "Please.

As she handed me my second drink she said, "Let me try something with you. Close your eyes and relax." Her voice was silky smooth and had a quiet, sexy, mysterious edge to it.

Without hesitation I did close my eyes and attempted to relax but I was far too nervous and curious to be relaxed.

She continued, "Now picture me as you looked at me walking away from your vehicle." I felt a slight smile come across my face as her wet lips touched against mine and we kissed.

As she moved away from my face, my eyes opened up slowly. She asked, "What did that feel like?"

I said, "Well, it was amazing. I didn't even…"

She finished my sentence for me. "You didn't even realize the difference between me and a 'real' woman." She did the air quotes.

The experience left me sitting there all kinds of confused and speechless, so I finished my whole drink in one giant gulp trying to figure out what to do or say next.

She said, "Honey, you are far too nervous. If you just relax you won't feel so confused." She paused for a moment to let that sink then. Then she asked, "Will you allow me to help with that?"

I said, "Sure." I had no idea what she had in mind, but I trusted her.

She grabbed my hand and took me back into the bedroom, then instructed me to take off my shirt and lay face down on her bed. I don't know if I was in some type of a trance or she slipped something in my drink, but I did exactly as she asked without any second thoughts behind it.

I felt the cold oil hit my back, and then she began to gently rub my shoulders and neck with her warm hands. I guess I became so relaxed that I didn't even realize shortly thereafter that she had removed my shorts and began to rub me down all over. I heard her gentle whisper saying, "Baby, turn over on your back."

I complied as I found myself lost in the moment, without even opening my eyes. The next layer of oil was applied to my front side as the rub down continued. I have previously visited Chinatown massage parlors and they didn't even compare to this experience. I was literally putty in her hands and completely helpless. I had completely lost all sense of time, responsibilities, and obligations; although I was completely aware of everything going on.

Next, I felt a gentle brush against my genitals which grew into a proper stroking as though I were doing it myself. I felt tension course through my body for less than a second, and then let go completely to return back to the state of relaxation that I was just in. The stroking then grew into a firm, moist feeling that was wrapped around my penis. My erection was at full peak with great anticipation for an eruption.

I heard the whisper, "Baby, are you okay?"

I responded with a faint, "Yes."

The next sensation that I experienced was as though I were penetrating a virgin. I felt her rising up and down on my fully erect manhood as I laid there experiencing pure bliss. Shortly thereafter, I exploded inside of her.

After laying there for a few minutes - wet, oily, and relaxed - the emotional drug had worn off and reality stepped back in. What had I just done? What just happened? Oh my, did I just sleep with a man? Did she slip something into my drink? Those were the questions that flooded my mind as I grew incredibly uncomfortable and immediately jumped up, halfway put on my clothes, and ran out the door with no explanation.

When I returned to my vehicle and pulled away, I felt incredibly disgusted with myself, but could not hide away the fact that I enjoyed it. What would I do with myself after this? The only thing I could do to overshadow the shame was to pretend that nothing happened and push it out of my mind. And go home and shower, repeatedly.

CHAPTER 45

MONEY BAGS

SATURDAY, OCTOBER 27, 2018 3:56 A.M.

I pulled into my driveway, utterly exhausted. I was staring at the digital clock on my stereo as I told Alyssa, "If I don't have a ride by four, I'm going to get some sleep." It had been a fairly busy night and my last ride ended a few blocks from the house. I needed the money, of course, but I also needed to rest so I wouldn't hurt myself or anyone else.

My phone pinged at 3:59 a.m. Of course. I seriously contemplated not taking it, but I made a deal with myself and a man is only as good as his word, right? I was happy to see that it was for the bar less than a quarter of a mile away. These local bar rides are typically pretty short, which meant I could come back home and go to sleep in good conscience.

The name on the ride is a man's name, Jeff, but two drunk ladies came stumbling out of the bar. They opened the door.

"For Jeff?" I asked.

"Yes, that's my husband," said the first woman.

I swiped to start the ride and verified the address. It wasn't a few minutes away. As a matter of fact, it was in a newer neighborhood called Skye Canyon, as far northwest as you can get in the city without reaching Mount Charleston. The estimated time on the navigation said thirty minutes. At least I knew it would be a lucrative ride. That bit of good fortune perked me up a bit. I just hoped I could snag an airport ride or something back close to my house, so I didn't have to make the return trip on my own dime.

The first woman, the more petite of the two, asked, "Can you take me to take my friend home, then bring me back? I can pay you cash or whatever." That made things much better.

In my ear, Alyssa said, "That's a come up!" She sounded excited for me. We had both been busy nonstop all night and she might have been almost as tired as me.

Being the responsible Rideshare driver that I am, I replied with the politically correct answer, "Of course. You can just add the stop in the app or update the drop off location once we get there."

"But we ordered it on my husband's phone and he's still in the bar drinking. Can I just pay you cash?"

I said, "We can see if he can update it once we get there, or we'll figure it out." I turned my availability off so they wouldn't give me another ride.

They jumped in and I started to drive. The petite woman appeared to be in her late twenties and was dressed in a chic, casual way with name brand everything, from her oversized bag to her jeans, shoes, and even her earrings. She had short brown hair that was meticulously styled and a long thin face with a nose to match. The other woman was about the same age, but not as kept. She wore basic mom jeans and a cute top with mid-length dirty blonde hair pulled into a ponytail. Her look made me think of housewives who didn't really get out much and considered the casual wear to be dressed up since their daily wear is sweats or yoga pants and baggy T-shirts. I wondered how these two ended up together for a night out, or how they even knew each other. They looked like they travel in contrasting circles and live drastically different lifestyles.

They were submersed in a drunkenly deep conversation that was interesting enough to keep me alert without having to interject and entertain them. Perhaps I'd be able to figure out their relation or how they ended up drunk together at four in the morning. My curiosity was helping me focus and stay awake, along with the knowledge that this trip and a cash payout for the return trip would round out my night quite nicely.

The petite one said, "Jo, it'll be alright. He said it was okay if you went out." I took a wild guess that she was talking about Jo's husband.

Jo said, "I know. But he never really means it's okay, even when he says that. I wouldn't have even gone if things hadn't been so crazy lately. I just can't take it. I don't know what I'm going to do."

Oh great, I thought. Was I in another domestic type

of ride? Was I going to hear all about how this man is beating her or keeping her captive and her friend is trying to talk her into leaving to save her? It might end up being more like an abused woman's crisis hotline type of ride. They would have been better suited with a counselor or something, but maybe they'd divulge some great insight on women and what they really want. I seriously doubted that I'd get anything out of it other than a little bit of money, but you never know.

Alyssa was laughing in my ear. "Sounds like you got you a *Housewives of Las Vegas* ride. Drunk chicks at four in the morning comparing war stories about their husbands."

My attention went back to the women in my car. "It doesn't matter what you've done, he can't hold you like a prisoner. You don't have to take that, honey."

Great. This sounded more like a women's empowerment thing when women can do whatever to a man and think that they still deserve the world. I think a lot of good men have been ruined by these types of women.

Jo started crying. "I know. But I feel bad. I don't know how to fix it. I'm not happy, Liz."

Liz scooted over and put her arm around Jo. The situation was no longer interesting but was making me slightly uncomfortable. I don't know what to do when women are crying and all emotional. I hoped they would just continue to talk among themselves. And I hoped the ride back wouldn't be awkward with Liz.

I tuned out the rest of the ride and started thinking about what needed to be done around the house and which bills needed my attention. Tuition was covered for my oldest daughter, but I needed to figure out how much I'd have to save up for Christmas. It gets harder and more expensive the older they get, even with fewer gifts.

My attention was brought back into their conversation with just a few minutes left until we arrived at Jo's house. Liz said, "I'm going to talk to him. He can't treat you that way. It's not fair to you or the boys."

Jo said, "Please don't. It'll just make it worse. I swear, Liz. Don't."

I wasn't sure what the proper thing would be to do if things went sideways. I mean, I didn't know any of these people. Their problems had nothing to do with me. But was it right for a man to just stand by if these two women were being bullied or hit by Jo's husband? Just like that last domestic dispute in my car, I wouldn't want to get involved. I was hoping this whole thing would just end. I mean, I could just drive off if drama started. I'd lose my money to get back home though.

Alyssa said, "That sounds like a hot mess." I wished I could tell her just how right she was. I grunted in agreement.

We pulled up to a new home in a tract of other new homes that looked identical. It was a quiet, well-kept neighborhood ideal for the younger families with above average incomes. Jo hopped out and Liz followed her. She left her bag in the car and called out over her shoulder, "I'll be right back. I just gotta pee."

I ended the ride and sat there, sitting in this neighborhood like a creep, for about ten minutes before Liz came back out. By then I almost had an attitude. I was deliriously tired and began to wonder if it would be wrong to just leave. I'd probably end up getting a returned item fee if I brought her purse back to her the following day. Or maybe I'd claim she had it. She was so wasted she probably wouldn't even know the difference. On the other hand, I didn't want to chance her husband filing a complaint saying I did or said anything inappropriate. I was tired and didn't have time to waste for these women to go back and forth with Jo's husband in their emotional intoxicated state.

I updated Alyssa on all that was going on while the two women were inside of the house. She laughed and said, "Yep. Sounds like a reality show. You always get the fun rides."

I thought she was crazy. There was nothing fun about all of that drama.

Liz finally reappeared and stammered, "I'm so sorry. That's a mess. Here, you can take me back, right?" She slid me a one-hundred-dollar bill. My eyes and attitude perked back up.

"I don't have change." I really hoped she had change, or better yet that she would just let me have the whole thing as a tip.

"It's okay. I don't either. Is that enough for you take me back to my husband?"

"Yes, ma'am." I suddenly wasn't as bothered by the ten-minute wait. I was actually ecstatic. That hundred dollars was one hell of a bonus for the night.

We started the drive back. She was on her phone, seemingly in and out of consciousness. Then she started rambling. "I'm worried about my friend. We went out to celebrate her birthday last night but she's going through it with her husband. He's being an ass. I'm just glad she actually went out. She hasn't been wanting to do anything for months now."

"It's good that you guys had that time together then." I figured that was noncommittal if she wasn't talking to me, but didn't want to ignore her if she was talking to me. I was only half paying attention as I was listening to Alyssa's chatter with her passenger. I was focusing on everything possible to keep me awake.

"Yeah. There's no cameras in here, right?" That was most certainly a question for me, though it was probably one of the weirdest things a passenger had asked me, and I've been asked some pretty out-there questions.

I almost wanted to say yes because I didn't know where that was going, but "no" had already escaped my mouth. I've heard about other drivers being shut off because of accusations of sexual harassment. I've been extremely cautious, even avoiding complimenting women because I don't want them to take it the wrong way. And after a few of my encounters with aggressive homosexual men, I feel bad for women knowing that they go through that all of the time. It also makes it difficult for a man though. I mean, sometimes I think the same comment could be considered a compliment if she's interested, or sexual harassment if she's not. It's really not fair to anyone to have to be so worried about being politically correct all the time.

"Good. Then I can talk. You don't mind, do you?" she asked. "It's just that I'm worried about her and need to talk it out."

"Not at all," I replied. I was grateful for the conversation to keep me going to get her back to the bar.

"She cheated on her husband last year. His best friend was having some financial issues and did flooring. They wanted new flooring, so he paid his best friend to come and stay with them and redo their whole house, even though it was all brand new already. She ended up giving his best friend head because he doesn't really show her affection or attention and the friend did. Plus, I think they secretly had crushes on each other for the whole ten years they've known each other. But she told him and came clean and hasn't done anything wrong before or since then, but now her husband thinks she was out cheating on him. But she wasn't."

"Oh, wow," was all that I could get out. I guess it didn't matter that I had nothing else I could think of to say because she just kept going, telling me all of this lady's business. That made me scratch my head. If she's your best friend, why would you share all of her personal business? Obviously, the lady was ashamed and didn't want to talk about it in my presence. Alyssa was right. They should definitely be on *Housewives of Las Vegas*.

"We all went to high school together. They moved out here shortly after I did. We're from a small town in Ohio. He didn't really want to settle down and do the whole kids and marriage thing, but she told him that she was getting older and wanted to settle down. If he didn't want that, she needed to move on. I guess he didn't want to let her go, because a few months later they were pregnant. Then married. Then another kid. Now they're both miserable and have a two-year-old and a four-year-old." She shook her head with a sad look and looked out the window.

Not sure if I should really say anything, but didn't want to seem like I was ignoring her, I said, "That's tough. Do you have kids?" I figured if we turned the conversation towards her life it wouldn't be so awkward. Or depressing.

"Hell no! You said there are no cameras in here, right?"

At that point, I was getting slightly uncomfortable. I didn't know if I should say yes as a precaution. I slowly shook my head no.

"Good. I have some blow. Do you want some blow?"

"No, thank you," I replied. She was all over the place; however, that kind of explained her behavior and the nasally sound in her voice. I was slightly relieved though, since it seemed like her erratic behavior and being drunk and high is why she kept asking about cameras. We were only a couple of miles from the exit to the bar anyway. I could end this weird ride and go home and finally get some sleep.

Her phone started going off. "Oh no. Oh my God." Her hands were flying around the screen of her large smartphone so quickly I wondered if she texted faster than court stenographers could type. Maybe even faster than Veronica. "Can we go back and get her? I think we need to go back. I'll pay you."

"Okay, so you'd like me to turn around?" I just needed to fully understand what this woman wanted me to do.

She said, "I still need to go back to get my husband. Is that okay?"

"Yes," I said.

She was already on the phone. "Honey, calm down. Breathe. Are you okay? I'm coming back to get you. Did he hurt you?"

I thought she was about to freak out. After their short exchange, she started talking to me again. "Is it okay if we go get my husband, and then go get her? I'll pay you, of course."

"Sure." My eyes and ears perked up. She could pay me all she wanted to. I was glad she didn't think the hundred dollars she had already given me entitled her to more of my time, even though I might have still done it. One hundred dollars for less than thirty minutes was a lot. On second thought, I was putting up with her and her erratic behavior; besides, if she had money to blow, why wouldn't I be entitled to be rewarded nicely for the service I was providing?

We pulled into the bar a couple of minutes later. She handed me another hundred-dollar bill. "Okay. I'm going to get him and have a shot; I'll be right back.

Maybe ten minutes, okay?"

"No problem," I replied. I don't even know if she heard me. She was lit and scurried off quickly. I'd be lying if I said I didn't contemplate just going home. I mean, what could she do? She gave me the cash and there was no record of this ride anymore. This was all extra. Then again, she might give me more for the ride back to this side of town again. Or rate me bad if I just took off.

I updated Alyssa on the current shenanigans. She said, "Wow, you won't have to work for the rest of the week after this ride." I shook my head. It must be so wonderful to be able to live off of less than forty hours a week and have no real responsibilities. I didn't get her. She just did whatever the fuck she wanted to do. She had no concept of real-life consequences. She makes just enough to cover whatever she has to pay or to spoil her boy toy of the moment and have people just give her all kinds of money. Her tips far outweighed mine on a regular basis. At least I got lucky with this cokehead tonight. I was starting to feel some of my financial stress ease up a bit.

A few minutes later, she came back out. "My husband already went home. It's right around the corner. Can we stop there really quick?"

"Yes, just give me the address so I can put it in the GPS please." What kind of circus is this lady involving me in? I should have just left her there and went home, I thought.

Four minutes later, we pulled into a gated community of ten exclusive, custom homes. She pulled out another hundred-dollar bill and handed it to me. "Just wait for a few minutes. I can't find my bag of blow. My husband will probably give you more, just don't tell him how much I've given you. He just won a jackpot for about fifteen grand last night."

She disappeared inside. The garage door opened to show a few guys sitting around a card table with beers. She zipped in and out and back and forth, moving as fast as a hummingbird. I didn't even mind the wait since I had three hundred dollars in my pocket. Of course, the knowledge that the husband hit a sizable jackpot and they were all drunk and high meant I might just get some more money out of them. She certainly made it sound that way. If she somehow lost her bag of blow in my car, I was sure I'd find it when I got up the following morning. That would be extra because I'm pretty sure I know a person or two who would gladly take that off of my hands, at a cost of course.

About ten minutes later, she climbed back into my car. She said, "Okay, we can go now."

"Are we waiting for your husband?"

"Oh, no. He's going to stay here with his buddies." I was kind of hoping the guy was going to join us because maybe he'd be just as generous, or more so, than his wife. Plus, that would eliminate any kind of accusations of some dude spending a couple of hours alone with his inebriated wife.

I pulled back out of the driveway and made my way toward the highway. She started telling me about how her husband is a dirt bike racer and shares the same first and last name with a famous R&B singer. She laughed hysterically, saying any time she makes reservations or orders anything people get excited, so she has to tell them he's the white one. Her conversation was erratic, bouncing between the husband, her friend's drama, not wanting kids, laughing then crying, and back through the rabbit hole she went. She mentioned talking to Jo's husband and asked if I thought it was a good idea, since I'm a man. I told her no, it's something they need to work out for themselves or decide that they want to part ways, without interference. I left out my opinion that her meddling in their business would most likely piss him off even more. The men I know seem to agree that what happens in the household stays there. We don't air our dirty laundry.

We made our way back to her friend's house while the sun was coming up. She ran inside as soon as we pulled up, before Jo could shut the door. Jo turned around to go inside after her, only it was locked. Oh boy.

Jo banged on the door and yelled for Liz to come out. Then she made her way to the car and climbed in the back seat, then slumped with defeat. A few minutes later Liz reappeared, with her back to us and a man, Jo's husband I'm guessing, standing in front of her. He was walking toward the door, forcing her to back up. As soon as she got on the other side of the door he slammed it shut. She couldn't get back in.

He was a slender man and looked like he had been beaten into submission. The look on his face and his body language screamed with despair and he looked like he wanted to just give up, curl into a ball, and die. I felt bad for the dude. I couldn't imagine my wife giving my best friend head, especially when he was staying in my home and I was paying him to work on my house. I'd probably kill them both. I'm not one to be disrespected like that, especially in *my* home and on *my* dime.

To forgive and forget and move on? No, I don't think so. I think my biggest dilemma might be who to kill first. And how. They'd both need to suffer and reap what they sew. They would have to feel my pain and pay for their disrespect.

Liz got in. Jo said, "What was that all about? You're making things worse." She started sobbing again. The loud, ugly cry sobbing. I reached back and handed her a package of tissues. She mumbled, "Thank you," and hung her head in shame.

Liz said, "I'm sorry, honey. I just needed to tell him that you didn't do anything wrong and that you love him and..."

Jo cut her off. "It's over." Through loud, gut wrenching sobs, she choked out, "he told me that he just can't do it anymore. He doesn't want to pretend anymore. He doesn't love me anymore and wants a divorce."

"Oh, honey. You're both drunk. Maybe he'll change his mind tomorrow. You should both get some rest, sober up, and talk tomorrow." Liz was rubbing her back and looking at her with pity.

Alyssa didn't even laugh or joke in my ear. She just

said, "Man, what a buzzkill." I agreed. It was incredibly uncomfortable. I was wishing that I had just left Liz at her house and took off with the three hundred dollars. I didn't even know if she was going to give me any more money. I was barely able to stay awake at that point and did not want to be anywhere near any of that drama.

"No, it's done. Once he makes up his mind like this, that's it. There's no going back. I'm going to pack up the boys and just go move in with my mom until I can figure out what to do."

"Honey, your mom is in Ohio! Don't do that. Come stay with me for a day or two until you guys can talk it out."

They went back and forth the entire ride back to Liz's house. My eyes were burning at that point from exhaustion. I was getting a headache, though I wasn't sure if it was from the lack of sleep or listening to their drama and sobs. Probably both.

As soon as we arrived at Liz's house, Jo said she was going to go home and get on the road. Liz said she couldn't because she was still drunk and had not gotten any sleep. It was a mess. Then Liz asked, "Will you follow us back to her house so I can drive her, and then take me home?"

I mumbled, "Of course," though I honestly wasn't sure that I'd make it. I wasn't in a position to turn down the hundreds this chick was throwing at me, but I was deliriously tired.

We pulled into the driveway at Liz's house and Jo jumped out of the car, ran across the driveway to the side yard, and jumped into her car. Liz threw her little name brand wallet at me and said, "Grab another hundred. I'll be right back; I can't let her leave."

She ran after her friend. I just sat there. I wondered how much of the fifteen grand was in that wallet. From the looks of their house, cars, and coke habit I would bet they had money before that jackpot. I could literally just drive off with her wallet and purse in my car. I'm sure I needed whatever was in her wallet more than they did. I mean, she was throwing hundreds around with a big bag of coke and dropping bills on alcohol in just one night. I stared at her wallet on my passenger seat.

I decided I was not going to go in this woman's wallet. She already hooked me up with three hundred dollars. I just wanted to go to bed. I was pleading with both of them in my head to end this drama so I could go home. If she didn't leave her bag and wallet in my car, I would have probably left without the additional money because I wasn't sure if I had it in me to make the six-minute drive home.

Finally, she walked back to my car. She pulled out another hundred and handed it to me. That was four hundred dollars for about two and a half hours. I was ecstatic. I bode the ladies good luck and farewell and made my way home. I passed out as soon as my head hit the pillow.

I woke up and my eyes sprung open. For the first time in a very long time, I was somewhat excited about waking up. I was excited because I actually woke up to having money. The responsible thing for me to do would be to take care of some other bills, and possibly treat myself to a simple meal, but I thought I'd like to really get myself a real treat. I'd really like to get myself another beautiful fish. They seemed like the one thing in my life that was peaceful and didn't seem to come with a lot of problems. I think I get some sort of pure pleasure from them that I just didn't get from anything else in life.

Forget it, I decided. I'm not even going to look at what I should do with this money to get myself ahead; I'm just going to go to the fish store. As much as I'd like to get a few more hours of sleep, I'm going to hop on up and get over to the fish store, anyway.

It's strange, because with this amount of money, I don't even think I have to look at the price before I look at the fish itself. I was going to shop like the Rockefellers shop and just put it in the bag.

I walked through, tank by tank, and didn't even glance up to check the price, even though I did feel the urge. I would imagine that even if I found two fish that I like, I could get both of them. Man, it was a great feeling. As I approached the last tank, I started to get discouraged. Nothing stood out to me. I hadn't seen a single fish that I really liked.

As I was about to give up my search, out of the corner of my eye, I spotted a silver fish that looked like a giant sword or butcher's knife. I thought it looked like a really unique fish. He swam up to the front of his tank toward me, as if he knew that I was there just for him. His mouth was really little, so I didn't even know if he would be able to make it in my tank. I wasn't sure if he'd be strong enough to defend himself.

The clerk walked over and asked, "Is there anything I can help you with?"

I asked, "Can you tell me more about this fish? What kind of fish is it?"

He said, "Oh, that's a jackknife. They're native to the western Atlantic Ocean along the coast of the US, Brazil, and throughout the Caribbean. They're also called donkey fish and lance-shaped ribbonfish." I tuned out pretty much everything he said past jackknife. Then he asked, "Do you have any other fish?"

I said, "Yes."

He said, "You can't add these fish to just any tank with any fish. The jackknifes are very aggressive and will kill other fish."

I said, "I don't think that will be a problem for me." I must have said it in a very arrogant way.

He asked, "Oh, really? What type of fish do you have?"

I said, "Only one is a real problem. He's a very ill-tempered pacu, who somehow thinks that he's in charge."

He asked, "How big is your pacu?"

I opened up my hand and showed him that he is the size of the full run of my hand, which is fairly large.

With some hesitation, he said, "Oh, I see. You may not want this fish."

I said, "Why? My pacu will kill him?"

He laughed. He said, "No. Quite the opposite. Your

pacu likely won't make it."

I said, "I'm willing to take my chances. I don't think he'll have a problem."

He paused and said, "This is quite a pricey fish." He looked at me questioningly. I realized I never even looked at the price tag. I nodded for him to go ahead.

He rang me up, and I looked at the total. Two hundred dollars. I gasped, as I was a bit beside myself. On the other hand, I came with the intention to treat myself, so that is exactly what I did. I told him, "Okay."

On the drive home with my new jackknife, I began thinking what if he was right? What if this beautiful jackknife does kill my pacu? He did say that the jackknife will be the most dominant and aggressive fish in my tank. I had grown to respect and appreciate the pacu. He was like a member of my family now. I think I would be upset if something happened to my pacu. Maybe I should have thought about all of this before I spent two hundred dollars on this fish.

Well, it was too late to worry about that at that point since I was pulling into my driveway with the jackknife.

I got him inside of the tank. He didn't take as long to adjust to the tank as the other fish have. He began swimming around inside of his bag almost immediately. The pacu was just watching him, not approaching him as he had with the other fish, which was understandable since the jackknife was nearly three times larger than the pacu.

I smirked at the pacu and said, "This should be interesting."

After watching the two fish size each other up for a few minutes, I released the jackknife from the bag and watched him swim freely. I left to get my work day started.

After working a long, hard day, I was anxious to return back home to see if the two fish had figured out their differences. Walking into the house, I didn't do any of my normal routine tasks, but went straight to my fish tank and witnessed the aftermath of World War III.

The interior of the tank was torn up. Nobody was floating upside down, and at first I didn't even see either of the two gladiators. They both couldn't have disappeared. As I took a closer look, the jackknife was down, hidden in one of the corners of the tank. He looked like he had several bite marks and scratches.

The first thought I had was, that is one tough pacu. It took a minute before I could even find him, as they had torn up the tank knocking over almost everything. There are giant rocks in there that weigh over five pounds, and even they had been moved in the battle. All of the decorations had been either dug up or were floating at the top of the tank.

In the opposite back corner, near some of the floating debris, I noticed the pacu. Man, he looked bad. I could only see the top half of his body, but just from that view it looked like he was missing part of one eye, a chunk of his fin, and had a major gash out of the side of his body about the size of a nickel. I felt bad for him. He looked like he had been thoroughly beaten. I couldn't even tell if the fish was breathing.

Well, I wondered to myself, which one is going to make it? Even though I felt kind of bad, I figured that this is what he gets for how he's tormented the other fish for so long. It was almost enjoyable to see him suffer, like sweet revenge being realized.

Over the next few days, the tank was quiet. And peaceful. The jackknife bounced back almost immediately, swimming around freely as king of the tank. The pacu stayed in his corner, clinging on to every ounce of life he possibly could. Looking at him each day, I couldn't help but wonder if it would be his last breath, or if he'd ever manage to swim another lap again.

As we approached the fifth day after the battle, I noticed a little bit more life in him. He definitely seemed to have lost a lot of his aggression. A sense of reassurance came over me, realizing that he would make it. I went on about my day. I was feeling confident that these fish would work out their differences or establish a mutual respect to coexist peacefully and bring some balance back to the tank.

That evening had to be one of the longest nights of my life. I could not wait to get home and just put an end to the day. The day was filled with some of the most difficult people I have ever dealt with. Every single customer had an issue, needed extra attention, or wanted to make me miserable. I sure hated life at that point.

I couldn't wait to get home to my two fish. I say two,

not neglecting the other fish, but because I was partial to the two being that they seem to have the most personality. As I entered the house I noticed a strange odor. It seemed somewhat familiar, though I couldn't quite put my finger on what it was.

Then it hit me. I thought to myself, there's no way. It can't be. I immediately ran up the stairs and made my way to my room. I found the pacu leaning half on his side on top of the jackknife, who was laying flat at the bottom of the tank. The smell was that of a dead fish.

I screamed, "What the hell just happened?" staring at the pacu, waiting for a response.

I know they're not mating. He swam about six inches to the left and the jackknife slowly floated to the top of the tank, upside down. I guess that was his way of answering me.

"This little bastard. This motherfucker just killed my two-hundred-dollar fish", I snapped, gritting through my teeth.

To top it off, I figured he's going to die, too. The gash on his side that was the size of a nickel had grown to the size of a half dollar.

I picked up my phone and called my friend, Adam. I said, "You're not going to believe what just happened."

I described the scene that I had just walked into. He explained, "Well, fish can actually drown."

"What?" I was dumbfounded. "How does a fish drown when they spend their whole lives in water?" I demanded, agitated. A fish drowning sounds like the most absurd thing I've heard in my entire life.

He patiently explained, "Fish breathe by swimming. They actually do need oxygen and get it while they're moving around swimming, taking in the water. They don't breathe when they aren't moving. So what must have happened is that the pacu couldn't outpower the jackknife, so he held him at the bottom of the tank so he couldn't breathe. And that slowly killed him."

We hung up. I was so frustrated. That's like saying that you suffocated because you had too much air. I immediately thought about what I could do to the pacu to torture him. But, since he was already probably dying too, I was actually the one who was losing. Twice.

In a fit of rage, I needed to release my anger and frustration. I ran back downstairs and went into my yard and just screamed at the top of my lungs. "Arrrrrrrrgh."

CHAPTER 46
SOME GIRLS HAVE ALL THE LUCK
WEDNESDAY, OCTOBER 31, 2018 11:00 P.M.

Holidays can be incredibly lucrative as a Rideshare driver in Las Vegas since more people are moving around the city and fewer drivers are working because they want to be with their families. I was not able to work on Halloween since I was with my younger kids begging strangers to give them candy that will rot their teeth and, ultimately, increase my dental bills. Alyssa was able to work though. She had an incredible night. I'm glad she did, since she really needed the funds - and to get her mind off of her on again, off again love triangle. Trying to be supportive, I encouraged her to share with me, though every detail that she shared just burned me more and more since I knew I really needed to be out there getting some of that holiday money with her. Not to mention the adult costumes and free entertainment.

Alyssa picked up three men from the Luxor about an hour before midnight. As always, she began by greeting them, confirming their name and their destination, which was the Crazy Horse strip club. Any time we get strip club rides, we light up. We know that we'll get the kick back from the club, which is a huge bonus. If you take enough guys to the strip clubs, you can make more that way than with tips and ride fare. Some drivers bank on it. The city is full of kickbacks, not just from the strip clubs.

She has a cute little way of starting her rides. Once she confirms their name and destination, she says, "You have temperature controls up here," and points to the backseat temperature controls in the middle of the ceiling between the front and back seat. "Please sit back and enjoy your ride. Let me know if you'd like different music, or if there's anything else I can do to make your trip more enjoyable." Every time I hear this, all I could think about was every time I get on a plane and the stewardess gets on the loudspeaker and I'm preparing to be thrust into the air to take flight. I almost want to sit back, close my eyes, and try to sleep through strangers elbowing me or bumping into me.

Most guys seem ashamed or intimidated when she confirms their destination as one of our local strip clubs, or when she picks up from them. She laughs. Because Alyssa is a bit free-spirited, she goes on to tell them which clubs are her favorites. I've told her that it can feel awkward for the men she's driving, so sharing her personal ventures and opening a non-judgmental sexual conversation helps relax the mood and invite them into a conversation. Most men fantasize about multiple women at the same time, or enjoying a strip club with another woman, so this can take the conversation in several different directions.

On the other hand, I look at it like why would a driver judge you for going to a gentlemen's club? We are in Sin City, after all. Do you know how often we take men - and sometimes women - to these clubs? I think Sin City is probably the most popular destination for bachelor parties, milestone birthday parties, graduations, and all kinds of other celebrations. The cliché bachelor party includes strip clubs and extracurricular shenanigans in Vegas, after all.

The guy in the front was a little friendlier than the two in the back. He drunkenly told her, "We've got money, and we want to see some titties!" He sounded like he had a laid back, good nature to him.

Alyssa laughed and joked back, "Well if you've got money, I've got titties."

All three men laughed, though the two in the back sounded more like nervous giggles. The one in the front got a little more serious and sober. He inquired, "No? For real? I'll give you a hundred dollars right now if you flash all of us."

Without thinking about it or hesitating, Alyssa pulled back toward the curb of the Luxor pick-up area. They had only managed to get about three car lengths away from the original pick-up. She undid her seatbelt, grabbed the bottom of her tight, little Halloween-inspired T-shirt and lifted her bra up with the shirt in one swift motion.

All three guys ogled, smirked, smacked their lips, and made little approving grunts. The friendly one counted out one hundred dollars in twenties. Alyssa lowered her shirt back down, buckled her seat belt, and proceeded on to the strip club. The three guys talked about her large breasts for the entire mile and a half ride.

After the happy trio exited her vehicle, ecstatic to start their night off right, no doubt, she parked to collect her kickback. All in all, she made over two hundred dollars in that short ten minutes.

While I was happy for her, I'd be lying if I said that didn't make me a little bit jealous. Actually, to be honest, I wasn't happy for her. She was just going to spend the money on a loser who didn't really want to be with her. I certainly needed the money, especially since I was just robbed of my two-hundred-dollar fish, and she showed a little bit of skin for five seconds and made two hundred dollars? Women just don't know how easy they have it.

Most of her other rides were people who were in costumes and pretty excited about the parties, costumes, and gossiping about their friends. I listened for another couple of hours before heading to bed, as I knew that I'd be awakened early with the sugary desires of young children who scored buckets full of candy.

CHAPTER 47
TIPSY TOPSY
SATURDAY, NOVEMBER 3, 2018 6:30 A.M.

What a long night. The sun was coming up, and I was utterly exhausted. I just dropped off what I thought would be my last ride at the airport. Maybe I should have put on my destination filter. Or maybe I should have just turned the app off altogether. I could barely keep my eyes open. Before I made a decision, I guess the decision was made for me. A ride came in. Money was definitely tight, so I went ahead and accepted it.

If I would have been paying more attention, I would have noticed the little line that said, "long ride: forty-five-plus minutes." I guessed I'd have to see which direction they were headed in. I thought I might have to cancel this one. I wasn't sure if I could stay up long enough to complete the ride.

The pick-up was in the fruit loop, which meant it could be going in any direction. I could only hope it was going toward my house. I thought really hard about cancelling the ride. I was beyond exhausted, but a long ride means good money, which would finish my night in a positive way.

I pulled up. Two incredibly flamboyant homosexuals approached my car. Man, I really hated these faggots. All I knew is that I was really not in the mood for them to hit on me. And God forbid if they were to actually touch me.

As they got in the car, I gritted my teeth and said, "Good evening. How are you guys doing tonight?"

They got in the back, thankfully. One ignored me, though the other said, "We're waiting on one more. Please don't leave yet."

The third man approached my car wearing what I think was a onesie. I couldn't get past the fact that he was wearing a skintight onesie, with the top half of the bodysuit down around his waist. He looked nasty and sweaty, and got in the front seat. I started thinking, he couldn't just sit in the back with the other two? I was sure they'd like to be squeezed up against a hot, sweaty, nasty man. But not me.

As the ride progressed, I began to see why he sat up front. He was the brother of one of the men in the back. And the other man was the boyfriend of the brother. Does that mean that homosexuality is contagious? Does it run in the family?

They were whispering to each other in the backseat and giggling like little school girls. So disgusting. The destination they put in was only thirty minutes away. I didn't understand why the app displayed a forty-five minute plus ride. The frustration mounting from the ride at least woke me a little bit. I was past exhaustion at that point. All I was thinking was how badly I just wanted to get these people out of my car.

You've got to be kidding me. The one in the front started snoring. What nerve. As we arrived at the destination, I noticed it specified "arrived at first stop" instead of destination. The estimated completion time of the ride suddenly made sense. I prayed that the one in the front would be the one who got out. I was sitting in front of the address, but no one was getting out of my car.

I said, "Sir, we're at your destination." That's when I realized I was the only one awake in the vehicle, except for the one in the back who ordered the ride. But he was in la-la-land, cuddling with his little homosexual boy toy.

He finally came to and mumbled, "Oh, okay." I was still praying that the one getting out would be the one in the front with the nasty little bodysuit on. I was wrong.

The one who climbed out was the little boy toy, after an incredibly long, exaggerated, noisy, sloppy kiss.

I confirmed the first stop on the app, which was deep in the north of Vegas, and realized that the last stop was back in the southwest, where we already passed about twenty minutes prior. I thought, this is fucking ridiculous. This is why the ride was so long. Instead of ordering his little boy toy a separate ride, or going home first like most people would, he rode all the way home with the little dude.

He tried to have a conversation with the one in the

front, but he was dead to the world, so he laid back to enjoy the music. Shortly after, the depth of bodysuit's sleep was confirmed as we hit a hard corner and he hit his head on the window. I thought he might have broken the window; the impact was so hard and loud. He didn't even budge. He just snored happily through it.

I guess he was the best kind of faggot to have in my car, one that was asleep and not bothering anyone, particularly me. I merged onto Interstate 15 south, which is under heavy construction. Every time I veered to the left or made a left turn, he seemed to hit my window. Right after the spaghetti bowl I noticed a sharp right turn with the construction causing a severe directional change. I slowed down to forty miles per hour, thinking he better not swing this way.

As soon as we hit the right turn, he fell onto me. I felt his sweaty body hit mine. It was fucking gross. What nastier feeling could there be other than this? I had nasty, faggot sweat all over me. Out of some kind of instinctual reaction, I overcorrected and went left, causing his head to smash hard into the window once again. His snoring was barely even disturbed. I nearly crashed into two other cars with the overcorrection. I didn't even care though. I'd rather have an accident than to feel his nasty sweat on me again. I wish I had a knife. I'd slit his fucking throat right now.

I did about fifteen to twenty miles per hour under the speed limit the rest of the ride because I couldn't chance him falling on me again. I thought about ending the ride. My thoughts were screaming at me, that I had to get these dirty faggots out of my car. Right now.

I barely made it to their destination. I didn't even have it in me to conclude the ride with any pleasantries because anything that would have come out of my mouth would have surely gotten me arrested, or at the very least banned from Rideshare. As they walked up to their house, all I could think was, good riddance. The world would be much better off without their kind. I turned my app off and went home. I needed a shower and to sleep this entire night off.

I often find myself coming home at night looking forward to enjoying the sounds of the water running above my head as I sleep. I need this in order to calm me down. It's a great way to decompress.

After having an exceptionally long night that began after an incredibly long day, I needed it more than ever. I shut off the lights, laid down, and tried to relax. All I kept thinking about was all of the aggravating people that I dealt with throughout the day.

I turned off the lights to the aquarium and turned off the TV because I was just over the day. I could not wait for it to be done and in my past. I appreciated my blackout curtains since they allowed me to forget that the sun was already up outside.

As soon as I turned off the lights in the aquarium and lay back down, I heard a loud noise as if someone hit the aquarium. I heard water splashing and a few drops of water hit me in the face. I thought, what the fuck was that? This was all that I needed right now. Did my tank just break?

I turned on the lights to try to figure out what just happened. I could see the water dripping down the side of the tank, but I couldn't see where it could possibly be coming from. I immediately started to panic, thinking the worst. Did the seam on the side of my tank just burst? How was I going to save my fish? Was this going to destroy my bed? My carpet? How much was it going to cost to repair? Where did I even begin to try to figure out how to repair it?

As I inspected the tank, everything looked normal. All was well. I couldn't find a leak, or any source of where the water could have come from. I decided to just lay back down. If I woke up in a puddle, so be it. I was too exhausted to keep looking for something that did not appear to be there. I cleaned up the rest of the water dripping down the side of the tank.

Once again, I turned off the bedroom light and the aquarium lights and lay back down. No sooner than my head hit the pillow, I heard the same sound, like the tank was being hit, followed by sloshing water and drops hitting me in the face. What in the hell could this be? I didn't get it.

One thing I did notice that time, upon inspecting the tank, was the pacu holding steady in the middle of the tank, just staring at me. None of the other fish were to be seen anywhere.

I asked him, "What was that?" I stared at him, truly expecting a response. He didn't say anything verbally, but his lips were moving very fast as he looked at me like I had lost my mind.

That time, my inspection was nowhere near as

thorough as the first. I took the same towel and cleaned up the water, then turned all the lights off and lay back down, again.

I kept my phone in my hand, with the flashlight on, underneath the covers. I was anticipating hearing the same noise again. Like clockwork, as soon as my head hit the pillow, the loud thud sounded again. I immediately shined my flashlight on the tank.

My light hit the tank just in time for me to see the pacu leaving the scene of the crime. He swam from one side of the tank rapidly, and he then quickly changed directions once he hit the corner of the tank causing the water to rise and spill over the side of the tank. When it all came together and I realized what he was doing, I stared at him and said, "You little bastard."

I got up and turned the bedroom light back on. "What the fuck do you think you're doing?" I scolded him, while he looked at me smugly like this was humorous. As I stared at him and yelled at him, he apparently felt the same way. He was in the middle of the tank staring right back at me, with his lips moving even more rapidly than I was spewing out my insults and questions.

I couldn't understand what he was saying, but his posture and the way his lips were moving made me think he was telling me, "Fuck you." This just enraged me even more.

I threatened him. I told him, "If you splash that water on me one more fucking time, I will fucking kill you." He was maintaining his position in the center of the tank, still moving his mouth rapidly, with a cold stare.

I told him once again, "I'm going to turn these lights off. And you better not splash me again."

I walked over to turn the bedroom light off again, maintaining eye contact with him the whole time. I lay down, and just as my head hit the pillow the sound came, followed quickly by the splash of water on my face.

In a fit of pure rage, I jumped up, turned the light back on and grabbed the net. I scooped him up and held him out of the water and told him, "Now you're gonna fuckin' die," as I watched him suffocating out of the water.

As he was sucking his last breath of air, something snapped in my head. This was a fish that I had become fond of and bonded with, yet I was sitting here watching him die, and gleaming with pleasure from it. It was not a quick, compassionate death either. I was watching a slow, painful, agonizing death overcome him. I released him back into the water.

My thoughts raced all over the place. I wondered, why did I enjoy that so much? Why was that bringing calmness to me? Watching him suffer caused a quiet excitement in me that I had never known before. What was wrong with me? Why did I want to do that? More importantly, why did I *enjoy* that?

All I had to do is drain the water down a bit, and even if he does his fast swim and turn move, it won't raise the water enough to splash me. Let me just close my eyes and forget that this whole thing ever happened.

CHAPTER 48

MORE PROBLEMS, MORE MONEY

WEDNESDAY, NOVEMBER 7, 2018 9:05 A.M.

I was actually starting to calm down a bit, thinking I was getting myself together. The bills were mostly on time; well, nothing was in immediate danger of being turned off. I knew that I had some larger expenses coming up, but I have things mostly under control. Tuition was due soon and the holidays were coming up, but I could get through it. Wednesdays are typically not the busiest day of the week, so I figured it would be a good day to stop off at the dealer for my routine oil change and maintenance. Thank goodness they gave me a couple of years' worth of free oil changes when I bought the car.

When I pulled into the garage the guy came out shaking his head slowly. I wasn't sure what he meant by that, so I simply said, "Good morning."

He said, "Good morning. Sounds like the

transmission, huh?"

Flabbergasted, I simply repeated his word that didn't seem to fit into my morning, "Transmission?" I was sure he had to have me confused with someone else. I didn't know anything about a transmission; I just needed my oil changed. What the hell did the transmission have to do with that?

He said, "Yes. Isn't that why you brought it in today?"

I shook my head back and forth slowly. Please tell me this is some kind of sick, cosmic joke. "I have an oil change scheduled," was all I could manage to get out. If that was his idea of a joke, he should definitely keep his day job. It wasn't funny. At all. It was cruel.

He said, "You might have bigger issues. Let's take a look at something." I handed over my keys and just stood there in disbelief. I had no idea how much a transmission cost, but I did know that I didn't have that much. My mind started racing.

After getting my car information and punching some keys on his computer he smiled and said, "Good news. You bought the warranty. This should be covered, but we'll need it for a few days to get it confirmed and have the warranty guys come look at it." A few days? How did an hour or so turn into being without my car for a few days? I figured I must have heard that wrong.

I just stared at him as though he were speaking Greek. I started to stutter, "But I...I just, how...but all I needed was an oil change." I must have looked like a complete idiot.

He looked at me with pity and confusion as he asked, "Didn't you notice that noise?"

"I mean, it sounded a little bit different. I just figured the oil was thin or something, I'm a little late on my oil change." I mean, seriously, what does a transmission sound like? It sounded like a car to me. An engine. The noises I had heard every time I have driven the car since I purchased it.

He said, "We'll get you taken care of as quickly as we can. Do you have a ride coming?"

"No. I thought I'd only be here for a couple of hours. How long will you need my car?" Something told me his "as quickly as we can" was far different from my definition of quickly. I didn't have the time or patience to deal with this. The only way I would be able to keep my head above water is to keep working. Even taking a slower Wednesday morning off was not really in the budget, just necessary to keep going. The weekend was nearing and I needed my weekend earnings.

He looked like he pitied me. That only further enraged me. For one thing, I don't need anyone to pity me. For another, that meant this was bad and even he knew it.

He said, "Well, we need to confirm the issue first. Then the warranty people will come look at it. It usually takes a day or so for them to approve or deny the claim once they come out. Then, if it's approved, we get the parts and make the repair."

All he really told me is that I wouldn't have my car today. Or tomorrow. Or anytime soon. I didn't even question him any further. There were so many variables in that explanation that he might have well said, "It depends. I have no idea, really." I sighed. What if they didn't approve it? Can they do that? Wasn't that the point of a warranty in the first place? If they didn't approve it, I had no way of making the money to pay for the repair. Let alone paying for the car. How come every time I'm almost able to breathe, I got knocked over the head, sucker punched in the gut, and pushed down again. I felt like I was drowning and there was no relief in sight.

I thought about all of the things I keep in my car. I asked, "Can I grab a few things?"

He said, "Of course."

I realized there was a possibility that I wouldn't see this vehicle again, so I started cleaning out all of my personal belongings. The chargers, gum, mints, notebook, the kids' books, etc. If I didn't ever see this car again that would mean I wouldn't be driving for money and my credit would take another hit. It was already shot so I wouldn't even qualify for a new car to keep working. It was a miracle that I was able to finance this car. I was going backwards. I didn't even think I would qualify for a loan shark payday advance at this point to pay for my car, a new car, or a transmission. I was just stuck.

He was walking around my car writing up the service ticket and pointed to the Rideshare stickers on my windshield. "You drive professionally?" he asked, taking me out of the spiral of despair in my head and bringing me back to my current circumstances.

"Yes."

"Oh," he said and looked down at his clipboard. What the fuck does he mean "oh?" What's he writing on his clipboard? I hear about these shops gouging people and charging all kinds of money for repairs that they may or may not need. Was he trying to turn my free oil change into weeks of repairs and thousands of dollars?

"What do you mean 'oh'?" I asked.

"That might be an issue. Did you purchase the commercial warranty?"

"Commercial warranty? I don't know. I don't think so. What's the difference? How would I even know?"

He explained, "Since you drive professionally your vehicle is considered commercial. If you didn't purchase the right warranty, they won't cover it. The last guy who had these stickers on his car got denied by the warranty company at the last minute because it was for business use, not personal. I can check for you."

"Oh my God. But I paid for the warranty. How can they deny it?"

The man shook his head. "I'm not sure how all of that works. All I know is, he was ready to approve the claim, and then denied it because he noticed that little sticker right there." He pointed to the tiny TNC sticker, which looks like a barcode, but it lets authorities and the airport know that we are Rideshare. What did he mean he didn't know how all of this works? If he's the professional and he doesn't know, how the hell was I supposed to make any sense of this? I wanted to shove my fist down his throat, but I realized that would probably do more harm than good since he was the only one who could get my car fixed for me at this point.

"So should I take it off?" I asked, nodding toward the stickers.

He looked at me, almost pleading with me. "Sir, I can't tell you to do that. That would be warranty fraud." He shook his head slowly, and then turned around.

At first, I thought he was being a dick. Like, why tell me all of this? Then just turn your back on me while we're having a conversation. That's rude. And disrespectful. He's had so much to say up until this point that I couldn't figure out why he suddenly had nothing to say. Then I realized he was giving me all of the information that I needed to make an informed decision.

I went around to the passenger side of the vehicle and began taking off all of the Rideshare stickers as quickly as I could. The emblems and the TNC sticker. It wasn't coming off that well. The stickers peeled off okay, but the obvious sticker residue wasn't cooperating. I was scraping the window with my fingernails.

He was kind of lingering but kept his back mostly to me. He walked over to the car and set something on the edge of the hood in front of the windshield then stepped away again.

What the hell was he doing, I thought? I looked at the small item he placed on my car. It was a small razor blade. I snatched it up and began scraping the glue off of the window. It worked quickly and efficiently. You couldn't even tell there was ever a sticker there.

I handed it back and said, "Thank you." I was sincerely grateful for that. He nodded slightly. Maybe he wasn't so bad. I needed him to be on my side right now.

I called Alyssa and asked if she could grab me and take me to my house to grab my old truck so I could pick the kids up from school on time. I really hated asking for help in these situations, but I didn't know what else to do. Without question, she came to get me. As soon as she got there I told her that I had no idea how long they would have my car. I think she saw my stress. She asked if I had time to grab lunch, her treat. She seemed to finally be ending things with her triangle lover. I just listened as she talked about how much better she was doing since she got a new place and was seeing him less. I appreciated the distraction, even though it didn't help much.

I felt like I couldn't breathe and had at least one thousand pounds of concrete pushing down on my head. Even taking the stickers off, they could still find a way to deny my claim. I had no idea a warranty issue had to be approved like that. That seemed like it should be illegal. I mean, they get to take my money when they sell me a warranty, then they get to choose if an issue is covered or not? I was definitely in the wrong business. Maybe I should start a warranty company.

I cashed out my earnings almost every day just to pay whatever bill was about to be shut off or buy groceries for my kids for that day. His non-answers about how long this shit would take made me realize it would be a long time. We weren't in immediate danger of anything being cut off, but that meant I only had a couple of days to figure out my next move before I was in that danger zone again. What was the pressure point before the big boiler tanks exploded? Because I thought I was at the human equivalent.

I wanted to choke the shit out of the guy at the dealership; he seemed so calm and nonchalant like he wasn't telling me the very thin wire that I had been balancing on just snapped beneath my feet. If it was just me, I'd be okay for a little while. I could sleep in my truck or whatever. But it wasn't just me. It was the family business. It was my five kids. The older boys were young men, so I didn't really have any financial obligation to them, but I did have an obligation to be the man they could look up to and follow in my footsteps. My older daughter depended on me for her education, so that she could do better than me and not end up like me or dealing with any loser men who couldn't support her. My younger kids, well, I was all they really had. I couldn't lose it. Who was going to look out for them?

The very next day I called to follow up on the vehicle. Patience is not a natural virtue of mine. The man at the dealership told me that they were going over the car and waiting on the warranty guy to come sign off on everything.

He called me back just before they closed to inform

me that they found over eight thousand dollars worth of issues. As he rattled down his list, I felt like I was listening to an alien speak to me in his foreign tongue while squeezing my head in a vice grip. I only understood one out of every four or five words. Once he finished his list, he informed me that the warranty person signed off on the repairs and all of them would be covered. He also told me they would be setting me up with a rental, which was also covered under the warranty. With a huge sigh of relief, I wondered why he didn't start with that news.

"How long will this take to fix?" I asked. I can't work in a rental. At least not with people. I could do the food deliveries. But those come in slower and pay less. I guess I should just be grateful that they were covering the repairs and getting me a rental. I mean, that was better than nothing, right?

"It all depends. We can't use any of the transmissions we have here. The warranty company will send us one. I'll keep you posted. But you're probably looking at least a week."

I was able to pick up the rental the following day. I knew I should be happy to have a car to drive, but I couldn't help but feel like the whole world was kicking me when I was already down. What did I do and who did I piss off to deserve this karma?

On top of everything else, I received a seven-page, hand-written letter from Veronica when I got the mail at the shop. Her handwriting is small and meticulous, but the words were repetitive and all over the place, which was her typical style.

She had never sent a handwritten letter, though. There was something different about this correspondence. She didn't waste any time getting to the nitty gritty details. It opened with:

"Scott, You are the biggest piece of shit I have ever met in my life."

I'm not sure what the purpose behind me continuing to read it was, but I guess it must have been a real page-turner. I progressed from a piece of shit to the biggest scum of the earth, along with treating her so poorly. She spelled out how she never wanted to see me again and just hoped I'd die.

I had to give her some credit, she was creative and imaginative in the ways she described her desires to watch me squirm, suffer, and cease to breathe. The flashes from my past came rushing back in like a tidal wave. Just another woman wishing I was dead. From my mother, to both of the mothers of my children, and now Veronica.

You'd think I would be used to it. Even though I didn't want to be with Veronica, I'd be lying if I said the words screaming at me from the pages of her notebook didn't sting a little. I had wanted her to leave me alone for a while. I guess I got my wish.

CHAPTER 49
THE A-WORD A-HOLE
SUNDAY, NOVEMBER 11, 2018 10:45 P.M.

Sitting there in the rental car was more torture than anything else I'd ever experienced. It was a quarter till eleven at night and I was scared to death to even look at my daily earnings so far. Sundays had never been this stressful in the past. It felt like forever between the requests coming in. I found myself looking between the phone screen and the clock. I think my last request came in almost thirty minutes prior.

After a few days of not working, due to my car being the shop, I got excited on Friday when I got to go pick up this rental car. It wasn't the same car that I drive, so I was limited on what I could do for extra earnings. Actually, limited doesn't even cover it. This was a fucking joke. All I was able to do was food deliveries. I'd always turned them down in the past because it seemed like they take longer and far less money is earned. My back was against the wall and I didn't see any other options, so deliveries was what I was stuck with.

Finally, the phone went off. I had a request that said it was twelve minutes away. Twelve minutes from the pick-up is fucking ridiculous. Oh, great. It's McDonalds. It seems like these food deliveries take at least twice as long as a regular ride, and they are never close. Well, if I didn't accept it I guess I'd just end up waiting around for another half an hour. So these few dollars would be better than nothing.

I arrived at McDonalds. I wasn't even sure what I was supposed to do. I'd only done a handful of food deliveries over the last couple of days. It seemed like there was no set pattern for them, they were completely different each time. Well, let's see what the instructions are. It said, "Proceed to the drive through and ask for the order by name and order number." I glanced over to notice that the drive through was the only thing open. Great, there was a line of like, seven cars.

As I sat in the line, waiting for the people in front of me to order, I wondered what happened to the optimism that I began the weekend with. I had a feeling that the food deliveries would be a bit slower than my regular rides, but since it was a holiday weekend I figured I'd end up okay since the kids were with their grandparents and I'd get an extra work day.

Oh, I know what it was that killed my optimism. It was that delivery that I did on Friday from Lawry's Steakhouse. I noticed that these food deliveries heavily rely upon the tips to make up for the slower pace and lower pay. I noticed that there was an option presented to the customer for the tip to be a percentage of the order amount. With the average dish being between thirty and forty dollars I was sure that delivery would be one for the record books. Little did I know what their policy was, until I arrived. As I approached the hostess, she directed me to the bar for takeout orders. The gentleman at the bar was kind enough to inform me that they don't prepare the order until the person picking it up has arrived. Of course, the customer ordered their steak to be well done.

In a great effort to fight off the frustration, I just reminded myself that this should result in a good tip. I kept reminding myself of that for the entire forty-five minutes that it took for the order to be prepared. I continued to remind myself of that for the twelve-minute drive to the drop-off location. I tried to remind myself even further into the delivery when I realized that I had to spend the next fifteen minutes parking and walking up to the hotel room because the drop-off location was at the SLS hotel.

I was no longer finding any comfort in any of that when I looked down to see that the delivery fee I received for the entire hour and fifteen minutes was five dollars and sixty-five cents. That five dollars and sixty-five cents would have been great, if this was the 1960s. A few hours later, the rest of my world came crashing down when I saw the whopping three dollar tip I got from that delivery.

Snapping back to the moment, I finally pulled up to

the screen to let the employee know that I was there to pick up the order. There was still a line of cars in front of me waiting for their food, so I still didn't know how much longer I'd be sitting there. The lady told me just to pull forward to the window.

I asked, "Is there any way I can just come to the door? There's a lot of cars ahead of me and I'm in a bit of a hurry."

She said, "I'm sorry, sir, but we're still putting the order together."

"Okay." I found some relief in that statement, hoping that it was a really large order because that would give me the potential for a greater tip.

Finally, there was only one more car in front me. I looked at the clock and realized that I had been in that line for nearly twenty minutes.

The lady handed me the order once I pulled up to the window. It was one little bag. I asked, "Is this all?"

She said, "No. There's one more thing coming."

A moment later she handed me a sundae. You've got to be kidding me. I looked in the bag. The whole order was the sundae and a small order of fries. The delivery charge on this had to be more than the fucking order cost. Oh well. Let me get this delivery out of the way so that hopefully the next one would be a more substantial order.

I pushed the button to go to the next part of this delivery, where the app showed me where to take the food. Oh, great. It was twelve minutes away. All I could do is shake my head and want to beat it against a brick wall at the same time. I dropped off the order and parked to wait for the next one.

That order took over an hour to drive to the restaurant, pick it up, and deliver it. I received five dollars and fifteen cents. At that rate I figured I was losing money. I was actually pretty sure of it. Well, wait! There might be a sign of hope. Before I could even turn off my engine, I got a ping for another order.

It was kind of strange that it didn't show the name of the pick-up location, it only showed the address. Maybe I spoke too soon about the struggles of food deliveries. I was only a few minutes away.

You'll never guess where the navigation brought me to. It was a 7-Eleven. I looked at the app for further instructions. It told me to go inside, make a mixed flavored Slurpee and get a pack of gummy bears. This had to be a fucking joke. I must have been in the middle of the Twilight Zone, or somebody's high paradise. It was the middle of the night, after all.

I will never try to understand the logic of some people. Because this made no sense, whatsoever. I don't even want to kid myself on the possibility of a tip out of a three-dollar order. I drove around the corner to the delivery location and the customer was nowhere to be found. Somehow, out of the dark shadows, someone just magically appeared. I handed the young lady her order and with a great deal of amazement, I looked at my phone to see how much I earned for this wonderful delivery. Not surprisingly, it was a whole four dollars. What a night.

I don't even have any completed thoughts on what that whole situation was. It was nearly one thirty in the morning and I was starting to get sleepy. I made a fatal mistake. I looked at my earnings for the night. For the five hours I had been working, I made a total of twenty-three dollars and some change. There was no way I could fucking do this. This was just not going to add up.

Just as I said that, another request came in. I think out of sheer habit, I accepted it. At two o'clock in the morning I could only imagine what type of request would be coming in for food. It was Jack in the Box, but at least it was only a few minutes away. I thought, I'm done after this. I should probably just cancel this one and go home. Out of habit though, or maybe for some sick kind of punishment, I continued on to Jack in the Box.

As I pulled up to the restaurant, the instructions told me to proceed inside. I didn't even know that they had a lobby that was open at this time of night. Yet again, there was a lovely line for me to wait in. As I waited, I heard a voice that sounded vaguely familiar. I glanced over my right shoulder and couldn't believe who I saw.

This is just the perfect way to end my night. I saw the gentleman that was just oh-so-helpful when I was at AutoZone a couple of months ago. He turned around and made eye contact with me, and I looked abruptly away. I wondered if he recognized me?

Well, nonetheless, I didn't want to deal with him. I would have better off if I had never seen him again the rest of my life. He shortly thereafter left the restaurant. They actually had my order ready when I got up to the counter.

I quickly left the restaurant with my order. I heard that same familiar voice say, “Hey! Hey you!” I ignored it. He said, “What’s the problem? You can’t hear me? I’m talking to you!”

I thought, he does recognize me. I said, “What? What can I do for you?”

He asked, “You drive Rideshare?” and pointed to the placard I had in the window.

He went into a long-winded story about how his ride cancelled on him, and then the next ride was rejected because there was some kind of an issue with his card. And now he was waiting to try to figure out how he was going to get home. He proceeded to offer me cash to give him a ride home. His whole story sounded like a bunch of bullshit. As I listened to him talk, I kept having flashbacks to how I was watching this same attitude and behavior for that entire night that I was trying to get his assistance, which ended up costing me time and money. I thought, I have got to get away from him.

I really could not believe the nerve of this guy. I told him, “No, I’m sorry; I have to take this order. I’m dropping this off.”

He said, “Where’s it going to?”

It’s none of your fucking business, I thought. “This order is going to the Hamptons.” I wasn’t sure why I even answered this clown.

“Oh, that’s perfect! That’s on the way to my spot.” He continued to tell me, “I got cash. Come on, I’m gonna pay you. It’s gonna be between me and you.”

I began to wonder if I could really afford to turn down any kind of money. Even after this order, I might make thirty dollars for the whole night. And, if I was already going that way, what could it really hurt?

I asked, "How much do you have on the ride?"

He said, "Come on man, I'm gonna take care of you. Don't worry." He pulled out a wad of money from his pocket to show me he was legit. From the quick flash that he did, it could have been all ones. I couldn't quite tell. Even if it was, it had to be at least twenty dollars or better.

"Well, I don't know."

He said, "Look, it's not that far out of your way. I'm only a block past that. We can even stop and drop off your order first."

"Ugh," I sighed. "Okay. Come on, let's go." I said and walked toward my rental.

He jumped in the backseat and I couldn't help but to relive all the time that I spent at AutoZone with him. I reminded myself over and over that it was just another ride. It's no different from all of the other obnoxious and annoying people that I've given rides to for money.

As we got going, I tried to remain professional. I asked, "How's everything been going?"

"Oh, everything's cool with me," he replied.

"Well, what do you do for a living?" I asked, thinking to myself, as if I don't already know.

He told me that he had a few hustles going on, but mostly he was in the music industry. I thought to myself, music industry? What the fuck does AutoZone have to do with the music industry?

I asked, "Oh really? What part of the industry are you in?"

In his cocky way he replied, "Oh, I do a little bit of this and a little bit of that."

I said, "Oh, so what has you out here in Vegas? I didn't think we really had a big music scene out here?"

Before he could reply, his phone rang. He answered and his whole demeanor changed. He says, "Yeah baby, what's good?"

After a short pause, he said, "You know, I just spent all night in the studio recording." I shook my head, noting he was wearing his AutoZone shirt.

As his conversation progressed, he told her how he just left a five-star steak dinner that he paid for with his mouthpiece. I thought to myself, mouthpiece? Besides all this bullshit lying that he was doing, was he trying to say that he talked himself into an expensive meal? I wondered if the girl he was on the phone with knew he was full of shit. Or that his five-star dinner consisted of value items from Jack in the Box.

I did my best to ignore the rest of his conversation. I pulled up to my drop-off location. I was really skeptical about leaving him in the vehicle alone. He just came off to me as a snake. At that point, I didn't think I had much of a choice. At least I could turn off the car and take my keys with me.

As I turned the car off, he said, "Man, you could leave the car running. I'm not gonna steal your shit."

I kept walking as though I didn't even hear him. As I got further from the car I heard him tell the girl that he was just talking to his personal driver. I didn't know I'd need my boots for this ride because this horse shit was getting really thick.

I dropped off the food and proceeded back to the car. I got in and asked, "Which direction are we headed?"

He directed me to go north on Nellis.

I said, "Just give me the address so I can put it in my navigation."

He said, "Man, it's just down the street."

I shook my head and started heading north. After two miles, I asked, "Do I just continue straight?"

He said, "Yeah, it's just a little bit further, just keep going straight."

As we approached the intersection of Washington and Nellis he directed me to continue straight and carried on with his phone conversation. I'm thinking, how is this only a block away? We've gone almost five miles.

I asked, "Are we getting close?

He shushed me and said, "Just keep going straight."

I couldn't believe in that short ride I was getting even more frustrated than I did when I spent the entire night at AutoZone. We were approaching Craig and I could no longer go straight. I could only go left or right. I couldn't even imagine where he was taking me to at that point. I looked over at him and asked, "Which way?"

He said, "Oh make this left, make this left."

He guided me into an apartment complex about a mile down the road. Even though I was incredibly agitated at the fact that this was nowhere near a block away from where I was going, I did have a sense of relief that I was finally going to get rid of this clown.

He immediately jumped out of the car, said "Thank you," and shut the door. Hard.

I rolled down the window and said, "Wait," since he slammed the door in my face. I asked, "What about my money?"

He pretended like he didn't even hear me. I turned the car off, jumped out and raced after him. I said, "Hey! What about my money?"

He said, "What? What are you talking about?" He turned his attention back to his phone call and said, "Hold on. Let me set this motherfucker straight and I'll call you back." As he hung up the phone, I finally had his undivided attention. He said, "What do you want for that little funky ass ride?"

I said, "Funky ass ride? You told me we were going a block past my delivery. You took me twenty minutes away. That wasn't no funky little ride in the least sense."

He said, "Here. I guess I do owe you a couple of dollars."

I was thinking, a couple dollars? I really could not believe the nerve of this motherfucker. He was standing in my face like I was bothering him when he pretty much begged to get in my car. He pulled out the wad of money that he showed me before.

He peeled off three dollars and extended his arm out to hand it to me. I looked down and saw the three dollars and stood there like a deer in headlights, in just sheer disbelief. He said, "Here. Take it."

I must have gone into instant shock because I was frozen, just standing still. It was as though time froze with me, moving in slow motion, and everything around me was intensified. I'm fairly certain I could even hear the blood rushing through my ears.

He said, "Here," once again trying to hand me the three dollars. I was still unable to move or react. I had plenty of words, but none were making their way out of my mouth. He dropped the three dollars on the ground at my feet and turned his back on me. He pulled his phone out to call the girl back as he walked away.

A sensation came over me that I had never felt before. The first thing I noticed was a giant rock on the ground next me, a short distance away from the three dollars that he dropped for me. I decided to pick that up, instead of the three dollars. As I quickly pursued him, sheer reaction took over and I struck him in the back of the head with the small boulder. One blow and he crumbled to the ground. Without any hesitation, I quickly dragged him to the car and threw him into the trunk.

THE END

MURDER MINDSET SERIES
A TRILOGY OF TRILOGIES

Three strangers.

Three vastly different walks of life.

Three disparate stories.

People that you'd come across every day.

However, there's a darkness brewing beneath the surface of these seemingly ordinary lives. The three are battling their pasts and trudging through their days.

In all, these three individuals each have their own trilogy.

But when their worlds collide, those who survive will never be the same.

Meet Scott. He's an average Rideshare driver in Las Vegas. He's there when he's needed. He helps people get to where they need to be. But, he's hiding something.

Scott, a forty-something single father, makes ends meet by moonlighting as a driver. He records his experiences in his journal. He's struggling to maintain normalcy while he begins to crumble underneath the surface.

Scott's story unfolds in three volumes. His journal shows how his Rideshare experiences add entertainment, joy, confusion, and ultimately darkness to his life. This darkness unleashed something that will wreak havoc in Scott's life and will affect all those around him profoundly.

Meet Serenity. She has the innate capability to blend in with the shadows or to steal the center stage and command all eyes to her.

She's a street performer on Fremont Street in "Old Vegas" during the evenings, and the self-proclaimed crusader and protector of the night during the witching hours. She sees her mission as righteously divine, though others might see it differently.

Serenity's story, told in three installments, shows how her journey gives her the tools, knowledge, and experience she needs to save others from the damnation that she knows is looming.

Meet Shyla. She's an incredibly intelligent, though often misunderstood, newly promoted police detective.

Shyla has dreamed of being a detective her entire life. She feels the immense pressures of being a minority in her field, feeling she must prove herself. She navigates the complexities of solving crimes, battling both the criminals and her colleagues, and expanding her personal life.

Shyla's story, comprising of three interludes, tells the tale of her doing her best to protect and serve the citizens and guests of the Las Vegas metropolitan area, one case at a time.

Coming Soon:

The Rideshare Chronicles: Volume II
The next ride could spell DEPRAVITY

Serenity's Salvation

The Rideshare Chronicles Volume III
The next ride could spell DESTRUCTION

Sign up for Amy's Happenings and get the latest scoop on characters and book releases at AmyJanece.com

ABOUT THE AUTHOR

Amy Janece is a long-time freelance writer, ghostwriter, and self-published author. She is the author of the Murder Mindset Series, described as a trilogy of trilogies, created by drawing on her years of self-employment. A jack of all trades, Amy has done everything from selling candles to trucking to driving rideshare. She currently resides in Las Vegas, Nevada.

For more information visit AmyJanece.com
Follow Amy Janece at:
Instagram.com/Amy.Janece
Facebook.com/AuthorAmyJanece

www.ingramcontent.com/pod-product-compliance
Lightning Source LLC
Chambersburg PA
CBHW060221030726
47499CB00004B/1138
* 9 7 8 1 9 5 2 9 7 3 0 0 0 *